GUKURAHUNDI

GUKURAHUNDI: VOICE OF THE LORD

Peter Abbot

Rock's Mills Press
Oakville, Ontario

PUBLISHED BY
Rock's Mills Press

Copyright © 2016, 2018 by Peter Abbot
ALL RIGHTS RESERVED. PUBLISHED BY ARRANGEMENT WITH THE AUTHOR.
ORIGINALLY PUBLISHED IN 2016 BY ROCK'S MILLS PRESS UNDER THE TITLE
VOICE OF THE LORD.

This is a work of fiction. Although the historical context is real, the characters do not represent actual persons.

Cover image: Basheer Tome.
https:/flickr.com/photos/basheertome/2665947256

Library and Archives Canada Cataloguing in Publication data is available from the publisher. Email us at customer.service@rocksmillspress.com or visit us online at www.rocksmillspress.com.

Give unto the Lord, O ye Mighty, give unto the Lord glory and strength. . . .
The voice of the Lord is upon the waters . . . the Lord is upon many waters.
The voice of the Lord is powerful; the voice of the Lord is full of majesty.
PSALM 29

O! Ancient crimson curse!
Corrode, consume.
ISAAC ROSENBERG, "ON HEARING ABOUT THE OUTBREAK OF WAR"

Robert Mugabe's . . . clan totem, *garwe*, the crocodile . . .
PETER GODWIN, *THE FEAR*, 2010

If yesterday I fought you as an enemy, today you have become a friend and ally. . . .
The wrongs of the past must now stand forgiven and forgotten. . . .
An evil remains an evil whether practised by white against black or black against white.
ROBERT MUGABE, ZIMBABWE INDEPENDENCE SPEECH, 1980

. . . three years after independence, Mugabe ordered his troops into the southern
province of Matabeleland to launch Operation Gukurahundi, "The Rains that Clear Out
the Chaff." They killed around twenty thousand Ndebele civilians. . . .
PETER GODWIN, *THE FEAR*, 2010

We accused and condemned the previous white minority government for creating
a police state and yet we exceed them when we create a military state.
JOSHUA NKOMO, 1985

What in our lives is burnt
In the fire of this?
ISAAC ROSENBERG, "AUGUST 1914"

I love you, great new Titan!
Am I not you?
ISAAC ROSENBERG, "SOLDIER: TWENTIETH CENTURY"

"I am the enemy you killed, my friend . . ."
WILFRED OWEN, "STRANGE MEETING"

. . . if way to the Better there be, it exacts a full look at the Worst . . .
THOMAS HARDY, "IN TENEBRIS (II)"

CONTENTS

CHAPTER	PAGE
I	1
II	16
III	31
IV	45
V	61
VI	76
VII	93
VIII	106
IX	126
X	142
XI	160

OCTOBER–NOVEMBER 1983

She was lying on her back with her eyes closed, beside the hotel swimming pool, in the late morning sunlight; alone.

He strolled to one of the lounging-chairs a few yards from her, and sat covertly watching the rise and fall of her breasts, the soft stirrings of her legs, thighs touching, parting. Was she aware of him, of the heavy stare behind his reflecting sunglasses? Abruptly she turned over, eyes fluttering open briefly to the glare. Auburn hair, cut short. Her slim tanned back curving down to the yellow swimsuit.

He had been sitting forward, hands on knees. Now, gazing steadily at her, he rubbed suntan lotion onto his chest, stomach and shoulders; then lay back, giving himself to the heat and to sexual imaginings. His penis tingled. Well, he could wait. His stillness matched hers. And anticipation of the hunt sweetens the kill.

A plump fair-haired girl came sauntering across the lawn; garish in blue shorts, red and white floral shirt, green plastic sandals. Her shadow brushed his face and he opened one eye to her petulant smile. "So here you are, I didn't know where you went, why didn't you tell me, hey? Did you get breakfast?" Thin high voice. Her round miniaturised face gaped back at her. Silence; his face impassive. "I'm hungry, hey—hope I'm not too late for breakfast. See you soon for a swim" as she went.

He closed his eye again; dozed. Heat gathered around them, two slim beautiful bodies unmoving as corpses beside the flickering pool. In the distance a dove called monotonously, calm fluid melody at ease with the radiant morning. Monkeys scurried and chattered in the mango-tree behind the far stone wall. Two waiters outside the dining room conversed quietly in their vernacular, Sindebele, with occasional subdued bursts of laughter.

A sudden loud splash roused him. He lifted his head. She was in the pool, surging through pale green water; her breast-stroke powerful, steady, economical. To and fro she forged, glitter in her wake. Ten laps, then she stopped, and clung with one hand to the far side of the pool, the deep end, shaking water from her hair.

Now. He took off his sunglasses, pushed them carefully beneath the chair, stood up slowly, stretched, ran lightly to the edge of the pool, dove cleanly, swept like a shark underwater until he could see the flicker of her body. Bursting up almost against her, he reached for the pool-edge and laughed into her face through a halo of sparkling droplets. Tiny red leaves bobbed and jostled on the water around them.

She smiled. Small freckled nose, grey eyes, wide mouth—she was even more attractive than he had expected, and he suddenly remembered an Irish girl he'd hooked up with for a few days, last year in France; remembered her lithe body beside him, beneath him.

She didn't speak, but suddenly launched herself backwards. He pursued her, caught up with her as she reached the shallow end. "Name's Paul. Yours?"

After a moment, "Oh, you're Australian—I thought you were South African." Her voice low, soft, warm.

"No, that's *Carla*—the fat girl, did you hear her talking to me? Met her coupla days ago. I'm from Perth, lotta Sith Effrikans there now. So you think I look like a Sith Effrikan, *hey?*"

"Well—you're blond and tall and tanned."

"And good-looking—with a great body?"

"Oh— Well— " Seems shy. Virgin?

"*You* have a great body." And he kicked backwards, scooping water at her with both hands. She yelped, threw herself after him, and they pranced around each other, flinging water into cascades that flashed slivers of rainbow. She pushed him. He fell back extravagantly, sinking to the green-tiled pool-bottom, drowning with frantic gurgles.

She caught him by both arms and pulled him gasping to the air. "Oh, I'm sorry, I'm so sorry, are you all right?"

He spluttered, survived, staggered about theatrically; seized her, led her to the edge of the pool. They pulled themselves up onto the warm cement and sat side by side, legs dangling in the water.

"And when did you leave the States?" he asked.

"Oh, I'm not American. I'm Canadian."

"Here for long?"

"Till tomorrow. And you?"

"I'll be moving on soon, maybe tomorrow too. Where you heading?"

"Bulawayo, and then—"

"Me too. Know what *Bulawayo* means? Someone told me—Place of

Slaughter. Their King in the old days, Lobengula, he was famous for throwing enemies off a cliff, lotta bleeding corpses. And after that?"

"I'm not sure. Great Zimbabwe. The ancient Ruins— I'd love to see them. Then Harare."

"Me too. Someone said to try and see Matopos, it's near Bulawayo, but sounds like just a huge pile of stones."

"With Cecil Rhodes buried on top of a kopje. Or just his heart? And they say it can be dangerous there now - guerrillas, the ones still fighting against President Mugabe and his government, they've been killing people in the countryside, haven't they? So I wouldn't mind missing Matopos. But we haven't discussed that yet."

"'We'?"

"Oh, we met on the plane, happened to sit together, and turned out we're flying back on the same plane too, from Harare, so we decided to travel together. Is this your first time in Africa?"

"Yeah. But I been in Zim coupla months."

"I've been longing to come, I want to see as much as I can. A week is so short. Zimbabwe! Even that name's exciting, don't you think so? Zimbabwe. Have you seen Victoria Falls yet?"

"Coupla days ago. You haven't?"

"We only arrived yesterday, and we had to get some sleep straightaway, we were so jet-lagged still. You could see the Falls from the plane as we came down to land, and of course you can see the spray from here, and you can hear rumbling too, or am I imagining that? So close— I can't wait— but Stephen said he'd like a swim first— Oh, here he is."

The young man strolling towards them was, Paul immediately assessed, no competition. Long brown hair falling ragged across a high wide forehead; granny glasses; baggy blue swim-shorts. Pale. Skinny. Paul jeered silently. What could any woman possibly see in him?

"Why so long?" she complained. "I thought we were going to see the Falls before lunch?"

He squatted beside her. "Sorry, Susanna. We'll go straight after lunch. Thanks for waiting. I slept so deeply, only woke up half-an-hour ago. Sorry." Posh English accent—Paul jeered silently again. Bloody Pom, one push and he'll piss his pants.

"Stephen, this is Paul. He's going to Bulawayo tomorrow too."

"Oh, are you? Glad to meet you." Stephen held out his hand, smiling, and Paul gripped it, extremely hard. "Travelling on your own?"

"Yeah."

"We could go by bus or train, but we're thinking of hitch-hiking. To meet local people, see more of the countryside, save money. Do you think that'll be difficult?"

"Easy, easy. Not many cars on the road but you get picked up without any hassle, everyone's friendly. I've hitched all over."

"Oh. And is there any danger, do you think? On the road to Bulawayo? Guerrillas? We were going to ask at a police station."

"That's all balls. Those guys aren't interested in *tourists.* Guerrillas'?—it's all just tribal, Blacks killing Blacks. Shona versus Ndebele: the two main tribes, they hate each other. And the Army's everywhere. Those Dissidents or whatever they call themselves, the ex-ZAPU guerrillas—they have to stay way out in the bush now. They don't have a chance in hell against Mugabe's lot, especially the Fifth Brigade, you heard about them? Just a matter of time, they say, before the Dissidents surrender. Someone told me Nkomo's run away to England—he's the Ndebele leader. Anyway, *I'm* gonna hitch to Bulawayo."

Stephen glanced enquiringly at Susanna, but she was looking away from him to Paul. "Well, would it be possible, do you think, to join forces? As we're going the same way on the same day?" smiling slightly at this unintended rhyme.

Having gained his object so easily, Paul put on a show of reluctance. "Yeah, well, harder to get lifts if there's more than two of us. Easiest when there's only one. Yeah, but then, why not?"

Stephen—"Great. That'll be great. What time do you think we should leave?"

"Early morning. Make sure we got plenty of time, so we won't be out in the bush after dark. Lions, leopards, elephants, poisonous snakes! So start early—just in case the lifts are slow."

"Great. Shall we talk about it some more later? I'd better have my swim—it's almost lunchtime, isn't it? Coming, Susanna?"

"No, I've had enough swimming for now. I'll sunbathe a bit longer while you swim."

"Hi!" Carla had arrived, slashes of scarlet bikini cutting into the luxuriant curves of her breasts and buttocks. She smiled at them brilliantly, swished her towel playfully.

"Oh, this is Carla. Sue and Steve. From Canada and England."

"Pleased to meet you. How're you enjoying Africa?"

"Very much," Stephen answered politely, "but we've only been here a short while."

"Well, it's *super.* You'll see. All the tourists say it's super. I missed breakfast, Paul, but they gave me coffee and toast, and anyway it'll soon be lunchtime, hey. Who's for a swim?"

Neither she nor Stephen was much of a swimmer, but they splashed about amiably and swam a few lengths. Two shrieking children joined them in the pool.

Meanwhile Paul pulled four chairs into a circle below one of the big multi-coloured umbrellas. "Come over here and make yourself comfortable" he called to Susanna. "How about a beer?"

She came over immediately, watched soporifically by four other hotel guests gathering under an umbrella on the far side of the pool for a pre-lunch drink. "No, I'll have an orange juice."

Paul flicked a finger towards a waiter. "Two Lions, one Fanta."

"Right, Baas. I get him."

She lay back in a shaded chair. "Actually, I'd better be careful about being in the sun. Last time I sunbathed I ended up with sunburn—and that was in Canada."

"You can use my suntan lotion" he offered.

"No, I'll be all right if I don't overdo it."

She looked across at him, intently. He grinned, and stretched out his legs lazily. Handsome, she thought, in a Robert Redford way. Short fair hair; firm chin; high cheekbones— He had put his sunglasses back on, so she couldn't see his eyes.

The waiter arrived with their drinks. As Paul turned to sign for them, she scrutinised him further. Yes, physically he was superb: tall, lithe, his athletic muscularity enhanced by the sunburnt brown of his skin and the minimal black trunks he was wearing. His arms were covered lightly with blond glistening hairs; and so was his chest— She was disconcerted, when she lifted her gaze to the glass he was holding out her, by the confident smile above it. More than confident, she told herself: arrogant. Knows how good-looking he is—of course he does.

And those sunglasses are repellent: shining armour of a predator, nullifying your gaze while empowering his own; throwing your smile back at you like a boomerang. Or was she over-reacting, forcing him into a feminist's male-chauvinist category because she was more attracted than she wished to be?—or yet wished to be? She sipped her Fanta, while he drank his beer straight from the bottle, fast.

"That's better! I sure was thirsty! Tell me about yourself?" Baritone voice, slightly husky. "Which part of Canada you from?"

"Toronto."

"What's it like? I'm gonna be in North America next year—States, Can-ada—look around before I go back to Aussie. *If* I go back."

"Well—it's a big city like any other big city, I guess."

"Just like Perth."

"Give me a chance" and she giggled. "I'm not a tour guide, you know, I just live there. On the Island, it's right opposite Toronto, we—"

"What's your father do?"

"He's a Prof, at U of T—the University. He teaches Philosophy. My mother's a high-school English teacher. They want me to go to university but I'm not sure I want to, not yet anyway—I want to think about it, look at the world, and then decide. My grades are good enough—to get me in, I mean—but I'm not brilliant like my brothers, and anyway I'm not sure I want to go on studying. I think I'd like to be a journalist, or go into television or some-thing. Anyway, I told them I needed time to think about it. Ever since I was a child I wanted to travel, and my parents finally agreed, so long as I went to a third-world country first, to see how poor people live—they're both left-wing, Amnesty International and all that, they read the *New Internationalist* and go on peace marches. So—here I am. My mother taught high school near Harare for two years before she met my Dad—you know, CUSO, students volunteer-ing overseas?—she loved it, so she was glad I wanted to come here, she still has friends in Harare, I'll be visiting with them before I leave. How about you?"

"Me?"

"Well, why are *you* here? What's *your* father do?"

"Dunno. Never knew him. Knocked up my mother, staggered off to the Outback, drank himself to death." He had told various stories when asked about his origins; this one always worked well on women; and it wasn't so very far from the truth, anyway.

He watched embarrassed sympathy flooding into Susanna's eyes. "Oh. How—? Did she bring you up all on her own?"

"Yeah. Slaved in a laundry. Ruined her health."

"And is she still alive?"

"Yeah. Married a skinny Pommy immigrant with five snotty kids, he threw me out when I was fifteen, said he never wanted to see me again." Which was untrue: his mother had been killed in a car accident when he was eleven, and after that he'd been brought up by her brother and sister-in-law, with their three much younger children.

Impulsively Susanna put a hand over his wrist. "I'm so sorry, Paul. That you had such an unhappy childhood."

"Oh, wasn't all bad—I had fun too. I'm not sorry for myself. Gotta keep moving." He took a long swig of beer, emptying the bottle.

"And what do you do?"

"Do? What job, you mean, in Aussie? Electronics—word-processors. Chucked it to see the big wide world. They said I could have my job back anytime—I'm an expert, see, they didn't want me to leave. But maybe I'll decide to live somewhere else—get a job there. So now we know a bit about each other. And here come the others."

Stephen and Carla had been drying themselves at the edge of the pool. They sat on the other two chairs. "Really enjoyed that" Stephen announced, briskly rubbing water out of his ears. "Invigorating, and now I feel ready for lunch and the Falls."

"What'll you have to drink?"—Paul.

"A cool drink for me—orange juice."

"How about you, Carla?"

"Same, thanks."

"You must be joking, Steve! Here you are in the Land of the Lion, and you aren't even gonna try one? It's a bloody good beer too. Much better than any of that piss you Brits call 'Best Bittah,'" ridiculing Stephen's accent. "I worked in a London pub for coupla months, you know. Bloody whorehouse, that was—couldn't even use the bog in peace, what with all the Queers standing round hoping for a piece of me. I won't say which piece."

Stephen frowned briefly. "No, honestly, thanks. I haven't got much of a head for drink. And we'll have to change for lunch soon."

"I think we'd better go right away"—Susanna. "They've started serving, I think. And I want to have plenty of time at the Falls. You and Carla can have your orange juice at lunch. All right?"

Twenty minutes later they were being served by a nimble deferential waiter in the dark dining room with its enlarged photographs of the Falls glowing under low lights on every wall.

"What do you recommend?" Susanna asked the waiter, glancing through the menu. "I'd like something Zimbabwean."

"Crocodile is good, madam." The waiters were barefoot, and wore red fezzes, white shirts and trousers, with red cummerbunds.

"Yeah, you should try the croc," Paul grinned. "Once."

"Have you had it?"

"Once."

"Well— Yes, please, Waiter, I'll have the crocodile."

"Me too," said Stephen.

Carla grimaced. "Not for me, thank you very much."

"Have you ever tasted croc, Carla?"—Paul.

"No and I don't want to, I'll have the mixed grill."

"Looks like chicken, tastes like chicken—tough chicken. I'll have the steak—rare."

"Yes, Baas. Rare." The waiter finished painstakingly writing down their orders and went off.

"You know where they get the croc meat?"—Paul. "From a croc farm right near here. You can go and pay to look at them in big ponds, all sizes from tiny lizards to humungous bloody monsters twenty feet long. Being fed raw meat to make them into food and handbags. Bloody weird sight. You should go just for the hell of it."

"We won't have time, unless we get there this afternoon after the Falls"— Stephen. "You said we should leave early tomorrow."

Carla turned to Paul, dismayed. "But *you* aren't going tomorrow, are you? Paul?" Plaintively: "You said you were staying another week."

"Yeah, well I changed my mind—*hey*. Want to come with us?"

Carla was tremulous. "You know I'm flying back to Jo'burg on Friday. You said you'd come with me, Paul."

"Well, postpone it."

"I can't. Daddy'd have a fit. He didn't want me to come but my Mom said I could. He hates Zimbabwe, thinks I'll get murdered or raped or something. I had to promise I'd stay right here at the hotel and phone him every night without fail. You said you'd like to meet him."

"Well, I will, later. When I get to Jo'burg. You tell Daddy that any job he offers me I'll accept, so long as I don't have to do any work—hey?"—grinning. "Ah, here's the food—I'm famished."

"But, Paul, I've got two days still, I'll be lonely—and I paid for you for a week."

"So let's make the best of this afternoon. How about you and me going to the Crocodile Farm while these two go to the Falls? And then we'll all go on the Sundowner Cruise."

"But I don't want to see crocodiles, thank you very much."

"Oh yes, you do. You'll enjoy yourself. Wait and see." He turned to Susanna, "What do you think of the taste?"

"Well—interesting. Chewy; not very tasty. 'Tough chicken' is about right. But I'm glad I'm trying it for my first real Zimbabwean meal. Once. My only crocodile experience!"

Paul— "I'll go and book for us all on the Sundowner Cruise—you two don't need to wait around. But be back before five—that's when the bus will collect us here."

"So long as it's agreed that we pay for our own tickets"—Stephen. "I've heard about it: expensive but don't miss it, someone told us on the plane. The boat goes up the Zambezi and you see the sunset."

"Yeah. And drink as much as you like, why they call it the Sundowner Cruise. Know what a sundowner is? You drink *up* while the sun goes *down*, haha. Ticket includes as much beer as you like."

"Well, thanks for seeing to the arrangements, Paul. Do you want any sweets, Susanna, or shall we get going?"

"Dessert? No, let's get going. We'll need the whole four hours, I'd think, especially as we have to walk there."

"Doesn't take long" Paul said. "Just go straight along the road towards the spray. Don't forget, see you in front of the hotel at five."

By half-past one, Susanna and Stephen had reached the Smoke that Thunders. "That's what it means" she told him, and read from the official guide: "'Dr David Livingstone is reputed to be the first white man to have seen the Victoria Falls, or *Mosi oa tunya* as the local people call them ("the smoke that thunders"), on November 16, 1855.' Just think, a hundred and thirty years ago he was standing right here!"

"Yes, I remember that. I read some books about Zimbabwe, a few months ago. When I was thinking about coming here."

She was looking at the booklet's map. "There's a statue of him near this end of the Falls. Shall we start there? Then we can walk right from one side to the other."

"Great."

She looked searchingly at him. "Why do you keep on saying that? 'Great.' The English don't say 'great,' do they?"

"You'd be surprised. All my friends say it. We're all of us citizens of the American Empire now—*baby*. Surely you noticed that in Canada? Anyway, isn't 'great' originally Irish or Scottish?"

They strolled along the path. There were only a few other tourists about. "I guess there are always *some* tourists here," Susanna said "but isn't October the tourist season?—it's the dry season, their winter, milder weather before their very hot summer. But I guess fewer tourists are coming now, because of nervousness about the fighting between ZANU and ZAPU—and the possibility of getting caught up in tribal violence—though it seems peaceful enough here, doesn't it? And talking of seasons, back home in Canada, it's Fall now. Red and brown and yellow—the colours, the foliage. So amazingly beautiful! And then it'll be winter. Snow—skating, skiing, I love all that. While here it'll be summer of course, and the rainy season, and then I guess all these trees around us will burst into leaf when the rain comes; though it's amazing how many of them have flowers and leaves right now, as if they know rain will be arriving soon. Sorry, I'm talking too much!"

"'*The trees are in their autumn beauty, / The woodland paths are dry. / Under the October twilight the water / Mirrors a still sky.*'"

"Wow, I know that! Yeats. That's one of my mother's favourite poems. She adores Yeats."

"'The Wild Swans at Coole.' '*But now they drift on the still water, / Mysterious, beautiful. / Among what rushes will they build, / By what lake's edge or pool / Delight men's eyes when I awake some day / To find—*'"

"'*—they have flown away?*' —But here we are in Africa, in *Zimbabwe*, and we have only a short while to see one of the wonders of the world! So—" They had slowed and stopped. "We haven't even reached Livingstone's statue yet."

They hurried on in silence towards the oversize bronze effigy gazing out, hand on hip, across the glory encountered in 1855. —Surely he had been stunned into disbelief, she thought, as she turned to follow the blank Victorian gaze. Surely flung himself to his knees, in wonder, lifting his face to his Maker? Not just *stood* like that, stiff and impassive. That couldn't be how it was!

And now the Victoria Falls. *Mosi ao tunya*, the Smoke that Thunders!—so much more impressive than I could ever have imagined! Green water sliding towards the jagged lip of the gorge, sliding inexorably, like—snow falling endlessly, endlessly, from a blank sky. Then, abruptly, turbulence, water jostling, churning, struggling to push back up into calm, but failing, and falling, hurtling downward in a white fury. And a deep roar lifting from the chasm, as if the earth itself can hardly sustain such intensity: as if it groaned, and tilted on its axis. That vast plunging, that deafening reverberating storm of endless surge. Voice of power, voice of triumph, voice of pain, voice of horror. We are drawn by it, to the vortex of good or evil—inexorably—as if our frail bodies can be detached from gravity, so that we too must fall, must plunge, down and down, into the heart of that immense darkness.

They walked hand-in-hand down precipitous slippery steps for another view of the Devil's Cataract; and along the winding path, paved with small stones, that led them along the edge of the Gorge opposite the Falls and flung them view after thundering view of that iron curtain of water, until they felt stunned by the immensity of it; and on into the Rain Forest, where spray flew up at them and soaked them, where rainbows sinuously formed and re-formed, and the trees and shrubs gathered thickly to drink sustenance; until they reached the far end of the path, Danger Point, where, leaning against smooth black wet shining rocks, they gazed down into the menacingly slug-gish whorl of the Boiling Pot; and then there was only the railway bridge, its grace and strength puny indeed, a merely human construct, a toy, in this immense display of nature's awesome authority.

Susanna felt sick, ecstatic. She spoke for the first time since they had left behind the toweringly imperturbable Livingstone. "No—words—they just can't begin to describe—something as huge as this—can they? '*We only live, only suspire, / Consumed by either fire—*'"

"'*—or fire.*' T.S. Eliot."

"That's the best I can do. A few words of poetry. Inadequate!"

Stephen kissed her, took her hands in his. She gazed at him, surprisingly unsurprised. Then they sat down together on a smooth boulder. He still held one of her hands.

After a pause, "Another of your mother's favourite poems? You know what *I* found myself thinking while I was looking down into the Gorge at the Devil's Cataract? '*And what rough beast, its hour come round at last, / Slouches towards Bethlehem to be born?*'"

"Oh. Yes. It *was* truly terrifying to look down into that—maelstrom. My mind just shrivelled. But—I wonder what time it is?"

He looked at his watch. "Going on for four." He glanced back at the Falls. "I'd like to do the whole walk again, wouldn't you? And yet, I don't think I could—too much to bear. And anyway, don't you think it's one of those things you should do only once in your life, so that the memory stays always—exact—intense?"

"No, but I do feel overwhelmed. Let's just sit and talk for a while and come back to earth slowly. Perhaps I've seen Niagara too many times and can't appreciate it any more. But—oh, this is one of the experiences that I'll never never never forget, whatever happens to me. And we'll always be linked by it, you and me, whenever we remember it, even though we hardly know each other."

"I'm gay," he said.

After a short silence, she stirred; but didn't drop his hand. "Why do you tell me that? Now?"

"Because I— Because I felt I could—felt I *must*. Because I came to Africa to face up to myself, to *become* myself. I felt—don't laugh, I felt I should come to Africa, to the very beginning of humanity, to where human beings—began— so I could begin to learn to be myself, after all the lying I've done, especially to myself, all the deceit. I've been living a lie for so many years! I'm almost twenty-two, and I know I haven't even begun to be what I am, or know what human beings really are and can be. I want to learn through *experience*, not just intellectually, theoretically, do you understand? So I had to start by telling someone something I've never told anyone before, a basic fact about myself. And now I have. I'm gay. I'm *gay*. Does any of this make any sense? Susanna? Coming out and coming home." He turned to her, gazed at her intensely.

"To be yourself, what you are. Is that what you mean? Well, I think— Telling me something so important to you is a—a compliment, I think that. But are you sure—about being homosexual? Have you—actually had sex with a man?"

He smiled, sardonically. "I went to an English public school, you know. Does it make any difference to our relationship, what I've told you? Can we stay friends?"

"Oh yes, Stephen. Of course. Though—" She smiled at him. "I guess I have to say I'm disappointed—not because you told me you're gay but because you *are* gay, or think you are. So we'll just have to be soul-mates, won't we? — And now, we should start back to the hotel." She studied the map. "We have to go back most of the way along this path, and then we come to the road."

After they had walked some way in silence, "What are you studying at Oxford, Stephen? You didn't tell me."

"History—Modern History. But sometimes I wonder if I ought to be reading English Literature. Conrad—*Heart of Darkness*—the fragility of civilisation. Hardy—*Tess* and *Jude*—victims of prejudice. Forster—*Passage to India*, destructive effect of colonialism. Joyce Cary—you should read his African novels, if you haven't—*Aissa Saved*, *American Visitor*, *African Witch*, and especially *Mister Johnson*, innocent Nigerian murdered by the British Empire. *Lord of the Flies*—Golding. And greatest of all novels— *Wuthering Heights*. My list of Great Books! But I admit that, like so many peace-loving people, I'm appalled and fascinated by violence, by war above all, the pity and horror of it. I don't know if I am truly a pacifist—well, I know I'm not—I understand why colonised people have to use violence to get their freedom— but I'm *almost* a pacifist, I hate violence, and always will. The First World War, the so-called Great War. Do you know the major English poets? Owen,

Sassoon, Edward Thomas?—and Rosenberg above all— But now *I'm* talking too much, sorry. Stop me, stop me!"

"Oh Stephen, I just wish my parents could meet you. They would love talking with you. My brothers aren't interested in art, literature, music, they're both into economics, finance—money, money. What will you do after your degree? Teach?"

"You might think so! Yes—but what I want to do most is research. If possible, on a topic that focuses on peace movements, especially understanding why they failed to stop both world wars, why they *always* seem to fail. But I'm eight months from Finals, and I'm taking two weeks off this term, as I told you in the plane—just to relax and get away from the tension, have a break. My Tutor approved. If I don't get a First I probably won't be able to do research anyway. My father's a civil servant—in the Ministry of Defence actually!—and Mum works part-time now as a dentist's secretary. He's worried I'll end up without a job, I think, and they'll have to support me while I write poetry or novels that never get published! I'm an only child."

"What do you think of Paul? Should we be travelling with him to Bula-wayo tomorrow?"

Stephen smiled. "Oh, yes, I could see he was attracted to you—to put it mildly. And I'm sure any woman—and probably, talking for myself, any man—would be attracted to *him*. He's so good-looking. Of course, he would have nothing to do with homosexuals—he more or less said so, didn't he?—obviously hates them—us. Very macho. But—I don't know, I think I feel a bit sorry for him, though that seems ridiculous. I wonder if he knows any more about himself, his real self, than I know about *myself*; for all his—charisma. I think there's some insecurity beneath those rants and rippling muscles, don't you think so? But I'm talking too much again. Stop me! What do *you* think?"

"I'm not sure. Haven't made up my mind yet. I confess I was a bit shocked by some of the things he said. But you're right, I do think he's attractive—physically at least. I guess we'll both have a better idea by this time tomorrow. Anyway, looks as if we've succeeded in coming down to earth again! With half-an-hour to go—just time to freshen up a bit. Did we even experience the Victoria Falls?"

They had reached the end of the path. The hotel was in view.

"Where's Carla?" Susanna asked.

"Got a bad headache. Says she's sorry she can't come."

The bus was packed with tourists exchanging anecdotes. "I woke up in the middle of the night and there was this elephant actually *leaning* against our tent, I thought we were *dead*"—"But it really *was* a leopard, I couldn't believe it, just what I came to Africa to see, there it was, just lying on a branch high up in the tree"—"Luckily I had my camera pointing in that direction because a Livingstone Lourie, you know it's very *very* rare, it had just flown up there"—

Stephen, just behind Susanna and Paul, was crushed against an emaciated blue-haired American woman who, with hardly any African preliminaries, launched into the story of her life. "I can never bear to say No to anyone, everyone takes advantage of me, my ex-husband—" Fortunately she was detained for a moment by her tour-guide when they left the bus, so the fourth chair at their table on the upper deck of the boat was occupied by an elderly Japanese man.

The engine rumbled, the boat swung out into the stream. Soon it was throbbing against the current towards the slowly sinking red ball of the sun, while cameras clicked and ecstasies proliferated. "Oh yes, that *is* a hippo near the bank, oh my *God*"—"Look, look, those must be waterbuck, surely they are, or are they impala, yes I think impala, oh aren't they *cute*"—"That's a giraffe on the right, in among the trees, can you see it, and there, over there, in the grass, is that a lion, can you see it, is it stalking the giraffe?"—

Stephen saw the crocodile first. He pointed at it speechlessly, un-believingly, as it flailed up towards them out of the darkness, almost in the wake of the boat; twisted heavily; and lunged towards the shore.

An excited babble from the alerted passengers. The Japanese tourist smiled broadly at Stephen, after clicking several photos. "Is cockodile. Good, good."

"Crocodiles make me think of sharks" Susanna mused, sipping her Fanta. "All that malignant cold-blooded destructive power. Evil. And yet—mys-terious. Beautiful."

"Oh, now you're being anthropomorphic—as well as quoting Yeats again!" Stephen responded energetically. "'Amoral,' I'd say, not '*evil*'—if we must impose human categories on the non-human. *I* think a crocodile's like some primeval god of the slime. Like—war, violence. If you rouse it, get in its way, if it's hungry—why blame the crocodile? You knew it was there, you knew it was there." He turned sharply towards Paul, "What do *you* think a crocodile's like?"

Paul had already consumed four Lions. He beckoned the waiter brusquely, seized another three bottles. "A cock looking for a cunt."

Stephen, embarrassed, said nothing, but Susanna was smiling. "That's cer-tainly—appropriate, I must admit, Paul. I hereby declare you the winner of our little crocodile-simile competition, and hereby award you your prize." She seized one of his Lions, hid it momentarily behind her back, then handed it to him with a smile. Immediately he poured its contents down his throat, gazing fixedly at her.

They passed Kandahar Island, long and green, its silhouetted palm trees; and now, as the red ball accelerated downwards, dwindling to the horizon, the boat slowed, its engines were silenced, it was allowed to swing and linger athwart the current to provide the passengers with maximum photographic opportunity. Murmurs of appreciative wonder counterpointed volleys of clicks.

Sunset! Like a stage-set, the placidly glowing river and a few high flaming clouds framed the momentous event, this daily drama of day's end. Someone, as the last slit of sun was swallowed, clapped softly—appreciatively or sardonically? Then the beat of the engines resumed and the boat slipped rapidly downstream as darkness gathered round them.

Susanna shivered. A chill was rising from the water as it glinted darkly past. She turned to Paul— "Well, that was fun, wasn't it? Worth every one of those dollars we couldn't really afford, don't you think?" But he was still drinking, and seemed now impenetrably morose. Susanna leaned across to the Japanese man, who had finally stopped taking photographs. "Did you enjoy it?"

He bobbed his head, eyes crinkling. "Velly good, velly good, yes. Sundowning. Cockodile. Good, good, good, good."

Paul suddenly slumped towards Susanna and spoke heavily. "You remind me of my mother. Specially—your voish."

"Oh—thanks." She noticed he was twisting the gold ring on the fourth finger of his left hand. "I hope she can sing better than I can."

"She— Your voish—"

Stephen, gazing into the heart of the water's darkness, thought: He's at the maudlin stage; hope he won't start puking over us.

The passengers disembarked in silence, subdued by the anti-climax of journey's end, queuing patiently for the gangplank.

Paul stumbled off the path into the darkness and returned zipping up his fly.

All the way back to the hotel in the bus—a different one, with grinding gears that the driver could change only with difficulty and both hands, while it plunged erratically from one side of the road to the other—he held Susanna's hand, and lay heavily against her, breathing stertorously, eyes closed behind the mask of his sunglasses.

II

Susanna and Stephen were up in good time for breakfast. Afterwards they knocked quietly at the door of Paul's room. No response. They went for a swim; knocked again; scrawled postcards, went for a walk to post them and to buy a few small gifts in the tourist shops of the town; knocked again; re-packed their knapsacks; and then Stephen went to knock yet again.

This time Paul appeared, pulling on a red T-shirt, above frayed jean-shorts and dirty white running-shoes. In spite of his irritation, Stephen smiled on seeing that the T-shirt was inscribed, in large black letters, 'KEEP IT UP.' Paul's face was sullen, unshaven.

"It's nearly twelve. Shouldn't we be gone by now? You said—"

"Oh—yeah. Yeah. Gimme ten minutes to shave."

"Well— Maybe we should have lunch here now? Then we won't have to worry if we don't get to Bulawayo till late."

"Yeah—right. See you there—you go ahead and eat."

Susanna was annoyed. "I bet he didn't even apologise" as they sat down at their table. "And he was the one who insisted we had to get going early. We could have seen the Crocodile Farm or the Big Tree if we'd known—it's an old famous baobab. Perhaps we should leave tomorrow instead—could we spare the time to stay here another day?"

"Talking of the Crocodile Farm, here comes Carla. Perhaps she'll tell us about it." But Carla, when she noticed them in the dining room's contrived gloom, veered away and sat on her own at a distance. "Oh. I wonder why she's cutting us. Maybe because Paul's not with us. What are you going to have, Susanna?"

She was studying the menu. "You know," she smiled at the waiter mischievously "I think I'll have the crocodile again, please."

"Well, *I* certainly won't—thank you very much. And it's unlucky to have crocodile twice anyway!" mock-seriously. "Gammon steak for me, please."

"Yes, Baas, Madam."

As the waiter went, "He's got such a sweet smile, did you notice, Stephen? And a kind expression. He's probably a grandfather and he loves playing with his grandchildren, all twenty-nine of them. I read somewhere that Zimbabwe has the highest birth-rate in the world, half its population is under fifteen years old. That's the main reason why unemployment is such a big problem. So let's leave a good tip."

"Twenty-nine dollars, one for each of the grandchildren."

"Oh don't be silly, Stephen, we can't afford so much."

"*Zimbabwean* dollars, not Canadian or American ones—that's not a lot for us. Well, we'll do it by twenty-nine percent then."

"Right. That's generous anyway? Here's Paul. And our food."

Paul had washed and shaved, sketchily; but seemed remote. "Steak" he ordered peremptorily.

"Yes, Baas. Rare."

"You too" observed Stephen, deadpan. "Ordering the same as yesterday. I've already told Susanna that's unlucky—and now you, which makes it *doubly* unlucky."

"So then you'll have all the luck to yourself, won't you—lucky you"—Susanna. After an uncomfortable silence, "Wouldn't Carla like to sit with us, Paul?"

He shrugged. "She knows we're here."

"Yes but—she looked as if she was deliberately avoiding us. Have we upset her somehow, do you think?"

"Probably Daddy told her last night to keep away from Steve." He turned to Susanna elaborately, smiling but indefinably hostile. "You must know the Boers hate the Brits. Too soft, too pansy—except for Maggie Thatcher, they like *her* because they say she's really a man."

Susanna and Stephen, discomforted, ate in silence. Obviously they've had a row, Susanna thought; but he's right, it's no business of mine. "Do you think— Perhaps we should think about going tomorrow, not today, Paul? We could leave early then, as you said we should."

Paul ignored her, slashing at his steak and swallowing bloody chunks of it half-chewed. He had finished his ice-cream while they were just starting theirs. "Come on then, let's get going" and he strode out of the dining-room.

They were walking unhurriedly along the main road out of the town. Hot, hot. A dry breeze. And not a cloud in the pale sky.

"Look, that's a baobab, isn't it?" Stephen pointed. He was sweating. "We must have walked about two miles. Why don't we stop there, in the shade?"

No cars had passed them, but, just after they had taken off their knapsacks in the tree's shadow, a few yards off the road, two came by, one after the other, driven by Whites: the first with a full complement of passengers, its driver gesturing apologetically; the second driven by a middle-aged woman who turned her head away very deliberately from Paul's thumb. Then silence, except for the whirr of cicadas, the dry susurration of dead grass, the occasional chirp of a bird.

While Paul stood on the left side of the road, Susanna and Stephen crossed over and sat down on dry red soil, leaning against the smooth trunk of the baobab, and surveying the panorama of rocks, dun grass and massed trees beyond Paul.

"What's that?" she asked, pointing to Stephen's waist.

"My flask. I happened to see it in an army-surplus shop a few days before we left. It's got khaki webbing to hold it to your belt."

"I didn't think you were into military equipment?"

"I'm not. I don't even usually look at the window of that shop, just scurry past. But it happened to catch my eye and I thought, Well, might come in useful in Africa."

They sat in silence for a few moments. Then: "*I've* got some useful things too" Susanna said. "Guides to the trees and animals and birds of Southern Africa. I bought them at the airport in Harare while I was waiting for you to come out of Customs and Immigration."

"Yes, you had quite a wait! They don't like British passports now in Zimbabwe. Understandable, I suppose. But having to empty *everything* out of my knapsack! I told you all about that, didn't I?"

"I want to get to know as many as I can, birds and animals and all. I'll get the tree book out—so many different trees, right here."

Stephen put his hand on her arm as she reached for her knapsack. "That's bad luck too," he said dreamily. "If you do that, we won't *never* get a lift."

"Don't be silly! Oh, you *are* a fool, Stephen! Well, then, entertain me by reciting some poetry."

While he pondered, eyes closed, she studied his face. Really, he isn't so bad-looking, though skinny as well as a bit shorter than me, and his nose and face and neck are too long, chin receding a bit; his adam's-apple prominent. Skin pale, and hair unkempt; but if he'd—she almost lifted her right hand, to smooth hair off his forehead. And he has a sense of humour; and he's sensitive and intelligent. She smiled wryly. What more could a woman want?

He spoke softly, and she leaned towards him to hear. "'*Snow is a strange white word; / No ice and frost and snow / From earth to sky / This summer land doth know, / No man knows why. / In all men's minds it is. / Some spirit old Hath turned with malign kiss / Our lives to mould.'"*

He opened his eyes and, turning his head slowly, gazed into hers. His eyes are green.

"'*Snow is a strange white word'*" she repeated, in a whisper. "Wow. That's—marvellous, isn't it? '*No man knows why.*' Is that all of it—the whole poem? Did you recite all of it?"

"No. It gets better—or worse. '*Red fangs have torn His face. God's blood is shed. / He mourns from His—His—*' what? Oh yes, '*His high place— He mourns from His high place / His children dead. / O! ancient crimson curse! / Corrode, consume. Give back this universe / Its pristine bloom.'*" He looked at her questioningly.

"Please," she said after a moment, "will you recite it all again?"

After he had finished, she leaned back against the tree, clasped her hands round her knees, and closed her eyes. They sat in silence. Then: "I don't want to say *anything*, Stephen. I feel as if I'm shivering inside. How can words do that? And I said yesterday something about that they couldn't, didn't I? I feel— it frightens me; the whole poem does; and that about some force stronger even than God, wounding God, killing God's children—'*Corrode, consume*'— how does it—?"

"'*Red fangs have torn His face. God's blood is shed. / O! ancient crimson curse!*'"

"'*Corrode, consume.*'"

"'*Give back this universe its pristine bloom.*' Do you know where that was written?"

"In Africa? '*This summer land—*'"

"Yes." He glanced at her in surprise. "Cape Town, in 1914. Rosenberg was there when the Great War broke out."

"And he was thinking it would be winter at home."

"Like you at Victoria Falls."

"Will you promise to send me Rosenberg's poems after we get home? I'd like to read them *all*. What was his first name?"

"Yes, I'll send them—I'd like to, Susanna. Isaac. Isaac Rosenberg. He was a poor Jew in the East End of London, he joined up for the money mainly. He was an artist as well as a poet—and a totally hopeless soldier—and he was killed on April Fool's Day in the last year of the War. He didn't have time to write many war poems but I think they're—the best—" He stopped, and when she turned to him she was surprised to see tears in his eyes. "Sorry," he said. "That's what war poetry does to me. As our esteemed Prime Minister Margaret Thatcher would say, I'm a Wet. Look at me weeping in the middle of Africa!"

"I'd like you to—recite more poetry by Rosenberg, and the other war poets, Stephen, but—I couldn't bear any more now."

They heard a car approaching. It surged by. Paul strolled over to them. "No luck. Your turn. I gotta take a leak."

Susanna and Stephen crossed the road, stood together near the edge of its tarred greyness.

"What's the time?" she asked.

"Well after two. Twenty-past. Let's hope we get a lift soon."

As he spoke, they saw a vehicle in the distance. It laboured up towards them, noisy and high off the road, belching smoke—a battered brown Ford pickup truck. When almost level, it suddenly half-pulled off the road and Stephen, waving his thumb, stepped back hastily.

The driver was an elderly White man, wearing a khaki bush-hat with a leopard-skin band. He leaned towards the open window on their side, keeping the engine running. "Where you want to go?" in a hoarse smoker's rasp.

"Bulawayo."

"Not going that far." A strong Rhodesian accent. "Turning off after a hundred k's. Want a lift to there?" Then he saw Paul, who was crossing the road to them. "But I can't take three in here, hey—one of you's has to sit in the back."

"He can only take us about a hundred kilometres," Stephen told Paul hurriedly when he reached them.

"That's—it's about a quarter of the way, I think," Paul responded. "We could wait and hope to get a lift all the way, but it's getting late and there don't seem to be many cars coming this way."

Stephen pulled a crumpled tourist-map out of a pocket. "And we should catch Hwange-to-Bulawayo traffic where he drops us off."

Paul went to the truck while Susanna and Stephen went to the baobab for the three knapsacks. "Thanks very much, sir, we'd be very grateful for a lift as far as you can take us."

They threw their knapsacks into the back. Stephen opened the door for Susanna, and looked questioningly at Paul while she climbed in. "Well—shall I get into the back, or—?"

"Yeah, if you want to, Steve" and Paul got in beside Susanna, who looked across at Stephen in surprised consternation as he turned to climb up into the truck's rear. Clearing away some dry cattle-dung, he settled himself on a sack of cattle-feed, his back against the cab.

The driver noticed that Susanna was looking at a battered Lee-Enfield rifle lying prominently along the dashboard. "Goes everywhere I go, Girlie. Did you think the Bush War was over? Maybe in the East. Not in Matabeleland. Farmers and miners and missionaries being killed down here again. You didn't know that, hey?"

The truck had roared and shuddered along for some miles before the old man spoke again. He reached across Susanna, offering his right hand to Paul—"Name's McGregor."

"Glad to meet you, sir. Paul Boyd. This is Sue—?"

"Mosonyi. Susanna Mosonyi. And our friend sitting in the back is Stephen Holmes."

"Mosonyi?" said Paul. "What sort of—?"

"It's Hungarian" Susanna explained. "My father went to Canada after the Hungarian Uprising. He had to flee—he was one of the student leaders - they would have executed him. He went to England first and studied for a doctorate in Philosophy. My mother's English. They met in London and emigrated to Canada in the sixties. I was born there."

The old man cleared his throat and spat from the side of his mouth out of his side-window. "Yah, yah, I remember the Hungarian Uprising. 1956. More than twenty-five years ago. Same time as Suez. The bloody Americans were so busy rescuing Nasser from the Israelis, they hardly noticed."

"And the Canadians"—Susanna.

"What about them?"

"The Canadians worked at the United Nations to get the British, French and Israelis out of Egypt. Lester Pearson."

"Never heard of him."

"He was Prime Minister of Canada. But he made his reputation at the UN as a peacekeeper."

"The United bloody Nations, hey. Now *there's* a collection of fart-holes. All they do is stir it. Look what they did here. I don't know what your politics are, Girlie, but in your travels you bloody look around at what's left of this country. Nothing but incompetence and corruption ever since the bloody Limeys gave it to the Munts in 1980. *Independence*, hah! *Dependence*, I call it—hands held out for money from the rest of the world, hey—only way they know how to exist. This country was independent up to 1980, a bloody fine country then—for *everyone*, Black as well as White. More freedom than anywhere else in Africa. By a long bloody shot. Smitty was a damn good man. Ian

Smith—you heard of Ian Smith, I hope? He was our Prime Minister, hey, a damn good man, but the slimy Limeys betrayed him. Harold bloody Wilson" and he cleared his throat. "Now they want to do the same thing to South Africa. Wreck another bloody fine country. So don't you tell *me* about the United Nations, hey, Girlie. And you better pray you don't end up in a hospital here—unless you want to die from all the bloody dirt. Myself, I can think of better ways to gap it, hey. What's your boyfriend think?"

"Well, there's a lot in what you say, Sir"—Paul.

"Where *you* from? You an Aussie? Sound like one."

"Yeah."

"The Aussies know a thing or two, hey. They don't get bamboozled so easy. Have their own problems with Munts, hey."

"But your Government doesn't support Apartheid, Paul" Susanna protested. "You have the same policy as we do in Canada: racial equality."

"'Racial equality'!" jeered McGregor. "'*Racial equality*'—That's a good one, Girlie. You won't find racial bloody equality *anywhere*. All it is, wherever you are in the whole bloody world, is getting yours and bugger the rest, excuse my language. You think you got racial equality in Canada? What about the Red Indians? You wait. No matter how much you give, they always come back for more. Because they're Munts—don't know nothing else. Don't know how to *work* for a bloody living, just how to steal what other people got, what other people worked for. And what about your Mories in Aussie? I bet *they* want more and more and more too, hey!" He snorted in appreciation of his extemporaneous joke.

"Aborigines," Susanna corrected him. "You mean Aborigines. Maoris are in New Zealand."

"Oh now you don't say, Girlie." McGregor turned towards her for a moment with a look of corrosive, consuming hatred—the truck swung off the edge of the tarmac, and flung up dust and stones. "The *Mahries* in New Zealand, and the What-the-bloody-hell-did-you-say-they-are in Australia, hey. Thank you, *thank you very much* for the correction, Girlie, I apologise for my ignorance. But let me tell you, they're all Munts, hey—*all Munts*—whatever else you call them. And they're all out for what they can suck out of the White Man." He gripped the steering-wheel with fury and glared out at the road.

After a moment, Susanna looked unobtrusively at him. Skin dark, leathery, lined; strong-browed profile under the dirty bush-hat; large red nose; beefy hairy arms; butcher's hands with stubby nicotined fingers; clean well-pressed khaki shirt and shorts; grey stockings gartered just below his knees; shiny black shoes.

Paul tried to rescue the situation. "This reminds me of once when I was in the Outback and no cars had come past for days, weeks, so I was getting desperate, *desperate*—no food, no water, hot as hell. Then a farmer gave me a lift, just when I thought I was meat for the dingoes—took me with him to his farm and gave me—he couldn't give me enough—food, beer, bath, bed. He even offered me his daughter!"

The old man coughed an angry laugh. "No, I don't believe it, Sonny— you're having me on. I wasn't born yesterday, hey. No farmer would be stupid enough to be that bloody generous. And don't you get your hopes up—even if I took you to my farm, my daughters are gone long ago—married, with kids, in South Africa."

"How many do you have, sir?"

"Two. And two sons—one son." The old man hesitated for a moment, then continued "My son Abe, he runs the farm now. I'm too old, only good for doing this sort of job, driving the bakkie, delivering vegetables. He does the farm-work."

Supervises the *Munts*, you mean, while *they* do the work, Susanna thought bitterly. She wished she could get at her guide to the trees which were flashing past unidentified, in their hundreds and thousands, as the road lifted out of the Zambezi Valley. And she wondered how Stephen was coping, all on his own, buffeted by the wind, blasted by the sun, crouched uncomfortably against the cab. She considered turning to smile and wave, but decided not to: that might be the last straw for this ugly old man; it would be dreadful if he stopped and threw them out, as she had thought for a frozen moment he was about to do; and it would be all her fault of course. Better just keep quiet from now on.

Paul was telling another hitchhiking yarn. "—and there was a woman, too, a real looker. So I had to sit in the back—like Steve is. The driver, he'd had a bit to drink, they all had, and after a while you could hear them yelling at each other, and the truck was jumping from one side of the road to the other, and the woman was looking back at me, she was terrified, just bloody terrified. The trouble with Abo's, they can't hold their drink."

"Yah, just like all bloody Munts."

"So then I banged on the window. And the second one took out a knife and showed it to me, but I carried on banging till they stopped. In the middle of nowhere. Then the two of them came round for me."

"Yah? So what you do?"

"There was a big piece of wood in the back. I slammed the first one on the head just as he's getting out, and he falls in the dirt, other side from the driver, and when the driver comes I'm ready for him. He didn't have much fight anyway, too drunk."

"Just like a Munt. No balls. So did you tie them up or what?"

"There was no rope—but they were right out. Lying there in the dirt. Then the woman jumps out and runs to me and throws both arms round my neck, kisses me, pulls me over to the bushes near the road." He paused suggestively, and the old man glanced at him admiringly. "And you—?"

"No, not there. In Aussie we don't do it at the side of the road."

"Yah, well here they do, the Munts. Look in any ditch. Why do you think the population's growing so bloody fast in this country?"

"So we took all their money and the truck and left them lying there in the dirt and drove on to the nearest town. And that night we had the honeymoon suite in the hotel."

McGregor was in a good mood now. He dug Susanna in the ribs. "You got quite a boyfriend, Girlie. I bet he's taught you a thing or two, hey."

Susanna looked coldly at Paul. "Yes," she said, "he has."

"Road-block coming up" McGregor warned. "Keep quiet, hey, and let me do all the talking."

Two Army trucks, painted the brown and green of camouflage, were parked opposite each other, facing away from the road, with their back wheels on the tarmac. Two empty petrol-drums blocked the passage between them.

As the bakkie approached, slowing carefully, a soldier with a rifle jumped out of the cab of each truck and stood in front of the petrol-drums; a third soldier, on the back of the right-hand truck, manned a machine-gun whose barrel swung slowly towards them, focussed on the nearing cab of the bakkie.

McGregor drew up in front of the two soldiers and switched off the engine. Susanna sat very still, not looking round. To her surprise, McGregor spoke in an ingratiatingly submissive tone. "*Molo! Wenazonke funa buka lo moto futi?*"

"*Aie.*"

"*Lungile. Ena kona muhle.*"

They came up to the windows, one on each side, and McGregor handed over his identity-card, and his registration and licence documentation. These were examined in silence by the frowning young soldiers, and handed back with a nod.

McGregor—"*Upi lo bafazi?*"

The two soldiers grinned briefly beneath their shadowing caps. *"Aie, aie, hayikona bafazi."*

"Wenazonke yola lo spatsholos?"

"Aie."

The soldier on their side looked into the cab, pointing enquiringly at Susanna and Paul. McGregor replied, and there was another nod. Meanwhile, the other soldier went round to the back and pointed to the knapsacks. Stephen handed them over, one by one, for examination. What are they looking for? he wondered. Weapons, presumably. In the cab, McGregor lit a cigarette, sucked it fiercely, and expelled an acrid smoke that drifted into Susanna's face as she turned to look behind. Stephen smiled and nodded that all was well.

A black Mercedes-Benz was drawing up. One of the soldiers strolled back towards it. McGregor started the engine as the other soldier gestured them forward while he rolled away one of the petrol-drums by its rim. McGregor waved, smiled, revved the bakkie into motion. *"Hamba gahle"* he called out as they passed the soldier.

When they had moved some yards beyond the road-block, Susanna glanced back for a moment, before McGregor cleared his throat warningly. She saw the passengers of the Mercedes-Benz, all Blacks, standing away from its open doors while the driver, on his knees, was opening a suitcase. Both soldiers, and the third, manning the machine-gun, were watching closely.

"What language were you speaking, Sir?" Paul asked. "What did you say to them?"

"Kitchen-kaffir. Can't use Sindebele with these boys and I don't know Shona" McGregor mumbled, round his cigarette. "Just said you were tourists, and asked them how they were getting along without any women. Helps to joke along a bit. But also they remember me—I came past this morning on my way to Vic Falls, and I come this way every week in this bakkie to deliver vegetables to the hotel and buy stuff for the farm. Never had any trouble with them, but some people have—you got to be careful; sometimes they been drinking or fighting or they want money, and then their fingers get itchy on the trigger if you don't give them what they want, or they decide they don't like you, or think you being cheeky. You got to be careful."

Hwange loomed on the right, belching black smoke from the stacks of its great coal mines. The road curved past it and steadily on up the escarpment and out of the great Zambezi valley, and they fell silent in the roar and shudder of the truck.

It was almost five as they approached the turn-off.

"Sure you don't want to come to my farmhouse for the night, Sonny?" McGregor asked Paul. "It's not far from this road—this here is my land already" and he waved expansively at the bush tumbling past on their left. "I got lots of beds—even"—and he winked—"double-beds. You and your two friends can spend the night, I'll put you back on this road early tomorrow morning, you'll be in Bulawayo by lunch-time."

"Thank you very much, Mr McGregor," Susanna said firmly before Paul could reply, "but Stephen and I have only got a short time in Zimbabwe, we must get to Bulawayo tonight."

"Your choice, Girlie, it's your funeral." He leaned forward and spoke to Paul across her. "But don't take no chances, hey. It's getting late, so you take the first lift, don't be choosy. There's no Terrs round here—they call them Dissidents now, but they're just terrorists fighting each other and doing what they did in the Bush War, murdering White babies, raping White women—like at that Mission last week, other side of Bulawayo, near Thabas Induna—murdered all the Whites there, the Missionaries and their wives and kids, even small babies, then they burnt the place down." He cleared his throat and spat out of the window. "But you never know what's really going on in this bloody country now. Can't trust any news: radio, TV, newspapers, it's all bloody Mugabe propaganda. Have to rely on rumours most of the time. But you'll be all right, Girlie," and he nudged Susanna, "this Aussie's a match for fifty Munts, hey. Here we are."

He turned left onto a dirt road and braked immediately in a flurry of dust. Susanna and Paul got out. Stephen threw their knapsacks down to them, and then climbed down himself, stiffly.

Paul put his head through the window. "Thanks for the lift, sir. We really appreciate it." He and McGregor shook hands.

"Look after yourselves, hey" and the bakkie was grinding off noisily.

"How're you feeling, Stephen?" Susanna asked. "It must have been awful in the back, the bumping and noise and wind and glare."

Stephen stretched, groaning. "Well, next time we toss for it, and I win. But it wasn't *all* bad. I communed with Nature! What with the engine-noise and the wind I couldn't hear a word you were saying—just see your mouths working away—like TV with the sound off. Puts human beings into proportion when we don't have our voices. So I just looked at the trees and the countryside, and the thatched huts we passed every now and then—meditated on the meaning of life, but don't ask me what that is. And we'd better get ready to hitch—can't afford to miss any cars now, can we?"

They walked back the few yards to the main road. It was empty—and remained empty for the next quarter-hour, apart from two cars heading in the other direction. Then the Mercedes came purring towards them, and flashed past their three raised thumbs.

There was a wide path opposite them, twisting away from the main road in continuation of the dirt road behind them; but it too was empty in the ruddy late-afternoon sunlight; and striped with heavy shadows.

"I think I'll stand in the middle of the road when the next car comes" Stephen announced. "This is getting serious, it'll soon be dark."

"*I'll* stand there"—Susanna. "You and Paul hide in the grass, with the knapsacks, and I'll have my skirt lifted to my armpits. Except unfortunately I don't have a skirt." She looked down with humorous regret at her white shirt and blue jeans. "Hardly sexier than your khaki bush-jacket and pants, Stephen."

But she was beginning to feel nervous. Apart from anything else—lions, leopards, elephants, snakes?—what would it be like to spend the night near Paul? It was already getting chilly, and they would have to help each other keep warm. Thank goodness Stephen is here! And we can make a fire and sleep round it near a tree, if we have to; perhaps we should start collecting twigs and dead branches, in case.

The silence grew heavier and heavier. "Well," Susanna said briskly, "let's not stand around doing nothing." She went across to her knapsack, rummaged in it, and came back with her *Guide to the Common Trees of the Highveld.*

"Now, gentlemen," she declaimed after a moment, gesturing floridly. "To you, I guess a tree is just a tree. However, let us look more carefully. Consider that tree across the road, with its beautiful white flowers." She was studying the index of the guidebook.

"What the fuck is this sheila on about?" Paul groaned. "Why don't you talk like a real person, Sue, and stop ranting away?"

"Her father's a professor"—Stephen, grinning. "Obviously runs in the blood. Or perhaps that's how he harangues his family. Look, I—" He had been shuffling and stretching for some minutes. "I'm afraid I have to—I'll try to be quick. Don't leave me behind! It's not your lecture I'm fleeing, Susanna," as she glared at him in comical outrage "it's just my gut. Either it was that gammon steak—I didn't think at the time that it tasted quite right, but I never know if meat's off—or it was the bumping of the fiendish vehicle, and its hellish fumes; or all of the above. But if I don't do something about it very soon—"

"Just a mo." Susanna rummaged again in her knapsack.

"He can use dry leaves," Paul laughed "like I've often had to do, in the

Outback. Don't spoil him, Sue—this is Africa!"

She handed Stephen a nearly-finished roll of toilet-paper. "Thanks. I'll be as quick as I can, and I trust you to resist all those lifts from Rolls-Royces while I'm gone." He walked off quickly towards the trees behind them, picking his way around thorn-bushes and clumps of rough pale grass.

"Well, to resume—"

"Oh let's talk about something else, Sue."

"Bored so soon? And I've just identified my first tree—well, second, after baobabs. Know what it is?" She pointed again at the tree across the road. "I looked up 'thorn' in the index because, as you have of course observed, that tree is covered with huge thorns all the way up its trunk as well as on its branches. There was nothing under 'thorn' but I just happened to notice, right opposite, in the other column," she turned to the back of the book, "'white thorn,' and that," paging to the front of the book, "is what it actually is! Number 29, 'Acacia Polyacantha,' also called 'hook thorn' or 'white thorn.' Don't you think 'hook thorn' is the best name? Just look at those thorns! The local people call it *munango* or *umohlo* or *umpumba*. 'It is a large handsome'—yes, look at it—'deciduous tree, up to twenty metres in height. The bark is pale in colour, inclined to be flaky, and may have strongly hooked thorns on woody bosses; these are sometimes on the trunk. The flowers are in white or creamy spikes and appear from October to March'—so it's only just blossomed, that's why the flowers look so fresh and pure—don't you agree they're beautiful, Paul? 'The fruits are light brown, flat pods, only eight to thirteen centimetres long; they mature from April to October.' Do you see them? Among the leaves. 'The roots are used by Africans to treat snake bite.' So it's also a very useful tree, not just beautiful."

Paul pulled the guidebook out of her hands, and threw it into the grass behind her. She stood rigid while he put his arms round her but, before his lips could reach hers, ripped herself away and struck out at him. He parried her blow and they stood facing each other tensely.

"How—dare you do that? Who do you think you are?" She had whitened into fury. "I won't tolerate that sort of behaviour. Do you think I'm some sheila you've picked up somewhere in the Outback?"

"Sue," he said. "Can't you see? I love you. Didn't you hear what I said last night?" He looked almost abashed.

"About having a voice like your mother's? You were drunk. And where do I come in? Don't *my* feelings and *my* opinion matter? You think you can do what you like to me just because you're a man and you say you love me?"

"It wasn't—I just wanted to kiss you. What's so wrong with that? It's natural. And you are—you must know you're a beautiful woman—as soon as I saw you—" He took a step towards her.

She flinched away, but after a moment relaxed and looked again at him. His face was held by the golden late-afternoon sunlight. "Oh, all right, maybe I'm over-reacting. You took me by surprise. We hardly know each other and you sure don't know what *my* feelings are. Let's leave it at that for now."

"No hard feelings?"

"Well— Let's just see how things work out. Why did you play up to that ugly old man?"

"The farmer? Mr McGregor. Ugly? Why did *you* attack him? He was doing us a favour. He didn't have to give us a lift. Least we could do is be polite. Maybe when he was a young man—"

"His mind was ugly, his *soul* was ugly."

A car came by, but from the wrong direction.

"And why do *you* keep those sunglasses on all the time?" she pursued. "Even now, when the sun will soon have set? Do you think it's fun talking to a pair of reflecting glasses? It makes you seem like a—you know, like a machine."

"Because I want to," he muttered. But he took them off, folded them, put them carefully into a pocket.

Yes, his eyes *are* blue, a pale blue, startling against his sunburnt skin. Funny, she had learnt the colour of his eyes only now. He hadn't, of course, worn his sunglasses when they were swimming yesterday morning. Maybe he needs to wear sunglasses to protect his eyes from the glare? She seemed to recall hearing in Canada that people with light blue eyes succumbed quicker than others to snow-blindness. She smiled slightly. Here I go, making excuses for him. And there he is, still looking like a sulky boy caught with his fingers in the cookie-jar. She was about to reach out and take his hand when the silence spoke to her. She jerked round. "Where's Stephen?"

"What do you mean? He went to drop a load."

"But that was ages ago. He should be back by now."

"Yeah"—reluctantly.

"He may be really sick. Oh God—maybe he's been bitten by a snake or— attacked by a leopard—" She ran to the edge of the bush and started shouting. "Stephen! Stephen!"

Silence seeped back, insistent after her sudden clamour. Darkness, too, seeping insidiously into the cooling air.

Susanna turned to Paul, agonised. He came to her, put an arm round her. "It's all right, Sue." Firm, confident, manly. "Don't jump to conclusions. I bet he's fine. We'll find him."

"Let's hurry then. Perhaps he's lost, walked in the wrong direction. It'll be dark soon." And she called again "Stephen! Stephen!"

They made their way through the tall grass towards the trees, Paul in the lead; following the direction Stephen had taken. The trees closed round them.

"We mustn't get lost"—Susanna. "Let's remember our direction so we'll know how to get back to the road in the darkness." She stopped and called again, as loudly as she could, "Stephen! Stephen! Stephen!"

"There's a path here, I think" Paul called back, relief in his voice. "I bet Stephen followed it and lost his sense of direction. Let's hope he stayed on it."

Susanna caught up with him and they started along the path. A few yards ahead of them, the dark figure of a man with a spear stepped out from the trees. Instinctively Susanna turned. A few yards behind them, there was another dark figure. He was, she saw with a shock, carrying their three knapsacks.

III

They came out from the trees into a wide vlei golden in the treacly evening light; and followed the man with the spear, while the one with their knapsacks followed them closely. Immediately they saw Stephen, sitting on a granite boulder, his back to them. To his right stood a third man. Like the other two, this one was shabbily dressed in a shirt and khaki trousers, and barefoot. He was carrying an axe with a crescent-shaped blade.

Susanna, coming up behind Stephen, put her hands on his shoulders. "Oh, thank God you're all right. We were so worried about you. Now we can go back and—"

Stephen's head turned slowly. When she saw the expression on his face, her voice sank into the surrounding silence. She looked past him. There was a fourth man, sitting on a boulder facing Stephen. Across his thighs, an AK-47 automatic rifle—which he now carefully leant against the boulder as he stood up. His decisive movement, and the obvious subservience of the other men as they gazed at him, asserted his leadership.

He spoke to the men, in a vernacular—Shona or Sindebele?—clearly giving orders. The voice was deep and dark. A Paul Robeson voice, Susanna thought; and indeed he had a look of Paul Robeson too: a largeness, not only in stature but in the aura around him. In the twilight, she couldn't discern his features clearly, but he seemed youthful—or in his maturity; certainly not middle-aged. Like the other men, he was barefoot, but wearing what looked like a soldier's fatigues—khaki streaked with dark brown and green—and a forage cap.

The three knapsacks were emptied in front of him.

One of the men jostled Paul against Susanna, and spoke quietly to them both, pointing down at their shoes. Now she noticed that Stephen was barefoot; his shoes lay beside the boulder he was sitting on. "He's telling us to take off our shoes" she told Paul.

"Well, *you* can take off your shoes" he retorted. "I'm not going to. Why the hell should we?" He folded his arms and stared ahead.

Again the man pointed at their shoes. Paul suddenly pushed past him and strode to the leader. "What's going on?" he demanded. "What do you think you're doing? We have to get to Bulawayo tonight. Take us back to the road."

No reply. The man near Paul, after glancing at him, squatted, and began to spread out, on the red sand, the contents of their knapsacks. The leader looked steadily into Paul's eyes. After a moment, Paul spoke again, a note of appeal threading the timbre of his voice. "Look, if you helped Steve, we're grateful. *He's* grateful. But we gotta get going. We're tourists—foreigners, strangers. We're hitchhiking to Bulawayo." He waved his thumb and pointed over his shoulder in the direction of the road, as it occurred to him that perhaps none of these men understood English.

The leader pointed silently at Paul's running shoes. Paul stared back at him, intransigent. Then the leader spoke quietly, brusquely. Paul was seized from behind, his arms pinioned. The man squatting near him turned swiftly, started untying the laces of the running shoes.

"What the—fuckin' bloody hell, what're you—?" Paul struggled and kicked out, striking the man's face. Then was on his back in the sand. His running shoes were removed, and simultaneously his mouth was forced open and filled with a rough fabric. He writhed on the sand.

Stephen called quietly to him. "It's no use fighting, Paul. Obviously they want us to go with them. We've got no choice. So calm down and don't waste your energy."

Susanna had taken off her shoes. One of the men piled all three pairs beside the knapsacks' contents. The leader was scrutinising these, moving some items to make a separate pile. He spoke again. Susanna and Stephen were pushed forward and Paul was dragged to his feet. They stood in a row, Stephen at the centre, as if about to be sentenced.

The leader passed to one of the men three sweaters and two hats: Susanna's wide-brimmed straw hat and a soft khaki hat that Stephen had bought at Victoria Falls. Obeying gestures, Susanna and Stephen put their sweaters and hats on.

Then one of the men pushed back into the knapsacks all the unselected items, while, with a hoe, the other rapidly dug a deep hole in the sand near a rock. As the knapsacks were taken over to it, Susanna spoke—"Oh please—my guide books. Please can I keep them?" She took a step forward impulsively, looking into the leader's impassive face.

It was now very close to nightfall; air chilling, a deepening greyness. Their knapsacks buried, the leader spoke again. One of the men slipped away. Another pulled up some grass and began carefully brushing the sand, to conceal the hole into which the knapsacks had disappeared, and any signs of human presence, especially shoe tracks.

The leader came up to Paul and removed his gag. Shivering, Paul pulled on his sweater. They stood waiting. Then four men appeared silently, three with what looked like rifles, one with a spear; they had been on guard, Susanna realised, some distance away. There were now seven men—eight including their leader. He spoke to them, and they gathered swiftly round the pile of knapsack items, choosing what they wanted in rotation.

Stephen glanced surreptitiously at his watch: it was just after six o'clock. Everything had happened rapidly, controlled firmly by the leader. What now? Stephen reached for Susanna's hand and held it gently. When he saw her face turn to him, a pale oval under her hat, he whispered, "All right? Don't worry. It'll be all right."

She nodded slightly, with a tentative smile he could just make out in the dusk; but her anxiety, like his, could not be hidden by words or gestures. "Dissidents? Terrorists?" she whispered; knowing in her queasy stomach they could be no other.

"I suppose so. We'll try to communicate with their leader when there's a chance. We must do everything they say for now." He leaned towards Paul. "All right?"

"Yeah" the whisper came back.

"Don't antagonise them in any way, Paul. Please. They look dangerous. They might kill us if we cause any trouble. We'll have to find out later what they want with us, when they're more relaxed."

The men had finished choosing from the clothes and whatever else had been put in the pile of belongings. One of them tied the remnants into a cloth and looped the bundle over his shoulder.

The leader spoke again, took up his AK and hitched it over his right shoulder so that it hung aslant his back. Then, followed closely by two of the men, he started along the path that had brought Stephen, Susanna and Paul to him. Gestured forward by one of the remaining men, and picking up the rhythm of the procession, they followed, walking swiftly in single file.

At first the path was smooth and sandy. The sifting coolness between their toes, the rhythmic tickling against their insteps, were strange but not unpleasant sensations—quite sensual, in fact, Susanna decided. Stephen, ahead of her, almost collided with the man ahead of him, who had stopped suddenly. They waited in silence; then found themselves crossing the tarmac of the road, rough and still warm against their feet. This could be the moment to cry out for help. But there was no sign of life, let alone traffic: no lights, no sounds or movement apart from their own swishing and breathing.

Now they were on a path swinging away from the junction of the two roads. As they walked on, Stephen lifted his eyes occasionally to the dark sky with its myriad sprinkling of stars. The moon was coming up over a horizon more sensed than seen—a new moon—*with the old moon in her arms* his mind chuntered automatically; but this scene must be similar to what the ballad was actually describing, that faint ring of light between the moon's horns, with its prescience of the cycle. The low landscape was not utterly obscure. Trees were deeper shadows, grass a paler shadow. Faint, diffused— but still there was light, enfolded, muffled, in the darkness—light that didn't seem to be descending from the stars and moon so much as exuding, a slow miasma, from the earth.

Stephen became aware that his feet were beginning to hurt. Every now and then he stumbled over a stone, and the path was becoming more uneven, less sandy. He wondered how the other two were managing. They walked on steadily. Seconds accumulated into minutes, minutes into hours. Occasionally a guttural cough or shrill cry, a nearby scurry, reminded him that this was Africa; but he felt no fear of being attacked by a predatory animal—he was, after all, held in a purposeful procession, with armed men ahead of him and behind him.

Now the path began to lift and fall, twisting into shallow valleys, or rising to low hills; rougher, stonier. Their pace slowed, but stayed steady. Stephen heard a sudden sharp gasp of pain from Susanna, just behind him; and later her breathing, like his, laboured when they climbed. Soon, he thought, we'll be too tired and our feet too tender, too sore, to continue at this pace.

The man ahead of him slowed; then stopped. The leader spoke softly out of the darkness. Relieved, Stephen half-saw, half-heard the man leave the path, piss, and sit down against a tree. He took Susanna's hand. "How're you feeling?" he whispered as they sat down together on the cold ground.

"My feet are sure hurting" she answered quietly. "I've cut the left one on a sharp stone, I think, or more likely a big thorn. I guess I stepped off the path a few times. I think it's bleeding. Yes, it is."

"Mine are hurting too. And it's hard not to step off the path occasionally in this darkness. Let's see." He lifted her feet onto his lap and rubbed them gently. She winced as his fingers found stickiness on her left instep. He pulled out his handkerchief, dampened it with water from his flask, and gently smoothed and rubbed the wound. "I wish I could see it. Seems quite a deep wound; probably caused by a thorn, as you thought. Let's hope it—" and he completed the sentence mentally—wasn't poisonous.

A movement nearby. "And how about you, Paul?"

"Surviving. Just gonna take a leak—I need it." He was a few yards away. "*My* feet aren't bad; still hardened maybe from walking barefoot in the Outback in the old days. But my legs are getting cut to ribbons by the thornbushes sticking out into the path. Shoulda worn long pants like you two. Wonder where are they taking us?"

"Well, you must have noticed we're going more or less towards the west or south-west"—Stephen. "I'm not sure, but I think we're going roughly parallel with the main road, in the opposite direction from Bulawayo, back towards the Zambezi. What do you think?"

"Yeah. Southwest maybe. But there aren't any towns that way, are there? Just bush and the Game Reserve? Surely we won't go into that? Too dangerous. But"—he leaned close to Stephen and whispered softly—"might give us a chance to escape."

Stephen spoke with quiet insistence. "I think it's too early to think about trying to escape. They'd catch us easily. And we'd make them angry. We can't risk that. Better to stay calm and obedient and try to be friendly and see what happens. Would you like some water? Just have a sip so we keep some for later." He detached his flask and handed it to Susanna.

After sipping from it, she passed it to Paul. "Do you think they might—decide to kill us?" she asked Stephen hesitantly.

"No. They could have done that straight away. In fact, when I finished crapping and must have walked in the wrong direction somehow, and found myself looking into the barrel of a gun, I thought that's exactly what would happen. I thought I was dead. Lucky, come to think of it, that I *had* just crapped—I got the father and mother of all frights! But I can't think what they want with us. A ransom? Perhaps they don't know themselves. I doubt if they were waiting for anyone just appearing by chance as we did. Perhaps they're on the run from the Police and that's why they travel at night, why they wait for darkness."

"Will the Police look for us, do you think?"

"They won't know for a while that we've disappeared, will they? No one's expecting us in Bulawayo. You have friends expecting you in Harare, Susanna—but not for a few days. And we wrote just today, this morning, to our parents. I promised to telephone my mother after a few days, to put her mind at rest—she wasn't keen on my coming to Africa, as you know; but she'll probably think I've forgotten or can't get to a phone. Perhaps no one'll know we've disappeared, Susanna and me, till we don't turn up for the plane in

Harare. What about you, Paul?"

"Here's your flask. Me? No one'll know, no one'll care about *me*. Except—" His voice rose, then sank to a whisper. "I've just remembered, Sue—your tree guide-book, remember? I threw it into the grass just before we went looking for Steve. Did you notice if it was with the stuff they put in piles?"

"No, how could I? It was dark and I was too far away." Her voice trembled, but strengthened as she went on. "Anyway, that's such a long shot. Who is going to find it—if it's still there? Especially if no one's even looking for it. And even if someone does find it, why would it seem important if no one knows we've been—abducted?"

Stephen—"Well, we must just try to keep calm and cool. I think we should try to rest now—that's what the men must be doing. We don't know how far he's going to make us walk—and he may not give us another break."

"How far do you think we've come?" Susanna asked.

"About ten miles, at a guess?" Paul replied. "Say fifteen k's. Can you see the time, Steve?"

"No, too dark."

"Say about three hours, we must've walked for about three hours. Ten miles would be about right."

After a pause, "Why don't we sit close together?" Susanna suggested. "That way we'd keep each other warmer. I'm getting cold."   Paul moved up against her, put his arms round her, while she dropped her head on Stephen's shoulder; and they dozed intermittently and uncomfortably until the men stirred in response to another quiet command from their leader.

The next trek was harder and slower, as the path and terrain continued to roughen. Stephen began to feel he was sleepwalking, though his feet were becoming ever more painful. He began to recite poetry silently to himself: *on the haunting flares we turned our backs / And towards our distant rest began to trudge. / Men marched asleep. Many had lost their boots / But limped on, blood-shod. All went lame; all blind; / Drunk with fatigue—* My dear Wilfred Owen.

A sudden scuffle some way ahead, a harsh cough, a subdued shout of surprise and pain—Stephen was shocked alert. More scuffling, heavy breathing. A loud long grunt. He heard the man ahead of him run forward, so he stopped, irresolute.

Susanna and Paul came up behind him. "What's happened?" she whispered.

"I don't know."

Three of the four men behind them pushed past swiftly, while the fourth remained close behind them. After some time, the men returned, talking quietly among themselves. The leader's voice came calmly out of the darkness, and the procession moved forward.

When they stopped again, after walking for what seemed about the same length of time, Stephen expected to be able to find out, or work out, what had happened; but all was silent, except for the sounds of breathing, and occasional groans, randomly shifting bodies.

"I don't know how much further I can go" Susanna whispered to Stephen. "My feet are so painful now. Especially the left one."

"Yes, mine are too. But it can't be much further. There's not much of the night left. One more three-hour hike, and then it'll be dawn."

"You think we'll stop then?"

"Yes. Yes, I'm sure. We'll have to rest, get some sleep. And food. *They'll* have to stop. Just try to keep on being as brave and strong as you are."

"Now you're patronising the little woman. I'm pretty tough, you know, Stephen. I'll probably outlast *you*." But he could tell she was glad of his sympathy and encouragement.

"Have another sip of water?" He passed her the flask. Paul was already snoring quietly, sprawled against Susanna, his right arm across her stomach.

"Have you thought," Stephen whispered after re-attaching the flask to his belt, "how amazing it is that the leader can find his way so easily in the dark? There must be many paths, surely, perhaps criss-crossing every which-way, in among the trees, and up and down and round about, and yet we seem to go on without any hesitation or uncertainty at all. I doubt if they can see in the dark all that much better than we can. I think he must know the way very well. Don't you?"

Paul moaned, grinding his teeth. "Maybe" she yawned. "Let's try to get some sleep now." She snuggled against Stephen, and soon her breathing settled into the slow emphatic rhythm of sleep.

Stephen, his back increasingly uncomfortable against the rough-barked tree, his bum stiff and itchy, his feet aching, thought: And here I am, somewhere in the wilderness of darkest Africa, abducted by terrorists who might decide to kill me at any moment; I'm frightened, confused; and in a way, in a major way—I confess it, God-if-there-is-a-God—I think I'm happy. Happy? Am I? Yes, happy. *The C Major of this life.* Who?—oh yes, Robert Browning. —He rubbed Susanna's arm very gently and she sighed in her sleep. He looked at the sky with its far brilliance of stars, its pale thin moon—*And nowhere did abide*— Journeying like us. He smiled. He slept.

Stephen was right. There was only one further three-hour trek to be endured. They all three moved stiffly, painfully, now. But the leader did not come back to reprimand them for slowing progress, as Stephen had feared.

Paul occasionally groaned and cursed, as he stubbed a toe, or a sharp thorn dragged across one of his legs. Susanna was definitely limping now, and Stephen could hear her gasping in pain. They crossed a wide river-bed, dry and sandy; then a dirt road; then, later, a railway line. The terrain was ever more rugged. Sometimes they climbed quite high rocky hills. And still they went on.

But now a very faint radiance began to sift into the cool dry air. Or was he imagining it? He hardly dared think that this might be the harbinger of dawn. But— Yes, surely. Trees were slowly pencilling themselves against an opaque grey background; the horizon creeping into definition.

Suddenly he saw himself, a very small boy at nursery school. With breathless care he was putting a cloth over an oily surface in a large pan, and then painstakingly pulling it up, until—there, revealed by unbearable degrees, floating upwards, a brilliant rainbow! She had been a harridan, that teacher, who tweaked your ear if you were slow with an answer; but he owed her this one vivid memory. Oh and another: she had screamed at him for some mis-demeanour and he had wet his pants in fear. Strange to remember that only now, after so many years—it must have sunk down very deep, infusing its humiliation into the crevices of his psyche—with who knows what effect? He trudged on.

Some time later, Susanna touched his shoulder. "Good morning" she whispered. And it *was* morning, even though they were marching west, away from it. The sky, fold upon fold of crinkling pink, rose before them into a vast cerulean dome. The landscape slowly suffusing, pulses of colour; blacks and greys yielding to greens and browns, and they to reds and yellows; and then a seethe of colour glowing ever brighter. Sunrise. Dawn! Marvelling, he almost walked into the man he had been following. The leader must have spoken again. It was time to rest. Rest!

Just ahead of them rose a kopje in the middle of a vlei. When they reached it, Susanna and Stephen sat down on a great granite shelf at its base, under a wide-spreading tree whose roots crawled around them over the smooth rock, like pale serpents. They were facing the rising sun.

Wasn't that a cock crowing in the distance, behind them? Surely not. He strained to hear, and looked enquiringly at Susanna. She sat very still. He saw that her left foot, whose ankle she had lifted to rest on her right knee, was badly swollen; and smudged with blood and dirt; the wound, and the veins near it, purple in pale puffy flesh. He leaned impulsively towards it, then glanced at her lifted profile, sensing both her pain and her pride, and lay back against the tree's smooth grey trunk; looked up into its rich canopy of small spade-shaped leaves, its nests of furred fig-like fruits at the tip of each branch. "What do you think this tree is, Susanna? A wild fig tree? Pity we haven't got your guide book, but that's my inspired guess."

When he leaned forward again to look at her profile, he saw that her lower lip was quivering. He could hardly hear her whisper. "I'll never know now."

With a rush, the sun freed itself from the clinging horizon and sprang upwards. A hard light flashed out, flattening the landscape into rigidity. Warmth fell heavily on them, promising heat.

"Ready for more Rosenberg?" Stephen asked softly. "Listen. '*The darkness crumbles away. / It is the same old druid Time as ever. / Only a living thing leaps my hand, / A queer sardonic rat, / As I pull the parapet's poppy / To stick behind my ear.'*" He caught hold of a stem of dry grass and plucked it, put it into his mouth, squeezing out its residual sweetness between his teeth. "'*It seems you inwardly grin as you pass / Strong eyes, fine limbs, haughty athletes / Less chanced than you for life, / Bonds to the whims of murder'—*"

The leader came round a big boulder further along the base of the kopje, walking purposefully towards them. Watching him, Stephen ended the poem very quietly: "'*Poppies whose roots are in man's veins / Drop, and are ever dropping; / But mine in my ear is safe— / Just a little white with the dust.'—*"

"I am glad to see you have survived," the leader said, as he reached them. He hitched his AK off his back, laid it carefully against a flat rock beside him, then held out his hand. "My name is Joseph." He was wearing a green shirt, not the military one of yesterday.

A sharp pause. Stephen's mouth slightly open. The chewed stem of grass dropped from it. Then he scrambled up and shook the proffered hand.

"You speak English" Susanna said.

"Oh yes, as well as you, maybe better. You are from Canada?"

"Yes."

"I know the accent. I was at Osgoode Hall."

"So you know Toronto."

"Sure. Parts of it too well. And"—turning to Stephen—"you're English."

"Yes."

"And your friend over there?" Paul, sitting cross-legged on a boulder some yards away, was rubbing his feet softly. His thighs and calves were striped unevenly with livid scratches, some oozing blood.

"Paul!" Stephen called.

"He's Australian" Susanna told Joseph.

"So you are a touring Committee of Inquiry from the Commonwealth of Nations?" Joseph smiled tightly. "The *Old* Commonwealth of Nations."

Paul came over. His astonishment was obvious when Joseph greeted him, offered his hand, and addressed them. "I'm sorry you must walk barefoot, but that is the common mode of transportation in the New Commonwealth—where wealth, you observe, is *not* common in countries like this one, impoverished by the Old Commonwealth. Some of my countrymen do travel about in Mercedes automobiles, true; but they are—excrescences. You will soon get used to walking barefoot. You will see. You will be stiff for a few days, and your feet will be swollen and sore long enough to teach you that to try to escape would invite catastrophe." He paused. "But you must be hungry; as I am. A little patience and you will be free to eat and drink and then relax for the rest of the day."

"What are you going to do with us?" Stephen asked.

Joseph smiled again. "You will see. In due time, you will see. Now you must wait here until you are summoned." He picked up his AK and strolled off towards three of his men, who were talking quietly near a stand of mopane trees. After a moment, the men followed him along the vlei, and all four figures disappeared beyond the boulders at the far edge of the kopje.

"Bloody shit!" Paul swore. "I wonder if he heard everything we said last night? Did you see the way he looked at me when he warned us not to try to escape?"

"He was observing us *all* very closely" Stephen commented.

"I bet he was listening—he must have crept up near us in the dark. And he let us think he couldn't speak English! Cunning lying bastard."

"If you're right," Stephen responded, "all the more reason to be very careful. He seems cool, controlled, calculating, and very strong. You can't mess around with a man like that—especially when he's got a gun and you haven't. I think he's the sort who would squash you like a fly if you gave him any trouble."

"Oh, aren't you being just a bit prejudiced?" Susanna objected. "What good evidence did we have for thinking that he couldn't speak English? None at all. Didn't we jump to that conclusion just because he's Zimbabwean, because he's Black? Once we get to know him, we may find he's actually a very kind pleasant generous person. We should at least keep our minds open."

"Well," said Stephen, "I'm certainly ready to give him the benefit of the doubt." He smiled faintly. "It's amusing even to say that, isn't it, when he has us so completely at his mercy. But I must confess I didn't get good vibes from him just now. He seemed so—cold, analytical, so lacking in sympathy. I think he wanted to frighten us even more than we are already frightened. And keep us ignorant. He almost seemed to be enjoying it. I don't think he—cares at all about us as individuals."

Susanna: "Why should he? We're Whites, we're privileged."

"You may be right, Susanna. My first responses have been proven wrong too often. So, as you say, let's try to keep open minds—and that's the best plan, practically, too: our lives may depend on getting to know him, getting his confidence and sympathy."

"Well, he was right about one thing for sure—don't know about you, but I'm fuckin bloody famished." Paul rubbed his stomach theatrically. "How are your feet?"

"Sore," Stephen answered. "But Susanna's are much worse than mine. Look at her left foot. Must be very painful. I hope he gives us a real rest now. I couldn't survive last night's trek again in a hurry. Here, let's finish the water." He handed the flask to Susanna.

"I wonder how far he intends to go?" she worried, before sipping. "Perhaps he'll tell us soon." She passed the flask to Paul.

"Or perhaps he won't tell us at all." Stephen squatted beside her. "Whatever happens, we mustn't get discouraged, we must always work together, help each other. That's our best chance."

"He's calling us" Paul told them, handing the empty flask back to Stephen.

From halfway up the kopje, Joseph was beckoning to them. They scrambled up towards him, Stephen helping Susanna from rock to rock; and, reaching the top, they found they were looking down, on the other side, at a group of thatched huts. Two women were walking away from this kraal, along a path that curved between other kopjes into the distance. The younger one, in a shabby drooping pink dress, had a baby tied to her back in a cloth, its head lolling, and a small child, a boy, holding her left hand. Balanced on her head was a bucket. The other woman, apparently much older, emaciated, wore a tattered blue sweater and long brown skirt; she walked jerkily, stiff-backed, behind the younger one; conversing loudly, volubly and, they could tell even from their distance, complainingly, under the bundle of reeds swaying precariously on her head.

As the two women dwindled into the distance, Joseph gestured again, and they clambered down the far side of the kopje behind him.

There were five huts, three circular and two square, constructed of the usual dagga, a dried mixture of ant-hill mud and cow dung. The walls were dark brown, with grey geometrical designs low on the outside. Closely surrounding the huts were rough wooden poles, to support the low-eaved thatch, which was dark with age; one roof was holed, decayed. Further away was a ragged reed fence with a gaping gate. Inside this enclosure were two big trees, an old grey ant-hill, and what looked to Stephen, as they were hurried past it, like a rack constructed of thin branches—to dry reeds or meat? he wondered.

Joseph pointed to the hut with the decayed roof, and they stooped through its doorway, under the low thatch. Some distance from the other huts, it was clearly used now as a storeroom: seven sheaves of grass were stacked against the wall. The mud floor was cracked and dirty, and the corrugated-iron door sagged open. Susanna and Stephen took off their hats as they reached the shaded far end of the hut.

"Well—what now?" Paul grumbled. "I'll tell you what *I* need—lotta food, a good shit, and a day's sleep, in that order."

They stood waiting as silence flowed round them. Then there was a small scuffle, and, clucking softly, a skinny speckled brown hen appeared, eyeing them beadily from the doorway. A few minutes later, they heard soft footsteps and the hen, which had begun to peck seeds from the floor, flustered off as Joseph appeared.

"I am sorry about the wait"—his deep warm voice. "But arrangements are now complete. Food has been provided. You, Australia, will remain here. Two of my men will bring you food and then they will stay on guard outside. When you need to relieve yourself, they will accompany you. Canada and England will come with me." Sunlight fell across him through the hole in the roof.

"Why—why can't we stay together?" Susanna asked.

"You will all be together again, later."

Stephen: "Can I ask you something?"

Joseph nodded. "Of course."

"What happened last night when we were on our way here? There were sounds, and the man behind us ran past and—"

"I will show you." Carefully he undid the buttons on his shirt and let it slip down his arms to the floor. "You see." Running round the left side of his chest, just below the nipple, was a livid blood-encrusted welt of four raked incisions in his smooth brown skin. After a moment, he stooped and slowly put the shirt back on. As he was doing up the buttons, "But—what was it?" Stephen asked. "What caused that?"

"A leopard. It sprang at me from a tree. It attacked me."

"And—what happened—did you kill it? There was no sound of a shot."

"No." Joseph smiled. "There was no shooting."

"So—?"

"The man behind me had a spear. I took it from him and when the leopard sprang again it sprang onto the spear."

"Dinkum?" Behind his sunglasses, Paul's eyes were alight with admiration. "Quite a story!"

"No. Just the truth. But it has a moral. You see, if you ever attack me, Australia, make sure you do not miss. There would be no second chance. Now give me your sunglasses."

"My—?" Paul looked round at the others. "But—I need them." Pleadingly, "The glare."

Joseph had his right hand held out. "There is no glare here."

"But—outside. I—have to have them."

The hand remained, haloed. After a moment, Paul took off his sunglasses and gave them to Joseph. "But—I'd like them back later. I'll need them."

Joseph put the sunglasses on. He smiled broadly. "And what else do you have? Turn out your pockets—you too, England. Give me that flask." He also took their wallets and passports; Paul's penknife; Stephen's crumpled map of Zimbabwe; but handed back Stephen's bloodied handkerchief.

"And your watch, England." While Stephen was unfastening it, Joseph called out quietly and one of the men appeared behind him.

Joseph pointed at Paul's left hand. "Your ring, Australia."

"But—" Paul's voice quavered. "It was my mother's ring. I—I can't—" But very slowly he wound it off his finger and handed it to Joseph, who now turned to Susanna.

"And what about you, Canada?"

"You took them. My guide books. Everything. I've got nothing to give you. Unless you want my clothes." She spoke dully, but with an edge of triumph.

"Nothing?" Joseph murmured meditatively, scrutinising her. "Nothing." *Nothing will come of nothing—* He turned from her and gave what he had taken from Paul and Stephen to the man, who went.

Then he bowed. "I must thank you all, you wealthy members of the Old Commonwealth. Your uncharacteristic generosity will be appreciated by my impoverished people."

IV

"I wonder why he didn't take *my* glasses?" Stephen mused. "I could do without them if I had to—for a while, anyway."

"Why do you wear them?"

"It's my left eye—nearsighted. The right one has perfect vision—or used to have. When I was a child I had a squint: the left eye used to swing inwards. Even now, if I'm very tired, that happens. But what a boring topic! In the middle of Africa."

He and Susanna were sitting opposite each other on low, roughly-made wooden stools. Between them was a grey tin bowl of gravy, into which they were dunking chunks of meat wrapped in dough. There were also two tin plates piled, respectively, with meat chunks and dough, and two battered enamel mugs of water. "How do you like this food?" he mumbled, chewing.

"Well—let's say that, compared with crocodile, at least it tastes like what it is, beef—from one tough ancient ox."

"I used to be a vegetarian, as a schoolboy—during my religious period. But I gave it up because I felt badly about the extra work it gave my mother—my father can't get enough meat—and because she worried that I wasn't getting adequate sustenance—I was so skinny! I tried to start being a vegetarian again at Oxford, but then I began to agree with my mother—you know what institutional food's like!"

"No, I don't, actually. I almost always ate at home, unlike most of the other kids. My high school was nearby, so it was easy to go home for lunch—in fact I liked to, it gave me a change from being pushed around by teachers. And I guess I'm a bit of a loner. When I did have to eat at school—for orchestra practice mainly, I play the clarinet—it was French fries and Coke, at the cafeteria. Gross!"

"'French fries'? What the civilised world calls 'chips.' *We* have fish-and-chips every Friday night at home. One of those ancient customs that survive, I suppose because hardly anyone remembers its original rationale. Tradition! Neither of my parents is religious—they never made me go to church, even though they had me baptised—and I was even confirmed, but everyone was Church of England anyway. Why are people so inconsistent?" He spoke spasmodically, between chewings and swallowings.

"Do you remember what he said this is called?" Susanna asked. "This white doughy stuff, he said it was made from mealie-meal, which is corn-meal, right? Did he say it was called—*sadza?*"

"That's right. And the whole thing's called something like 'sadza and sechebo'—I suppose it's their equivalent of fish-and-chips. *Sechebo* must mean 'meat,' including this gravy we're dipping the sadza into? I quite like it, even though the meat's so tough."

She smiled. "You're good at cheering me up, Stephen. Thanks. I'm so glad he put us together. But I'm worried about Paul. Why would he be separated from us? Do you think they're—hurting him?"

"We'd hear, surely."

"But the other hut isn't that close." They listened for a few moments to near silence. Only the hen's distant cluckings.

Stephen: "Anyway, it's pointless worrying—we can't do a thing about it, just wait and hope. And Paul can take care of himself."

"I'm not so sure. But I guess he's probably fast asleep, as *we* should be. It's about ten o'clock—mid-morning, wouldn't you say? And we still haven't fin-ished our sadza and sechebo—see, I got it right! Are you nearly finished?"

"Yes. Why?"

"Because—I want to relieve myself."

"Well, you just have to poke your head out of the doorway and one of them will come—that's what he told us to do."

"But I want *you* to come with me, Stephen." She glanced at him, embar-rassed.

"Oh. All right, if you want me to."

"You won't have to—I mean, you'll just *be* there, with your back turned of course."

"Of course." At last, with a flush of shame, he understood. She was the only woman among ten men—as well as being a prisoner, vulnerable, fright-ened. Hard enough for *me* to keep cheerful! "Sorry, Susanna. I wasn't think-ing. I'm a male chauvinist." And there was her wounded swollen purpled foot too. Please don't let it be infected.

"No, you're not, Stephen. You're a hero! *Stephen Hero.* Wasn't that the first version of that awful novel by James Joyce, *Portrait of the Artist as a Young Man?* I remember our English teacher saying that. See, I'm trying to impress you! We read it last year, my last year at high school, and I hated it!

Now *he* was a male chauvinist—James Joyce! Look at how he treated women. And all that selfishness and coldness and arrogance, you almost wished he wouldn't make it to write novels. But of course he already did—Joyce—if that makes any sense! My teacher said I didn't understand it, it was a masterpiece—but I think *he* didn't even *want* to understand it. But I thought about it now only because of your name, and I think you look a bit like what I imagine Stephen Dedalus looked like."

Grinning, "Thank you. Susanna—I think."

They had both finished eating, and now—gratefully, despite its muddy taste—drank their water.

"Well, shall we—?" She nodded her head at the doorway.

"That wasn't so bad, was it? Thanks for coming. I sure *do* feel relieved! A childish joke, I know—sorry. Now to get some sleep!"

"Yes, please." Stephen yawned. "It's getting really hot now, isn't it? Soporific. Thank goodness it's not humid as well."

"Should we take it in turns?"

"Oh, why? We both need all the sleep we can get. Who knows what lies ahead, tonight. We might need—lots of energy—" He glanced involuntarily at Susanna's foot.

"I hope we won't have to walk miles and miles again, Stephen! It was bad enough limping just now into the bush—there and back. Even with you to lean on."

"Don't worry about it. Please don't, Susanna. He can't possibly expect us to do a hike like that again, any of us. He knows we're—effete Whites. And if he does, we'll talk to him, Susanna. And if he still insists, then we'll take turns, Paul and I, to help you. So please—"

"Thanks, Stephen. Stephen Hero." She kissed him lightly on his forehead, pushing aside his lank hair. "There, I've wanted to do that for the longest time."

"What—kiss me? Any time!"

"No—you dummy! Get your hair out of your eyes. Now, how will we sleep?"

They looked round the hut. Red walls—mud and cow dung plastered over a lattice of branches—rough and uneven. The floor, also of dagga, was smooth and swept very clean. Six reed mats, all rather dirty, surrounded the fireplace, at the centre of the hut, in which the remains of a fire still smouldered—source of a pungent, pervasive smell of wood smoke. Two small openings at the top of the wall, right under the eaves, filtered a soft grey light and a small breeze into the hot gloom. "How can anyone *live* here?" Susanna murmured. "These poor, poor people. Look at how little they have."

Poor naked wretches— But are we really looking at evidence of a life of deprivation, of quiet desperation, of mere existence? Stephen asked himself. Or rather of simple sufficiency? Surely it's impossible to tell. Even if I could communicate with the usual occupants of this hut—a subsistence farmer presumably, and his wife and children, perhaps a mother-in-law too, six people, judging by the mats, all of them eating and conversing and sleeping in this one small room which the two of us are filling—in which we can't walk more than five paces and can barely stand upright even at its centre—if we could ask them whether their lives are happy, fulfilled, would the question seem relevant to them? Even meaningful? Our ancestors lived like this. It's the immemorial life of rural people, the peasantry, around the world. So isn't it simplistic, romantic—even impertinent—to pity them? He glanced apologetically towards Susanna. Or am I being callous? Cynical? Ignorant? He scrutinised the hut again. *Is* it even human to live as these people must live—uncultured, unexamined lives? Or is it we in the West, with our clutter of possessions and our so-called sophistication, who have lost our souls and our sanity?

Yes, the furniture is utterly sparse and simple. The two roughly-made stools on which we have been sitting; and a small graceful stool with three curved supports, carved out of a single piece of iron-hard pale wood; and an even smaller dark narrow stool-like object with a curved top— They had debated its purpose earlier until Stephen pronounced it perhaps a head-rest. An un-doored cupboard constructed of mud and wood, against the wall; on its shelves a can of olive oil, and tin bowls and plates. Opposite, against the wall, two shabby women's dresses and a black shiny man's suit, on wire hangers suspended from the uneven wooden poles that, radiating like spokes, support the thatched roof. And that is all.

Susanna was gazing at him. "Well?"

"Well." He yawned. "I think I'm going to sleep on three of those mats and you can have the other three." He pulled the thin grass-mats on top of each other into two adjoining piles.

"What about the head-rest, Stephen? You must have *that*."

"No. Thank you very much, as Carla would say—I wonder what *she's* doing? I wouldn't be able to hold my head straight for a week afterwards! How can *anyone* sleep with a head propped up on that? You'd need to be a contortionist—or a Zimbabwean, I suppose." He yawned again.

She winced as she sat down gingerly on her pile of mats. "Here, let me see that foot again" Stephen ordered. He held it gently, then caressed the wound with his still-damp handkerchief. She winced again, and when he looked up he saw that her eyes were closed in pain. "Susanna—I'm so very sorry—what can I do to make it any better?"

"Nothing. You can't do anything. It's throbbing so much, and feels so hot, like a furnace. I just hope I haven't got blood poisoning or something. I've been trying to put pressure on it when I've been walking and standing, but—it's so—" She bit her lower lip. "Why did this happen to me? I feel so ashamed. I always tried to keep fit and healthy—I played hockey for years—with boys too—had lots of falls on the ice; and I skate; and swim; long walks almost every weekend on the Bruce Trail in summer; and camping; and when I was a child my parents used to take me with them on peace marches. I thought I could walk *any* distance and now—look at me! A crock. And you'll both think it's because I'm a woman."

"Nonsense, Susanna. This could have happened to any one of the three of us. *I* could have trodden on that thorn, or Paul. It's nothing to do with *you,* your strength, your endurance—and certainly nothing to do with being male or female. It was just chance."

"But it happened to *me*. Not to you, or Paul. And I made myself as fit as possible before I came here, too—went jogging every afternoon, even got my hair cut short like this because my Mom said that's better for the tropics. And I don't know what will happen to me now if my foot isn't treated soon. It *must* be poisoned!"

"Well, can I talk to him about it? We'll both talk to him when we see him—or should I call one of the men to ask him to come now?"

"No. Let's try to get some sleep first. We're both exhausted. You never know, it might be much better when I wake up. Then I'd feel a fool if I go on making a fuss."

In fifteen minutes, she was curled asleep on her left side, her head against Stephen's shoulder; breathing fitfully and occasionally moaning softly.

He lay on his back, gazing at the centre of the dark thatch circling above him. —s*till point of the turning world*— And then, as his mind began to drift, he saw again Joseph's brown muscled torso splashed with sunlight, the four blood-etched gashes, the rise and fall of his smooth rounded torso, the swell of his shoulders modulating to the powerful curves of agile arms and hands.

Out of the thick darkness a leopard flashed towards them, claws slashing the air, eyes flaring, fangs agape. —*burning bright*— A spear, honed tip glinting, was lifting steadily upwards. *—in the forests of the night—* But then the leopard's leap slowed to stillness, while Joseph's face swung smilingly into the sunlight, and his smooth brown muscular arms lifted towards Stephen.

Joseph spoke, in his low warm voice. Stephen lifted his head. Smooth brown arms extending to him. "I have brought you some tea. You have been sleeping for over five hours."

Stephen became aware of Susanna stirring beside him. "Five hours" he repeated stupidly. "I feel horrible. My eyes are— And my mouth feels like a cesspool. Thank you," taking one of the proffered enamel mugs.

"The tea will help you wake up. And here is your food." One of the men had come in behind Joseph with a tray of rice and meat. After it had been put down in front of Stephen, Joseph spoke quietly to the man as he left.

Susanna sat up slowly, grimacing. "I had such a vivid dream. I was in bed—at home—it was winter—snow falling outside—but I was warm—and so happy." She spoke quietly, closed her eyes, frowning in concentration. "My mother and father and brothers came into my room, laughing—yes, Christmas— and then I thought 'I've come home, and I'll never go away again.' But of course I will."

Stephen: "Why don't you have your tea, Susanna?"

"Oh." She looked up at Joseph uncertainly, then took the mug he was holding towards her. "Thank you."

While they drank the weak milkless tea in silence, Joseph watched them steadily through Paul's sunglasses. Behind him, the man came in again, put down a white plastic bucket, and went. "Water" said Joseph. "To wash your hands and faces after you have eaten."

Susanna, smiling gratefully at him, "Oh, that's great, thank you so much. You are—being so kind and thoughtful. Thank you."

He bowed. "You are guests in my country, so of course I wish you to be happy. Have you finished your tea?" He held out his hands for their mugs.

"Can you tell us what will be happening next?" Stephen asked quickly. "Will we be staying here tonight? And when can we be with our friend?"

"You will see. I will return in ten minutes." He stooped through the doorway with the two empty mugs.

They could see, beyond his silhouetted figure, that it was late afternoon now: richly golden light. The long shadow of a tree pointed towards their hut across the hard brown soil. Strangely, it seemed brighter in the hut, now that the sunlight was slanting at a low angle, rather than striking straight down in a midday glare.

"He seems pleasanter and friendlier now," whispered Susanna. "Thank goodness."

"Yes—" Stephen was less confident. "I nearly said something about your foot, but then I thought better not, until I could find out how it feels now and what you want me to do."

"I'm glad you didn't. It feels a bit better, not throbbing so much. I think. But I won't know how it really is till I put my weight on it, I guess. If he tells us when he comes back that he wants us to walk a long way tonight, then I guess I will need to talk to him. Perhaps he'd let one of the men take me to a doctor, or a hospital if there's one somewhere near here. I wish he'd tell us what it's all about, what he's going to do, why he— Surely he'll tell us soon? It's horrible not knowing, isn't it? That's almost the worst thing."

They ate for a while in silence. "I don't like this food so much" Susanna commented. "Cold clammy rice, and this sure is a scrawny stringy chicken. Still, it's filling my stomach, I shouldn't complain. What shall we talk about now? What about art?"

"Art?"

"Who's your favourite painter?"

Stephen tried to focus his mind on the topic. "Well—I'm not sure. Turner, Constable."

"Oh, I could have guessed!" she crowed. "How appallingly jingoistic, Stephen. You should be ashamed of yourself!"

"All right—I'm ashamed. Who're yours?"

"The Group of Seven, but you wouldn't know about them. The Impressionists, especially Monet. I've got a book. You know his paintings of that cathedral, at different times, in different light? Awesome! And there's one, I think by Monet, of a young woman walking through a field, and there are poppies in the grass, and a row of trees in the background—poplars, I think, yes I'm sure they're poplars -swaying and shimmering. Do you know it? That picture always makes me feel so cheerful and optimistic. I'd love to see the original and just stand for hours in front of it. What about music?"

"What's all this—an inquisition?" Stephen's uneasiness, apprehension, had increased and he was trying to work out why. And he felt irritable. Perhaps sleeping, or trying to sleep, during the day has disturbed my balance, my sense of reality. Everything feels unreal—*I* feel unreal. "Actually, I prefer the Post-Impressionists—especially Cezanne. And medieval art"—brusquely. "Less emotion, more form."

"Oh." She felt rejection in his tone. "If you'd rather not talk—" but he smiled an apology. "I just thought we might as well fill in the time and talk about things we enjoy. We used to play this at home—a family game: Who's your favourite singer, favourite film star, hockey team, and so on."

"All right." Stephen tried to suppress his disquiet. "So then— What's your favourite—name?"

"Boy's or girl's?"

"Boy's."

"Daniel. I love that name. If I ever have a son, that's what I want to call him."

"And Joseph? Paul?"

"No and no."

"Do you know what 'Paul' means? I once looked it up—before my confirmation, which was in our local St Paul's Church. 'Small,' if I remember correctly. Small Paul. We'd better not tell him!"

"My turn. What's you favourite girls' name?"

"Susanna."

"Oh Stephen, that's despicable! Surely not! It sure isn't *mine*."

"Well—Emily—for Emily Bronte, of course. But I do like Susanna. Do you know the story in the Bible? In the Apocrypha, I think. A cheerful story, for once. I remembered it as soon as you told me your name. A powerful man lusts after her and threatens to accuse her of being a prostitute if she doesn't give in to him, but she doesn't, and then—what happens? Oh, I remember, she's rescued by Daniel, I think that's right—he of the Lion's Den—no wonder that's your favourite name! He exposes the wicked man and everything ends happily—except perhaps for Daniel, because Susanna was already married, I think. So he has to be content to be just a hero."

"No, I didn't know that! What a coincidence—about Daniel, I mean. And it *is* a good story—except that it's sexist, a male point of view—didn't you notice? Poor little Susanna has to be rescued by the local hunk! Not my type of Susanna. Anyway, want to know why my parents called me Susanna? Nothing at all Biblical. Ever heard of a song called 'Suzanne'?"

"Oh—yes, as a matter of fact I have. By Leonard Cohen, the Canadian poet and singer?"

"Right. But how did you know?"

"A Canadian in my college, a Rhodes Scholar—he and I used to have coffee quite often in each other's rooms, late at night—talk about essays we were writing and so on. And he would play his Canadian tapes. 'Suzanne' always made him deliciously homesick, he said. So he played it over and over—I think I know the words by heart!"

"My parents play it too, occasionally. It was one of their all-time favourites—they said that when I was born it was one of the big hits. And they were immigrants, newly arrived in Canada, so I guess it had a special meaning for them—new life in a new world, something like that."

"And did you know that Shakespeare's daughter was called Susanna? And the heroine of Mozart's *Marriage of Figaro*? File under 'Trivial Facts.'"

"Wow! No—but maybe my Mom or Dad did. Talking of music, who are your favourite classical composers? I'll start this time. Schubert. I learned the piano for a while, before I started on the clarinet, and I loved playing one of the 'Impromptus.' And I love the *Unfinished Symphony*. Mozart's *Clarinet Quintet*, of course—I played the slow movement at a school concert. And my Dad used to take me to orchestral concerts regularly—by the TSO, Toronto Symphony Orchestra. Debussy, *La Mer*. Mahler, *The Song of the Earth*, awesome! Richard Strauss, *Four Last Songs*. Those are some of my favourites."

"Stop, stop! I give up. What a romantic you are, oozing emotion at every pore. I should have guessed!"

"And you?"

"Bach of course! Among modern composers, Vaughan Williams, if you'll excuse the jingoism, but he *is* a great composer. And Stravinsky. If I had to choose one modern piece of music as my desert-island listen-forever favourite, it would be *The Rite of Spring*."

"I don't know that. Should I? Actually, my Dad is crazy about classical music, he's got records and tape recordings of almost anything you can think of, and he doesn't mind me listening to them. It's just my pop music he hates—I have to listen to that in my bedroom through earphones. I don't know if he's got that one you mentioned."

"*The Rite of Spring*—it's by Stravinsky."

"Oh yes, I've heard of *him*. Lots of discords and so on."

"Yes, and violent clashing unpredictable rhythms. Harsh, wild. Destructive and yet also creative. Almost unbearably exciting! There was a riot when it was first performed, it's ballet music—Nijinsky danced in it, I think. There are lots of recordings."

"Then I'll get one as soon as I get home, if Daddy doesn't have one, but I'm sure he has it if it's such an important piece of music?"

Stephen gazed at her, mock-serious. "All I can say is that anyone who doesn't know and adore *The Rite of Spring* is either geriatric or married with twenty-nine children. Or a male chauvinist."

"Oh, now you're being silly again, Stephen. You're not allowed to make fun of me. I thought we were being serious—having a serious conversation."

"Have you finished your sadza and sechebo? Shall we summon our waiter and ask for the bill? Joseph's late—he said ten minutes."

"Then we'll tip our waiter and ask him to show us the way to the washroom? Yes."

When they returned to the hut, Susanna limping painfully, they found Joseph waiting, seated on the pale stool, his back to the doorway. They passed him, one on either side, and turned to face him uncertainly. The man who had accompanied them came in behind them, and gathered up the bowls and plates. As he left, Joseph spoke curtly to him.

Then: "Sit down, please." They sat on the other two stools, which had been placed side by side opposite his. "I hope you are both feeling well-fed, vigorous, and happy?"

They nodded. His gaze, behind the dark reflecting glasses, seemed to be directed at Susanna now; but he spoke to Stephen, in a quiet confidential tone. "Is Canada your girlfriend?"

"Well—"

"Yes," Susanna said sharply.

"I asked *you*, England, not her."

"Yes."

"Show me."

"Show you?"

"Yes, show me. Kiss her."

After an uncomfortable pause, Stephen turned to Susanna, kissed her lightly on the cheek.

"That does not prove anything. Kiss her on the lips."

"I— Why —? What's this for?" Stephen protested. "I don't see—I thought you said you would be telling us now what's going to happen. You said you—"

"Kiss her on the lips."

Susanna was looking at Joseph, clearly uneasy. Joseph leaned forward and spoke softly to Stephen. "Does she want you to fuck her?"

Stephen flinched. He swallowed. "Why don't you ask *her*?"

Joseph leaned forward again and struck him hard, back-handed, across the cheek. Stephen's glasses flew off and struck the wall. "I asked *you*, England."

"I—don't know."

The second blow was even harder. Stephen nearly fell off his stool. His head jerked back; tears came to his eyes; his cheek reddened. Susanna whispered urgently "Yes—say yes, Stephen."

"Does she want you to fuck her?"

"Yes."

"Then why don't you fuck her?"

"But— I don't— I can't just—"

"Stand up." Stephen obeyed, shakily. "Take off your clothes." When he had only his underpants left, he looked pleadingly at Joseph; then took those off too. "Now take off *her* clothes."

Susanna stood up slowly, looking fixedly at Joseph. Clumsily Stephen unbuttoned her white shirt. When he drew it over her head, she put her arms round him and nuzzled him on each cheek, whispering very softly into each ear "Do everything he says, Stephen." Her eyes, when he looked shamefacedly at her, pleaded intently.

He unzipped her jeans and pulled them down, and then pulled down her panties. They stood protectively near each other. Stephen looked at Joseph. He felt his cheek twitching and knew he was close to tears. Susanna was trembling.

"Make her kneel down with her forehead on the head-rest" Joseph said calmly. "You are in Africa now. You fuck like Africa." His face was taut, implacable, below the sunglasses.

"No— Oh please— " Stephen begged. But Susanna was doing what Joseph had ordered. After a moment, Stephen knelt down too. He reached forward round her waist to her breasts, and fondled them, gently, anxiously, willing his penis to stiffen. But still he could not achieve even a partial erection. At last he turned to Joseph, and said tremblingly "I can't—I can't—"

"Get up then." Stephen stood in confused shame, hands over his flaccid penis. "Get dressed."

Susanna remained motionless, her forehead on the head-rest, back curved, buttocks pushed upwards. Then she sat sideways on the mats, an arm across her upper legs, looking steadily at Joseph.

When Stephen was clothed, Joseph spoke again. "Does she want *me* to fuck her?"

Stephen's legs trembled. Tears came to his eyes. He felt feverish. "No—I—"

But Susanna suddenly spoke, in a dull harsh voice. "Oh, say Yes, Stephen, can't you see what he's doing. He's just playing with us. Can't you see he's going to do with us what he wants to do. We're his prisoners, he can do what he likes with us."

"Does she want *me* to fuck her?"

Stephen swallowed. "No. All right - I suppose - "

"Very well. I think you are right. England expects every man to do his duty, but you have failed to do your duty. So, because she wants me to fuck her, I *will* fuck her. I will do what you wish. I will take your place. Now take my clothes off."

Weeping in spasmodic gulps, Stephen undid the buttons of the green shirt, baring Joseph's wounded torso; pulled the shirt over the outstretched arms; undid belt and zip and drew the trousers down.

"Tell her to lie down on her back. Because I am taking your place, England, I will fuck her the White way."

Susanna lay back on the mats, her arms at her sides; closed her eyes and turned her face away from them.

Joseph moved to Susanna, pushed her legs apart with his feet, knelt, and stooped quickly to enter her. She whimpered, then yelped before her upper teeth clamped on her lower lip. Now he lay flat on her, reached upwards and clasped her shoulders.

—beast with two backs— Stephen turned away; his sight mercifully blurred; trying not to hear, not to know, not to be there.

Joseph stood up and dressed in silence. Without looking at Stephen, or Susanna, he stooped through the doorway.

Stephen gathered up Susanna's clothes, and sat down on the floor beside her. Wordlessly he lifted her head and cradled it in his lap, rubbing her forehead gently. His mother had always consoled him like that when he had been a child.

After a while, the heaving gasps and moans of her weeping diminished and her breathing evened, became gradually regular. Her head turned, her eyes opened and gazed blankly upwards, past Stephen's face, tears brimming slowly and running down her cheeks. "There, there; there, there," he intoned softly—again as his mother had done when, as a very small boy, he had fallen and hurt himself.

Ten minutes passed. Then a long quivering sigh, and she raised her right hand. Stephen took it, and put it to his lips. Kissing her knuckles gently, he continued to intone "There, there; there, there." He looked down her body, and saw that blood and semen had run down her inner thighs and onto the mats. With his left hand, he pulled the dirty handkerchief out of his pocket, leaned over her, and very gently mopped her skin. She sat up, still staring blankly ahead. He gathered up her shirt and, as if automatically, she lifted her arms for him to slip it over her head. Then he drew her panties, and afterwards her jeans, up over her calves; and she lifted her buttocks so he could pull them up to her waist.

At last she spoke. "Could I have some water, please?"

He looked round. The plastic bucket still stood near the doorway. He brought it over, and scooped up water in his right hand for her to suck. "Enough?" She nodded. Then he sat again beside her and laved her cheeks, washing away her tears; laved her eyes and forehead.

Then: "Susanna—" he gasped, and found himself weeping. Great gulping shudders burst up from his lungs. "I'm so sorry. I feel so ashamed. I should have—shouted out—I should have tried to stop him, I should have attacked him—"

She put her right arm round his neck and drew his head down to her breast. Then, in silence, ran her hands through his hair. "You couldn't have stopped him" she whispered. "It wasn't your fault, Stephen. It wasn't your fault. You couldn't have stopped him. If you'd tried, you might have made it worse. He might have killed you—might have killed both of us. You couldn't have stopped him."

And she went on speaking, quietly and firmly now; out of a painful ease of determination. "I want to say something. You saw it all, everything that happened. You saw how—in spite of myself— He knew what to do. It was—so painful but also— You mustn't think, please, that I wanted it, or could ever have wanted it—sex—like that. He forced himself onto me—into me. And my body responded. But that made it all the more—hateful and humiliating. It was so—humiliating and destructive and— He could even force me to give him—the physical responses of my body. Do you understand? I feel so—"

"Yes, Susanna, I think so." He wanted to say he admired her courage, her strength of mind and will, her honesty, her capacity for wisdom and charity, her maturity; but he found himself coughing instead; his throat dry, constricted, aching.

A shadow lengthened through the doorway, and Joseph followed it into the hut. He stood looking down at them. "Now that she is a woman, I have decided to release Canada, on condition that she does not give any information." Stephen looked up at him. Susanna turned her face away. "I have decided she needs treatment for her poisoned foot. In hospital."

"Oh"—Stephen, hoarsely. "When will we—?"

"Not you, England. Only Canada. I will take her to the main road so she can get a lift to Bulawayo."

"But—she can hardly walk. If I come, I can support her—as far as the road—"

"No. The road is not far. Only a few kilometres."

"Only a few—! But she's been limping very badly. She's in a lot of pain. How can she—?"

"She must be ready to leave with me in five minutes. I thought you wanted her to be treated in a hospital, to be cured, England?"

Susanna spoke, dully. "How did you know that?" He turned away without replying. "You've been listening to us, haven't you? Were you just outside the doorway? Yes, you were, listening to every word we said. What a strong honourable man you are. To spy on your prisoners! To abuse them, hurt them—"

"Susanna, don't," Stephen begged. "It won't help."

"No," she whispered. "Nothing will help."

"Five minutes" and Joseph went.

After a moment, Stephen: "But you do need a doctor and treatment in a hospital, Susanna, for that foot, as soon as possible." He put his mouth against her ear and breathed hurriedly "And this might be the only chance for all of us. You'll be able to tell the Police. And they'll be able to rescue us, Paul and me. Otherwise—what chance is there for any of us?' Then he spoke aloud again— "So I think you should accept his offer, Susanna. We should be grateful that he's—that he's concerned about you."

Susanna gazed into Stephen's face, her expression inscrutable. Then, slowly: "I guess I have no choice."

He helped her to stand up. She was in obvious pain; winced and gasped as she put weight on her swollen bloodied foot, then limped towards the wall and came back holding her wide-brimmed straw hat. "I won't need this" smiling very faintly. "Give it to Paul, with my love. Tell him I think it'll suit him."

"*I'll* have it, Susanna. He wouldn't wear it. But I'd like to have it, if you don't mind. I'll give him *my* hat instead."

"Well—I'm ready. Are the five minutes up? At least I don't have to think about luggage, do I? Travelling light. We'd better say goodbye, he'll be back here any minute."

Stephen put his arms round her, kissed her on both cheeks. "Don't forget us—once you're there, in hospital, being looked after by doctors and nurses—" His voice faded. He gulped.

"I won't forget you, Stephen." She brushed the hair off his forehead and kissed him quickly and lightly on the lips. "My friend. Stephen Hero." They stood looking intently at each other.

A shadow at the doorway. Susanna smiled at Stephen, turned carefully, lowered her head, and limped into the dwindling sunlight.

They were slowly approaching the kopje from which, that morning, she had first seen the kraal. Joseph, the AK suspended below his arm, was some four paces behind her.

"Follow the path. It takes you round the kopje."

She tried to ignore the pain between her legs, the pain of her foot. A few kilometres is a long way, she told herself bleakly, especially when you are limping slowly over rough ground. I must pace myself, force the damaged foot to do its job. And I must try to ignore the other pain.

She remembered a camping trip when she had been a girl of twelve. They were near the tip of the Bruce Peninsula, her father, her brothers and herself, hiking in single file. To their left, ragged ranks of cedars advanced to the escarpment, almost to its edge, where the Trail clung. To their right, the cold green restless waters of Georgian Bay slapped against rocks far below. She had swum in those waters the previous night, on her own, glorying in the chilly purity of their clasp, glorying in her strength as she pushed her body out into the blackness, against the surge of the swell. Suddenly she was stretched on her back—fortunately where three stunted trees stood between her and the precipice, and where the jagged rocks of the path were buried in dead leaves and moss. Her father pulled her to her feet, "All right, Sue?" Her brothers, called back by him, teased her scornfully: "Bad luck, Susie. Poor old Susie." What can you expect of a *girl?* "We warned you it would be tough"— they knew how to rile her. "Lucky we're not far from Tobermory," her father sympathised. "We can take turns carrying you." "No, you won't!" she spat back. "I'll walk there myself." And she did, gritting her teeth so they wouldn't hear her gasps of pain, as she limped ahead of them. It took many weeks for her ankle to heal.

They were rounding the kopje now, passing into its shadow. The granite shelf on which she and Stephen had sat watching the dawn approached, then receded, on her left. The vlei stretched ahead, spread smoothly in the sunlight. Her shadow swayed ahead of her. The dry grass here was high. Its graceful tresses were golden waves.

Then they were walking through a grove of mopane trees. "Turn left"

Joseph said. After she had obeyed, Susanna glanced back at him, puzzled. They had left the path; she was limping over stubble. Now they emerged from the shadowing trees. The stubble was black: there must have been a bush-fire here some months ago. "This is a shortcut to the road" he said. More trees, some of them burnt or partly burnt. She concentrated on finding as direct a route as possible among them. Then she was limping out into another wide vlei; this one in shadow, its once-graceful grass also stricken into black stubble.

Evening was near; the orange light ebbing swiftly; but of course he will know his way in the darkness. The vlei flowed up towards, then between, two kopjes.

As she limped, Susanna began to hum to herself. It was a moment before she recognised what she was humming. Then she grimaced thinly: the last of the *Four Last Songs*. Stephen would have been amused. And that was another way they could have filled the time enjoyably—if they'd had more time together: identifying each other's hummed favourite melodies. But could you hum *The Rite of Spring*?

The butt of Joseph's AK slammed into her skull. She fell forward, twisting on her damaged foot. Her widened grey eyes gazed up at him. He smashed the AK down on them, again and again, until her face was an oozing pulp of flesh and tissue and bone and blood.

In the thick red light of sunset, he hurriedly scraped her grave near a boulder, using first the butt of the AK and then his hands; dragged there her still-twitching corpse; covered it with sand and rocks.

V

Stephen picked up his glasses. One of the lenses—the left one, unfortunately—had fallen out. It shone up at him, undamaged. The metal frame was twisted and a tiny screw had been torn loose, so the lens wouldn't stay in. Well, he thought, after struggling clumsily, for a few minutes, to repair the frame, I'll just have to do without, for a day or two. Then I can get them fixed in Bulawayo before we go on to Harare—won't be time to visit Zimbabwe Ruins now, and anyway Susanna probably won't be up to it. He folded the damaged frame carefully and put it, together with the lens, into the right-hand pocket of his trousers. And how will I locate her, anyway?—but at least we will be on the same flight to Gatwick from Harare.

He went to the doorway and sat down cross-legged under the eaves. The sky was afire. Massed cumulus clouds, purple, pink, grey, yellow; above them a ceiling of cirrus modulating from yellow through orange to dull red, against deepening blue. The sun invisible behind this evanescent flare of beauty. Susanna will be looking at it, glorying in it as I am, he thought—seeing it more clearly than I can. Then he remembered that she would be walking in the opposite direction: east, towards the dawn. Well, that's the right direction, symbolically speaking! How long will it take them to reach the road? Three or four hours at least. However fast Joseph may want to walk, Susanna won't be able to, so they'll have to stop every now and then for her to rest her foot. Then the return journey will take Joseph how long, around two hours? —longer probably, if he waits to be sure that she gets a lift to the nearest hospital. Say, seven hours in all? That will be most of the night.

But his mind dragged him back to its grindingly painful debate. Why had he just stayed silent? Why hadn't he shouted out? Attacked Joseph, seized him, pulled him off? But no, I could never behave violently, could I? That just isn't in me: I'm a pacifist, aren't I, more or less? Evasive, Stephen; evasive. Not just *violent* action—*any* action, *hey*, that might threaten to disturb your little universe? *In a minute there is time / For decisions and revisions which a minute will reverse—* But you made no decision at all, did you? Face yourself,

61

Stephen. You were divided, complicitous. You were a coward. Neither Stephen Hero nor Stephen Martyr: just plain Stephen Coward. However hopelessly, you could have done *something*, Stephen. But *I am not Prince Hamlet, nor was meant to be—* Bitterly, *I should have been a pair of ragged claws / Scuttling across the floors of silent seas— My* Love Song too, Susanna, not only Prufrock's. I betrayed you. He gazed unseeing at the red sea of the sunset, the final blood-stained linger of light. In the silence— Then he was weeping again, in a desolation of shame. I betrayed you. Silence. But not despair— please, not despair.

A man stood in front of him, in the gathering darkness, beckoning. Caught in dread, Stephen waited for him to speak; but the man merely continued to beckon. As the silence stretched out, Stephen became aware that it was not silence after all: there was a chatter of birds, a faint scuttering in the thatch above him. *Let us go then, you and I, / When the evening is spread out against the sky—* "I'm coming" he said, scrambling stiffly to his feet. "Just let me get my things."

In the grey hut he stumbled against the stool on which Joseph had sat, then felt his way to where he had dropped the hats and sweater. He put the sweater on, wincing as his arm brushed against his sore and swollen cheek. Then he stood for a moment looking round the darkling hut, with intensity. Remember this place. This place of my shame.

It was twilight as he followed the man across the enclosure towards the dilapidated hut where they had first been incarcerated. Clouds, deep purple and grey, were falling into blackness. The man pushed open the hut's decrepit squeaking corrugated-iron door. Stephen went in. The door was shut behind him.

"That you, Steve?" Paul's voice came querulously from the far side of the hut, and Stephen could just make out that he was lying on the floor with his head on one of the sheaves of straw.

"Thank God you're all right, Paul." Mingled with his relief Stephen felt a surge of affection that surprised him. "We were worried about you. We wondered why they kept you separate, what they might be doing to you."

"Nothing. Did a lotta sleeping. Eating. He came here a few times, Mister fuckin Boss Man. And I went out a few times with Tweedledum and Tweedledee to pee or shit. That's all. Boring as hell, and no one to talk to. You can see a bit out of the hole in the roof if you stand on tiptoe, but not much, and anyway bugger-all was happening, so I didn't spend much time doing that.

Just lying here or sleeping, passing the time. Where's Sue? She still in the hut he took you to? What you think he's fuckin playing at?"

"He's taken her to the main road so she can get a lift to the nearest hospital. Her foot's really bad now—purple, swollen, still bleeding, seemed to be infected." He knew as he said this that he would never tell Paul about the rape.

"But that must be bloody miles."

"A few kilometres, he said."

"And he took her himself? On his own?"

"Yes. But I don't know if he was on his own—I didn't see. He decided she needed medical attention. Thank goodness. She really does, Paul. Badly. She was in a lot of pain. But"—he moved closer to Paul and lowered his voice to a whisper—"she's also going to tell the Police about us. And where we are."

"No need to whisper. They don't understand English. Except for fuckin' Boss Man, Joseph. And anyway, I've only seen two of them around. One has a spear, the other has an axe. An axe, you better believe it! With a curved blade."

"We can't be sure they don't understand some English" Stephen said quietly, then squatted down close to Paul. "We'd better be careful anyway. Joseph was listening to Susanna and me."

"Dinkum? How do you know?"

"From something he said."

"When he came here, I think it was just to check on me. All he did was stand in the doorway and look. Wouldn't reply to my questions, didn't say a bloody thing. Just stood there." Bitterly, "Wearing *my* sunglasses. I said he was creepy, didn't I? But he's a fuckin' sight worse than creepy."

"Keep your voice down."

"I wouldn't bloody mind if he was listening to every fuckin' word I say! *My* sunglasses. *My* ring on his fuckin' finger. *My* shirt on his fuckin' bloody back."

"Your shirt? I didn't know that."

"Well, it is. Musta been with the stuff they stole from our knapsacks, remember? He musta got it from one of the others after the leopard messed up his terrorist uniform. Three things of mine he's fuckin' wearing. Pisses me off. I want them back, and tomorrow I'll *get* them back, I'll *demand* them back. You'll see."

"He's wearing *my* watch, you know. Not everything's yours." Stephen paused. "Better be careful of him, Paul, truly. We don't want to—upset him. Especially before the Police find us. He might—"

"Fuckin' bloody bastard. *Bastard.*" Paul's voice was shaking, hoarse with fury. "Who the fuckin' bloody fuckin hell does he think he is? Just because he's fuckin' Black, he thinks he's got the right to fuck-up anyone with a White skin, because of what *he* suffered—or *thinks* he's suffered. That's what I think it is, all this—some sorta weird revenge. I think he's round the fuckin' bend—totally fucked-up." Paul cleared his throat, coughed. "And you know why he can do it? You know what's the only difference between us?" Stephen was silent. "His fuckin' bloody AK. His weapon. If I get my hands on that—then you'll see who's boss—fuckin' bloody fuckin' coward!" breathing harshly, voice trembling.

"I wouldn't try it, Paul. Really, I wouldn't. It's much too dangerous. He's—you can see he's not the sort you can meddle with. He could kill us, easily." I say it over and over. But does he hear me?

"Yeah? Think so? Just because we're frightened of him—correction, because *you're* frightened of him—doesn't mean he's some sort of fuckin' Superman. *I'm* not some sort of *Queer*."

They were both silent. Stephen felt his way to the sheaves of straw, and dragged one over close to Paul. Harsh dry smell.

"Steve."

"Yes?"

"You think we'll be marching tonight?"

"Not while Joseph is away. And he can't be back until after midnight, can he? Perhaps we won't be marching at all tonight. Who knows?"

"So let's make a run for it. Soon as there's an opportunity. They won't be able to see to catch us at night. By morning we'll be so far away that they'll never catch us, and anyway, surely we gotta meet someone eventually, even in the bush, and then we ask the way to the nearest Police-station, or one of those Army check-points."

"Well—I don't think it'd work, Paul—even if we survived a night in the bush on our own. Remember the leopard. We'd be defenceless, no weapon, and we don't know anything about the bush."

"*You* don't. I've been in the Outback, I know all about the bush, thicker bush than this—how to survive in it like the Abo's do."

"But we might not even get that far. I don't think we'd get very far at all before they caught us. They know this country. *We* don't. We'd probably walk in circles."

"Right. I get your point, Steve. You'd rather stick around with fuckin' King Kong."

"That's not fair, Paul. You know I—" Stephen's voice faded into silence. What's the use?

After a pause, "You think it's on the level, Steve? He's really taking Sue to the main road?"

"Yes, he suggested it *himself*—before we could even ask."

"Yeah, but— He's taking a risk, isn't he? Being seen by the Police or Army. When he's keeping us fuckin' bloody prisoners all day—in case anyone sees us, why else? And does he strike you as the type who takes risks to help anyone—especially a White?"

"Well, he may just possibly be a bit more humane than—"

"Godzilla? A bit more humane than Godzilla?"

"Actually I think it's mostly because he saw that she couldn't walk any further with us, and needs medical treatment—she would be a liability—whereas, now she's gone, there's *less* risk."

"Yeah. Well—just wondering."

Stephen swallowed. "Anyway, we'll know he did what he said he'd do, and she's all right, if he comes back after seven hours or so." He lay back, his head on the prickly straw.

"You like her, Steve, don't you?"

"Yes."

"I could see that. Why I kept out of your way. Give you a chance to get to know her."

"Oh. When?"

"But you *really* like her? Want to fuck her?"

Stephen was silent. They lay side by side, looking up into the darkness. Stephen turned his head away from Paul, but his cheek was too tender to endure prickles of the straw, so, restlessly, he turned back.

"Steve. You a Queer?"

"I'm homosexual - yes."

"Yeah, I had that feeling. Funny how you can tell. So why—"

"Why am I interested in Susanna? Why do I love her?"

"*Love?* You can't love a woman if you don't want to fuck her."

"Why not? How do you know? Anyway, I do. Take it or leave it. But it's love as a friend, of course, not as a—sexual lover. Because I admire her—because I like and admire—all that she is. Intelligent, generous, sweet-natured. Of course I know she's not perfect—who is? Thank goodness she's not. She's impulsive, she's—headstrong, has her own opinions and feelings and doesn't hide them. She's a feminist. I enjoy talking to her, I enjoy just being with her. Anyone would. Whatever she does and whatever I do, I hope I can stay friends with her. She's a truly beautiful person—in mind and spirit, not just body. She's also so—optimistic and innocent—" and he found himself weeping silently as he heard again the two bodies beating against each other. Biting his lower lip to hold back any sound, he gazed into the thickening darkness. Then, after a few moments, "There. You asked."

"Yeah, right. I like her too. So at least we agree on that, Steve. But I want her body. Not just her mind and spirit. *Real* love. She's a *woman*, you know— a sheila. And women want sex. Or perhaps you don't know that and never will. Not just 'a beautiful person,' Steve."

Again silence. Stephen twisted against the rough cracked floor, trying to find a comfortable position for his stiff back and shoulders. Better to lie on some of the sheaves of straw? No, much too prickly. And that sharp smell right in one's nostrils. He wished he felt sleepy.

Paul spoke again. "Funny, here we are, lying next to each other, and you're a Queer. Never thought that would happen to me. Once in London, after the pub closed, the one I was working in, we were walking along, me and some Aussie mates who came for a booze-up— And we see this couple holding hands. Men. *Technically* men. Holding hands and gazing into each other's eyes!" He paused.

Stephen didn't respond.

"So what do you think happened?"

"I don't know"—heavily. He knew.

"We beat them up. Nobody around, so we dragged them round the corner into a dark alley and beat them up. Just to teach them not to do that in public. Anyone can do it in private, that's what I think, that's their business— but not in public. See, we didn't beat them up because they were Queers, but because they were doing it in public. Anyway, didn't take long. Fuckin' cowards. Blubbed like a pair of sheilas before we even touched them, 'Please, don't hurt us, we aren't harming anyone,' all that shit. We let one of them get away after a bit, then we worked on the other one, paying special attention to his cock and balls. Not for long, in case a bobby heard and came round the corner. Funny thing was the other one. Didn't know whether to stay with his girlfriend, so he just ran backwards and forwards whimpering."

Stephen lay nauseous with—anger? pain? despair? What's the use? What can one say? But one must. He spoke slowly, quietly, tonelessly. "Sometimes I think that all the pain and violence, all the wars and repression, all the racism, hatred, prejudice—sometimes I think it all comes from sex. Not sex itself, because the animals have it and they don't murder their own kind. And it's basically good, it creates new life, and it's enjoyable of course. But sex as we human beings mess it up. Why do we mess it up? Because of human nature, what religious thinkers call Original Sin? But it also has something to do with the act itself. We make a mess because our minds take the wrong message from what our bodies do. Does that make any sense? We see the heterosexual act as—as a paradigm of violence. Phallus penetrating vagina; Punch pounding Judy. Somehow we think that what we do in sex is by definition violent, *must* be violent. But must it? Surely not. Your sort of sex, Paul, *must* it be violent?"

"Too deep for me, Steve. All that philosophy shit is for the birds. But you're right what you just said. Fucking's violent, gotta be."

"I didn't say that. I was asking *you* if it *had* to be violent. You're straight - heterosexual, and you've done it, haven't you?"

"Yeah. I've fucked quite a few times, yeah, and I bloody hope there'll be quite a few more times. Even Carla, I fucked her that afternoon when you and Sue were at the Falls. She didn't want it, we didn't have any condoms, so she wanted to wait, but I—"

"You were violent with her, you hurt her? Why? You go on insisting that sex must be violent, Paul. But *why* must it be violent?"

"Because you're the fucker. Man's the fucker, woman's the cunt, she's a hole, you got to get your cock in her and—pound away, like you said. It's Nature. It's the way we are, the way we have to be—it's why you're *here*, why you were born, why you're even alive. You can't change that."

"But why do we have to think of it that way? Isn't that where it all goes wrong? Even D.H. Lawrence got it wrong. Why can't we see the heterosexual act as—not the man penetrating, attacking, firing his gun, his AK, into the woman. *She's* part of it too, the woman. She's active, not passive. If you both want sex, then she's active too, isn't she?—she's thrusting, she's into you, she's taking the seed into her body, actively, not just passively receiving it. It's mutual, it's a—it's a good act, a mutually beneficial act, it's life-giving, it's enjoyable, it's *creative*. Not just—what you say it is. It doesn't have to be rape, always rape. Intrinsically rape. Does it? Can you see what I mean?"

"Yeah, now you're talking positions. The woman on top. But that doesn't change anything. The man's cock is still in the woman's cunt. That's what I said. Man's the fucker. You can't change that. How can you?"

Stephen lay back against the straw. "Yes. How can you change that?" He felt close to weeping; close to despair again. "And if that's true, Paul, then—perhaps human nature could never change, or be changed, now, after all these centuries of thinking and acting like that. Perhaps violence is endemic, per-haps it's *always* there in *all* of us, perhaps it *defines* us as human beings, even if we don't want to know that. Especially defines men because, as you say, we're the fuckers—but affects women too because"—bitterly—"they're the ones we fuck."

"Not you. Steve. You don't fuck women, you only fuck men. If you fuck at all."

"So there will always be wars, won't there? Always. Look at how we use that word. 'Fuck off, fuck-up.' Violence, destruction—not love, not the joy of new life. A swear-word. A curse, never a blessing."

"Tell you what, Steve. I could use a good fuck right now. Gotta real hard-on. I bet you're sorry you can't see it. If you had a cunt instead of a cock, I'd be inside you, pounding away right now. Filling the world with violence." He laughed lazily, contemptuously. "But don't get your hopes up—or your cock. I won't touch you. I'd rather toss myself off than touch you. In fact, that's just what I'm doing."

Stephen looked into the blackness. Even *talking* about sex brings more violence. Anger. Just when he seemed to be more sympathetic, even seemed willing to talk to me, to tolerate me in spite of his hostility to homosexuals. 'Queers'! I should have kept quiet. What's the use. What can one say, how can one communicate across such a chasm? And for a moment he saw again the seethe of water plunging over the Devil's Cataract, pouring down and down, swallowed into the heart of darkness. But Paul seems quite edgy, now, too. I suppose the strain is getting to both of us. Thank God Susanna's out of that. And he imagined her limping painfully through the darkness towards the road, and tried to project waves of love and encouragement towards her.

But— Why am I homosexual? His mind suddenly filled yet again with that question, and he tried, yet again, reluctantly, to answer it. Perhaps it has something to do with what I later realised was my first knowledge of the heterosexual act. Waking up in the darkness—how old was I? Five? Moans from the creaking bed on the other side of the room, his parents' bed. He was in their room, the old cot, because he'd sleep-walked and woken up scream-ing. He screamed again. The bedside light flashed on, and he saw that his father had been beating his mother. Her face, crushed under his father's, looking at him sideways, urgent and affectionate, as she called across the room "It's all right, darling, it's all right, go to sleep, it's all right." Then dark-ness again and he heard his father whisper complainingly to his mother and his mother answer quietly, submissively. No further sound until his father's snores filled the room. Was that the deciding moment - why otherwise do I remember it so vividly? The moment that made me irrevocably homosexual? Or was it somehow pre-ordained? Genetic? Was I *born* homosexual? But I am not ashamed of who and what I am. I am *not* ashamed. I am not an aber-ration. I am a member of a proud and creative community which has suffered for far too long, and is still suffering, but is now insisting on, and beginning to achieve, social acceptance. I am not ashamed. I will neither apologise nor explain.

As he lay, stiff as a corpse coffined in the blackness, he became aware of Paul's heavy regular breathing.

And he must have fallen asleep too. Because he suddenly jumped awake. Joseph was talking. His deep warm voice. The darkness as thick as ever. What time was it? As his mind lurched to reality, he needed to know. "—five minutes," Joseph was saying. "You have five minutes. Move now. *Move.*"

Paul groaned, "What the fuckin' hell—"

Stephen sat up. "Where are we going? What time is it?"

"No questions. Get up."

Stephen felt for the two hats; jammed Susanna's on his head and pushed his own into Paul's hands. "Put it on. We'll need hats later, in the sun."

Soon they were walking again; over the hard cold soil of the kraal, then out beyond the enclosure and to the left—west again, he thought, or southwest. Perhaps, Stephen decided, it was slightly lighter than it had been the previous night? With his blurred sight, he could just pick out the moving figure ahead of him—Paul. He turned his head—yes, and a moving figure behind him.

The cool air was sweeping him back from sleep into this other world, of night shadows, of shifting darker and lighter shadows. Soon—but how soon?—these shadows would be eaten by the sun. He must try and work out what time they had left the kraal. He looked up at the glittering canopy that moved, swaying slightly, with them. The moon, still a pale new moon but marginally bigger and brighter. If I knew anything about the position of the moon in the night sky, then maybe I'd be able to work out the time exactly. But surely its being low towards the west means that dawn can't be far off—in which case we must have left the kraal at say three in the morning? That would be about ten hours after Susanna and Joseph left? His heart lifted.

The path was meandering and uneven as before, but he had the impression it was generally moving downwards. Then it was *definitely* moving downwards, quite precipitously. They were crossing a river-bed in a wide valley—larger, he thought, than the one they had crossed the previous night; sand and stones, but are those pools of water glimmering in the distance? It's beginning to seem like a dream, or a nightmare, an imagined landscape. Unreal. Then they were climbing out of the valley, sometimes having to scramble over large rocks. The path seemed to level for a while, then mount sharply again. Stephen's breathing laboured, and he began to feel faint. He fixed his eyes on the shifting paler shadows ahead - Paul's legs. Which stopped suddenly.

Thank God. A rest. He pissed, away from the path, and sat down, feeling gingerly for a smooth place on a low boulder. He was beginning to feel very hungry and thirsty. Surely there's a hint of light now, in the sky and around them? His feet were so tender, and he rubbed them; but not as sore as he had expected. There was an abrupt movement close to him, and Paul's soft whisper was warm against his ear. "I'm off. You coming?"

He found Paul's ear. "Don't. They'll catch you. It'll soon be light."

"We've been going further and further away from the main road. This is our last chance. Are you coming?"

"No."

"Right. Try to keep them thinking I'm still with you. Make a bit more noise, talk, that sort of thing. If they find out, distract them if you can. Tell them I went south."

"I'll do my best. Good luck."

And Paul was gone. Stephen listened anxiously for the sound of a stone rolling, a twig snapping; but stillness lengthened. He scuffled about occasionally, whispered. When he heard movement ahead along the path—the trek resuming—he walked forward quickly, but not too quickly, until he was close to the figure ahead.

They went on, across rugged country. Light was flowing into the sky now. Large shapes—kopjes—loomed to left and right. As they descended into a small densely-treed valley, there was an abrupt stir of movement, and across his blurred gaze flashed a dark brown shape. A buck, disturbed at its morning drink. He began to feel thirsty himself. He heard a splash, a small thump. As he walked on, his tension grew. Perhaps they would stop soon. But Paul's chance of escape probably depended on how long they kept walking now. The first trek had been shorter than each of the three during the previous night—say two hours? This one would be even shorter. Dawn was close now.

The man ahead turned to the right, off the path. But that's Joseph, surely, Stephen noticed with surprise. That slanting stripe must be the AK slung against his back. He was striking off towards a very big ragged kopje. Where was the man who had been just ahead of Paul? Could he have realised that Paul wasn't behind him and set off in pursuit? Stephen glanced behind him. Yes, the other one was still there—the one with the axe—which Stephen could see quite clearly, held across the man's stomach.

They climbed the kopje. Light was flooding in rapidly now. Stephen's throat constricted and he raised his left hand involuntarily to his swollen cheek. Soon Joseph would stop, turn, and look at them—at him. He clambered clumsily, carefully, over several boulders, and found himself in a sandy amphitheatre, surrounded by yet more boulders. In a great sweep of granite ahead, there was a cave. From its blackness Joseph emerged.

"When?" Stephen's arms, twisted behind him, were searingly painful. Oh God, they'll snap off if he twists them again. "*When?*"

He struggled to speak. "I—don't know. I don't know—what the time was. A while ago." His arms were twisted; and twisted again. He screamed, and fell into a vertigo of blackness.

He was moaning, lurching up towards consciousness. Opened his eyes into a slam of sunlight, threw his head to the right, then, recoiling with a whimper, to the left. Susanna's hat, fallen from his head, was there beside him, on the sand.

Later, he looked up again, through narrowed eyes, cautiously. Sun heavy on his face. He was lying on his back, in the amphitheatre. His arms, across his stomach, ached excruciatingly. When he tried to move them, he found they were tied together just above the wrists with a piece of flex. A headache was stabbing him behind his right eye. At least I didn't give them any indication of when Paul went. A pity, though, that Joseph hadn't first asked about direction; so I could have misled them. But even then, they would surely have assumed that Paul would make for the road?

He could smell wood smoke, and hear a gentle crackling. By twisting his neck, he could just see that a fire had been made at the mouth of the cave. A pencil of smoke rose above it. Suddenly a shadow fell on Stephen's face, and Joseph was looking down at him through the sunglasses. "He will not escape. They will find him—if a leopard does not find him first. It was stupid. You were stupid."

He moved away and Stephen blinked as the sun crashed down on him. "Can I have some water?" he croaked.

"Soon. And some meat. I will cook it."

Stephen heard hacking sounds, and later smelled meat roasting. They must have killed a buck. Then Joseph was untying his arms. He sat up, trying to rub their soreness away. His hair was full of sand.

"Come and eat, England. I did not ask if you like your meat rare. It is all rare in this restaurant."

Stephen followed him unsteadily to the lip of the cave, and leaned back against one of the big boulders nearby. The fire had been smothered. Joseph handed him a tin mug of brown water and he drank greedily, trying to ignore its dead muddy taste and smell. "Thanks." He handed the empty mug back.

"Now the main course." With a pen-knife Joseph was cutting chunks of bloody meat off a haunch that had been seething on a slab of stone balanced just above the fire. He handed one of the tin plates to Stephen, then squatted.

Stephen found a rock to sit on, a few feet away. They ate in silence. Rather a Neanderthal-like meal, he thought wryly, as he tore the venison apart and stuffed it into his mouth; but I'm hungry enough to eat an elephant. "Could I have some more?" he asked, and Joseph sawed off another chunk. He was almost—companionable, Stephen thought; despite what they had recently done to each other. A few moments ago he had even made what sounded like a joke; though perhaps it hadn't been intended as one. But this is the man, Stephen's brain warned, who raped Susanna. Again Stephen heard the beating bodies. But also this is the man who took Susanna to the main road for medical help— And the man with the AK—who can slaughter me at any moment if he chooses to—and slaughter Paul too, if they recapture him. I must try to forget about the rape—at least while I'm in his power. I must try to reach him, communicate with him, keep him calm. But I want to know, I need to know—

"Was she all right?" he asked. "Susanna. Did she get a lift?"

Joseph chewed and swallowed. "Yes. A car came quickly. It was going to Bulawayo."

"Did you speak to the driver?"—incredulity in Stephen's voice.

"No, of course not. I was in the shadows nearby, I could hear."

"Oh. But that's *wonderful*" and Stephen's heart flew upwards. "So she'll be in hospital now, under a doctor's care— Oh, that's *great.* I'm so glad." He reached out spontaneously towards Joseph; then gasped, drew his arm slowly back, smiling apologetically. "Thank you. For taking Susanna to the road. Thank you."

"And you show your gratitude by letting your friend run away to be eaten by the wild animals of Africa? Well, it does not matter. They will find him. They are good trackers. He did not run away before we stopped for the rest— they said he was with us at that time—he cannot have gone very far."

"Did she— Was Susanna able to walk all the way? Did you have to carry her? Did she send any message?"

"She said she would see you soon. She was limping, you know that. But she was brave, she would not let me carry her. She sent you her love, and said you should trust me."

"Yes. Thank you." Stephen hesitated. Then "Why did you—?"—*the beast with two backs—* But no— Perhaps he couldn't control himself, hadn't had sex with a woman for some time, so— No, Stephen, don't try to find excuses for him, you mustn't. Just put it aside for now.

Joseph was staring at him, chewing slowly. He took off the sunglasses, and held them loosely in his right hand. I've never looked carefully at his face, Stephen thought. Of course he's had those sunglasses on most of the time, and that somehow makes it hard to define the rest of a face. As if the main piece of a jigsaw is missing. But look at his face now, while you have the opportunity. Under the green-and-brown forage cap, a wide brow; delicate ears; strong nose, almost aquiline, with the wide nostrils of his race; a scar on the left cheek; lips full, but often clamped in a hard line; jaw square, not receding slightly like mine but not, he smiled faintly, advancing pugnaciously like Paul's. And the colour of his skin: how to put into words that subtle sheen, that gloriously rich dark colour—

"So what do you think? Am I good-looking?" His deep resonant voice. His deep-set brown eyes, beneath raised eyebrows, fixed now on Stephen's eyes. Then he put the sunglasses on again.

Stephen flushed. "Sorry. I didn't mean to stare. But it's a pity your eyes are invisible."

"A touch of mystery?" The lips curved, then opened wide in a slow warm smile. "That is just the intended effect, surely? Why Hollywood actors wear sunglasses? Anonymity—and mystery."

"Where are you from? Are you from around here?"

Joseph chewed thoughtfully for a moment; then "Yes."

"I thought you seemed to know this area well."

"Yes. I was born here. In the hut where you spent yesterday." *—the beast with two backs—*

"Did you—?" Stephen hurried on. "I mean, do you have any relatives here?"

"Yes. My mother and my sister. And my sons." The two women we saw leaving, with two children, as we watched from the kopje yesterday?

"Which tribe do you belong to?"

"The people in this part are called Kalanga—they speak Shona. And the Ndebele are to the east and all the way to the other side of Bulawayo—their language is called Sindebele. The Shona were here when the Ndebele arrived from the south in the middle of the nineteenth century and conquered them. The Ndebele were warriors separated from their people, the Zulus. Then the Europeans, the Whites, came a few years later. But you know about that, and the Bush War, the war of liberation, the war that made our country free and independent three years ago, 1980. Some call that war the *Chimurenga*, the second Chimurenga—it is a Shona word meaning 'rebellion.' My father is Ndebele; my mother is Kalanga. So I speak both languages. And I have relatives in both tribes."

"Did you grow up here?"

Joseph paused a moment. "Of course."

"And then?"

"Questions, questions. I think you should tell me the story of your life too, England. Then I went to Europe and North America, then I came back here." He smiled sardonically. "Maybe we will exchange biographical details later. Have you had enough to eat?"

Stephen nodded, and handed Joseph his plate. "But I'd like some more water. And then I need to—defecate."

"Help yourself. Over there. The water I mean." Stephen followed the gesture, saw his flask standing in the shadow of a rock.

"Where does the water come from?"

"Can I trust you not to run away?"

"Yes."

"Then you can go on your own. To—defecate."

"Thank you. By the way, where are the other men? There were seven with you to start with, but only two with us last night."

"I sent them to their homes. I do not need them now. It was time for them to go. Any other questions?" sarcastically.

"Yes." Stephen was trying to widen the channel of communication. "Who killed the buck, and when and how?"

"One of the men. When we disturbed the buck, it was drinking at the river—there is some water, a little. Mpofu, the one with the spear, he was bringing the buck here when I saw Australia was gone. I was angry with you also because I had to wait until he came with the buck before I could send them after Australia. How are your arms?"

Stephen shrugged. "Well—I won't be able to write any letters for a few days. Even if I could see well enough without my glasses."

Joseph smiled slightly. "Now we wait."

"And one final question."

"No."

"Please tell me what your plans are. What's this all about? What are you doing with us? Now that you've let Susanna go—I'm very grateful of course for what you did, your kindness and generosity—but now you've done that, what's the point of keeping me—and Paul?"

"No. Not now. Later we will discuss all these matters, not now. You will see. When Australia is back with us. Then we will hold a Commonwealth Conference about this important topic, and others. We will be two Whites and one Black debating—the right proportion to come to rational and ethical conclusions, do you agree?" He smiled again, tightly. "Now we wait."

VI

It was only when Stephen was pulling up his trousers that he thought about his glasses. Cautiously he pushed his right hand into his pocket, and was dismayed to find shards of glass. As he pulled the pocket inside-out, the frame, badly mangled, fell from it. But the loose left lens, which had been at the bottom of the pocket, had survived. He dropped the glass fragments and frame in the sand and powdery clumps of dry grass at his feet; and put the lens back in his pocket.

He wandered across the sandy amphitheatre to a group of boulders, enjoying the breeze and warm sunlight on his face. His right cheek was still painful when he ate or spoke, but less swollen; he rubbed it softly, finding that the itchy stubble of his beard was roughening. Flies and mopane bees were becoming an irritant, seeking out his eyes, settling to bite neck and arms—he was glad his legs were protected from their attack. Oh, but my feet ache, ache!—he tried to watch for small stones, so he could avoid painful contact.

Reaching the encircling boulders, he closed his right eye and leaned close to one of them. How well can I see? Not well, and I'm squinting again. The rough grey surface, blackened in places, was mottled with smooth streaks or crinkled rosettes of lichen—red, ochre, yellow. He ran the fingertips of his right hand over the rounded granite surface, trying to register the variations of its texture. The thick grey sand on which he was standing must, he decided, have been shed by the matrix of this boulder, to accumulate, millennium by millennium, particle by chipped particle, as the kopje gradually evolved. First a fiery thrusting of stone from the rocking earth; then a long cooling; then weathering; then the first plants—ferns?—lichens?—scrabbling for purchase. A slow sifting of time around me; aeons, aeons; within which humanity's tenure on earth is a flicker of froth on a surging wave.

He stood upright, feeling dizzy as he always did when the vastness of the universe impinged on his imagination. In that context, my situation is trivial, meaningless. What does it matter whether I survive or not, whether Joseph kills me or not? The whole human enterprise—none of us, none of us, matter, except to our own inflated infinitesimal selves—as we fall in flakes off the grey granite-face and sink into limitless grey sand. Or is that my uncertainty and fear talking?

He looked around. Try to notice everything you can, every detail, however wavering; concentrate the mind, distract it. I see stone and sand. Clumps of dry grass. Some flat-topped trees, mostly bare of foliage. A few small trees and some bushes. Surprisingly prolific, this vegetation, perched on granite. But then the whole of our myriad mad world has grown from stone, is rooted in stone, has very gradually transmuted stone into unending diversity and complexity. Think of it, the ineffable miracle of it. The endless unfurling of creation, wave after wave of fecundity, beating against— What? *For* what? Banal thoughts, Stephen, we've all thought them. Concentrate on the actual, the real; the now; what you can see and touch; what *is*.

He looked down the shaded western side of the kopje. A blurred slash of scarlet leaped at his gaze. He clambered laboriously down to it, between two boulders, over rocks, using his still-aching arms only when steadying himself against trees as his feet slithered away from him on the piles of dead leaves gathered in every space between boulders. Faint acrid scent of those leaves; and a dry aromatic smell that he was beginning to identify as distinctive of this kopje-and-vlei landscape.

The scarlet slash was a flower—no, a great corona of blossom, a constellation of tiny spiky brilliant stars rearing out of the sand like a fan. The most exotic bloom I have ever seen, or could have imagined! And no plant sustaining it? Just, when you stoop and look under it, a low green spike, a dwarf's fist thrust through the sand, proffering this impossible bouquet. *You must sit down, says Love, and taste my meat—* Stephen squatted, bent over the flower in wonder. If only Susanna could see this! My clamour of silent voices. I hear them. *Ripeness is all—beast with two backs—Corrode, consume—*

Stop. No more. *That way madness lies—* My head aches. So, stop. He turned to climb slowly back up the kopje towards the amphitheatre. Sensing that he was being watched, he swung his head from side to side. For a moment, saw no movement. Then a small brown animal slipped behind a rock. And a bird, no less peculiar than the crimson flower, but comic in its lolloping flight, suddenly alighted high in one of the bare trees ahead of him. As he approached, its huge red clown's beak lifted and tilted; a theatrically angry pale eye glared down at him; and then, with a whoop, it suddenly threw its shiny long-tailed body into the air.

The tree, he saw now as he clambered up towards it, was not after all quite bare: a few withered papery leaves clung to its branches, and so did a multitude of small seed-pods. As Stephen reached up for one of the pods—light brown, four delicate wings spreading out from the sheen of its seed-case to sketch a tiny paper ball—he sensed rather than saw a sluggish movement—Looked down and—

His heart clutched, spasmed— His right foot was descending upon, almost touching, a blurred scaly barrel, grey and brown— A row of black-and-orange V-shaped markings along a slow undulation, a sluggish heaving— And the snake's heart-shaped head rose delicately—enquiringly—

Stephen's foot, leg, his whole body, rose with the snake's head— And he was rolling down over rough stone— And then floundering in a soft mass of dead leaves.

He lay there for some moments, heart and head pounding, left arm crushed painfully below him. Then, very cautiously, he got up. The snake, when at last he crept painfully towards the tree, was gone. A puff-adder, must have been a puff-adder. He recalled the warning he'd read in a book before leaving England, and shuddered. One of the commonest and one of the most dangerous of Zimbabwe's many varieties of poisonous snakes: if you were bitten by a puff-adder, you died quickly, in excruciating pain as its venom bloated your body. Is that why it's called a puff-adder?—because it puffs up its victim, rather than itself? But one of the most horrific deaths one can imagine. He let out a long breath, and realised that he had been breathing only shallowly, as shallowly as possible.

He climbed on towards the crown of the kopje, stiffly and with extreme caution, his headache pulsing so harshly now that he had to stop and lean against a tree or boulder every few steps until the jagged pain diminished.

At last he came into the brisk sunlight, and into the amphitheatre. Heat was gathering. The sun was already high. He drank the last of the water from his flask.

Joseph was sitting on one of the big boulders, in the same position as when Stephen had first seen him. Quite still. Gazing straight ahead from under his military cap, the AK cradled on his lap. But his eyes were invisible again, behind Paul's sunglasses.

Have they caught Paul? Are they still pursuing him? Or is he talking rapidly, vehemently, to a Policeman or Army officer, turning to point across the brown bush, the vast veld, to this kopje and its unmoving sentinel? He walked to the foot of Joseph's boulder. "Can you see anything?"

"No. Nothing. They will come soon. You will see." Is he worried? I hope so. The longer his men are away, surely the more likely it is that Paul has escaped; also the more likely that he or they will have been seen by, or reported, to the Army or Police.

"What's the time?" That tic of his old life, that pointless need to note minuscule specks in the endless pour. *I wasted Time and now doth Time—*

The sunglasses were directed at him. "Would you like to have your watch back, England? You can have it if you want it." Joseph raised his left wrist and held it out; the watch glittered. Stephen hesitated, looked down at his feet, at the pocked sand. And would he give it to me anyway? "No. I don't need it."

After a moment, he looked up. Joseph's gaze was lifted again to the distance. A taut faint jangle of cicada shrieks was beginning to impose itself on the morning. "But I do need more water. Can I go down and get some? Then I'd like to sleep. I've got a bad headache."

"Yes."

Stephen made his way carefully down the eastern side of the kopje, and then through the high dry grass. The river was not far away, in the wide valley that spread east from the kopje, all of it under Joseph's surveillance.

He came to a series of small dark sour-smelling pools separated by sand and rock. Surely fed by a spring? Are there springs in Zimbabwe? Otherwise, where does this stream come from, picking its lethargic way through a parched wilderness? Yet this isn't truly a wilderness, Stephen corrected himself, remembering the crimson flower on the kopje; you could even imagine it to be a Garden of Eden. He looked around him, squinting into the brightness. Golden waves of grass spread in every direction—*orient and immortal wheat, which never should be reaped, nor was ever sown—* Water-boatmen skittered away as he squatted to push his flask down into the dark water, down until water could glug slowly into it. The glassy water at the surface is fresher, purer, than the water in the slimy murky depths—or is that ignorance and wishful thinking?— After all, isn't that why we are, again and again, snared by evil? The delusively attractive surface. Joseph. Joseph. Handsome face, smooth voice, beautiful body— Why evil can take us by the throat. *Too deep for me, Steve— Man's the fucker—*

He stood up; turned back towards the kopje. *—banality of evil—* The phrase is itself banal, threadbare. Like violence, evil's in *all* of us— But is that really so? Is it? And anyway that's another cliche, Stephen. Is this a debate where all arguments are platitudes? Are all moral debates inconclusive at best? And what is evil? And why am I chuntering along like this? I'm confused. I can't think clearly. Observe, just observe, Stephen! Evil will look after itself.

He raised his eyes again as he walked. Now I am walking as I walked a few hours ago in the rosy dawn. Eyesight flickering, he looked to right, then left. Stones, big stones, small stones, half-buried stones, heaped randomly. *Burnt black by strange decay, Their sinister faces lie, The lid over each eye. The grass and coloured clay More motion have than they, Joined to the great sunk silences—* Yes, Susanna, Rosenberg again! Who else could have perceived that, could have written that? *—great sunk silences—* Now *that* is truth: those words, those images. Everything dead as far as any eyes can see, in the nightmare trenches, in the horror of No Man's Land; yet life persists, the dead still live? All right, not the truth. His voice, his truth, and now my truth. The glory of literature. Final answers impossible, even if we persist long enough, penetrate deep enough? *Man's the fucker—*

He lifted his eyes to the kopje and, even with the blur in his eyesight, and the hard glitter of the sun, thought he could discern the black shape of Joseph crowning its summit.

He woke to voices. The cave was dark. It must be afternoon.

He stumbled out into the amphitheatre. One of the two men, face streaked with sweat, was kneeling forward on the sand, body slouched in exhaustion; was talking softly, with small gesticulations; his curved-bladed axe cast on the sand beside him. Whenever he paused, Joseph spoke abruptly, asking what must have been harsh questions, for each one provoked another explanatory and seemingly apologetic flow. Stephen's spirits rose. He must have escaped. He's done it! Paul's done it. Thank God-if-there's-a-God. Maybe the Police are on their way here—he's leading them here, he's pointing ahead towards this kopje—

When Joseph turned his head away from the man dismissively, Stephen asked, as casually as he could, "What's happened?"

"Come and see." Joseph stood up on his boulder and offered his hand to Stephen. They looked down on the vlei, partly in the kopje's shadow now. The second man was walking towards them, into the shadow, spear held across his chest. A few paces ahead of him, arms tied together above the wrists, stumbling painfully—Paul.

Stephen clambered quickly down off the boulder, gasping when he wrenched an arm in his haste. He went to the edge of the amphitheatre, and on down the kopje.

As Paul came up towards him, struggling from stone to stone, Stephen could see how battered he was. Legs and feet bleeding from a myriad cuts and scratches; filthy; his shorts and red T-shirt torn, the latter so badly that his chest, also severely scratched, was partly exposed; his fair hair dirtied, tangled and matted; the hat, Stephen's hat, gone; a gash across his sweat-and-dust-streaked forehead running almost to his right eye; and both eyes bloodshot.

Stephen reached out a hand to help him up. "Here, Paul—"

"Fuck you, Steve"—whispered without looking at him. "Go to fuckin' bloody hell. Outta my way." Reaching the amphitheatre, he fell to the sand, his chest heaving. After a few moments, rolled over, propped himself against a rock, and stared defiantly up at Joseph, who was still sitting calmly on his boulder.

"You have caused us much trouble"—Joseph, quietly. "And you are lucky to be still alive."

"Fuck you. Fuck the whole bloody lotta you." Paul coughed, spat into the sand. "So why don't you fuckin' kill me? Why don't you fuckin' kill me right now?"

"Later." —Contemptuously. "We will talk later. You need food and water." Joseph came down from his boulder and undid the flex binding Paul's arms. Stephen brought the flask; after a resentful glance at him, Paul seized it and drank greedily.

"And meat." Joseph gestured Stephen towards some rocks to the right of the cave. There he found, on a tin plate covered with a cloth, chunks of meat cooked that morning. They were cold; fat and blood were congealed on them. Paul wolfed them down. Then he sat back against a boulder. Stephen sat down cross-legged near him, beginning to feel hungry himself.

"And now," Joseph said "are we ready for our Commonwealth Conference? I promised you one." He smiled. "Or shall we call it an *Indaba*? Yes, I think so. We are not meeting in some expensive Hall in London but in the open air, here in poverty-stricken Zimbabwe. 'Indaba' is the appropriate term. You know what it means? A formal discussion. Our Indaba."

Paul looked up dully as Joseph climbed back onto the boulder and sat there, sunglasses flashing down at them. "There was a famous Indaba once in my country. In 1896, during what the Whites, the Settlers, called the Matabele Rebellion—the first war of liberation; the first Chimurenga some call it now. My people, when they saw that the Whites were taking all their land and turning them into slaves to farm it for them, rose up and fought for their freedom. They lost in the end. They did not have rifles and machine-guns. And they were tricked. The great Cecil Rhodes went to the Matobo hills, where the rebellious chiefs of my people were assembled. He talked smoothly to them, and he made many promises—but of course most of them were not kept; he persuaded them to give up their rebellion. Now here we are almost a century later. And I am Cecil Rhodes. I have weapons—my AK, my men's spear and axe. And you have no weapons. I am sitting as he did, the great

Cecil Rhodes, up above you; and you are sitting as my forefathers did, down below me. Can I persuade *you*, I wonder, as he persuaded *them*? Are my words and my weapons strong enough?" He paused. "What do you think?"

Stephen cleared his throat. "I think the analogy is not a complete one. Cecil Rhodes and the Whites won in 1896, and your forefathers lost; but now his descendants have lost, and you have won. Your numbers were more important than their weapons—or even *your* weapons. There were just too many of you."

Joseph rubbed his nose. "We have not won. Only some of us have won. Some of us are no better off now than in 1896. And some of us are being slaughtered by those who won. Do you know that? You will not hear about it on our national radio and TV, or read about it in the newspapers. Do you know what is happening, right now? Not very far from where we are sitting. Do you know that defenceless men, and women and children, are being slaughtered every day by Mugabe's wild dogs, his Fifth Brigade? Just like your people slaughtered us a century ago. Worse. They are being slaughtered because they are Ndebele, only because they are *Ndebele*. In Harare they are calling it *Gukurahundi*, as if the people of Matabeleland are dirt, nothing more than dirt, to be swept away." He paused, meditated. "No, you are right, England. The analogy is not exact. I do not want to be your Cecil Rhodes any more than I want to be our Robert Mugabe. But I tell you we have *not* won, none of us have won, until all our land is ours again. Mugabe says all are equal now in Zimbabwe, even while he slaughters those he calls his enemies; but we are not equal, no Black man can be equal, until all the land the White settlers took from us is ours again. Maybe Mugabe thinks England will pay the White farmers to give us back our land, but I know the English—they will not keep whatever promises they make. But there are many of us who fought to get our land back, and we will force Mugabe to take the land back from the Whites and give it to us. You will see."

"But—You can't just—"

"Yes, we *can* 'just—'" We will take it, all of it. *That* is justice. The land is ours."

"What about law and order? What about—the consequences—Zimbabwe's economy—?"

"Whose law? Whose order? It is our land, I tell you. And we will take it. We are already taking it. And that will not stop. It will not stop till every White farm is ours, *all* our land. You will see. Where were law and order when you took our land from us, England? It is our land, and we will take it, and that will be the only 'consequence.'"

After a few moments of silence, Stephen: "But what are we in all of this, Paul and I? We are visitors to your country. We have come to admire it and learn about your people. Yet we are prisoners. Why? What harm have we done to you, or your people?"

"You are White. That is enough. You are from the rich West, which continues to plunder Africa's resources and suppress Africa economically so that we can never be self-sufficient, never be fully free. And you say to the White farmers who oppressed us, and still oppress us, you do not know how much—that they can keep our land, and we must accept that? Yes, it is enough that you are White."

"All right, I concede some truth in what you say. But we are individuals too, I am an individual. We are not just 'the rich West.' Since I was a schoolboy, I have opposed Apartheid and Colonialism in every way I could. That's the main reason I wanted to come here and not to South Africa. Only when South Africa is free—"

"And Australia? What about you, Australia?"

Paul stirred, looked up wearily. "What?"

"Are you opposed to Apartheid and Colonialism like your noble mother-country here?"

Paul groaned, closed his eyes again.

"I didn't say I was noble, or my country was noble"—Stephen, sharply. I might be back at school, he thought, bellowing away at a Debating Society meeting, "Mister Chairman, it seems that once again the Proposer of the Motion has completely missed my point." He shifted his position on the sand, stretching his legs out so he could rub his feet. "There were many sins," he continued, "and failure to expiate them. I know that. But then, was Colonialism so very bad, so entirely evil? Did no good come from it? None at all?"

"You mean Shakespeare and the Houses of Parliament and judges in wigs, and roads and hospitals and big buildings, and electricity and posh Mercedes cars?" contemptuously. "Oh I think we could have survived without all of those—in fact I think we would have done better without them. We had our own culture, our own government, our own way of life. It would have been preferable for us to evolve our own"—sarcastically—"*lifestyle.* You English are always so pompous, so superior. But I know all about you, I know what you really are. I lived with you for over a year. I know all about your class system and your dirty little secrets. Like Dick Whittington—you see I even know about him!—like him I walked the pavements of your New Jerusalem, and did I find gold? No, I found dirt, dirt, dirt, dirt. You are vicious, a vicious people. Behind your oh-so-good manners, your gentle smirks, your so-called benevolence, your complacent anti-Apartheid marches—yes I marched in two of those—behind it all you are the same England of Cecil Rhodes, stealing, lying, murdering. At least in the 'good old days' you did it without apology and deceit."

"Without deceit? How can you say that? When you know that the whole Imperialism thing was deceit from top to bottom. We all know that now. Deceit and self-deceit. Public schoolboys masturbating in India for the greater glory of Britannia. Bashing the natives because they could, because they had machine guns, and of course because the natives had gold and diamonds."

"And land. Now who can see no good in the Empire? Whose side are you on, England? Make up your mind. This is an Indaba."

"On the same side as you, if you could hear me. And my name's not England. My name's Stephen Holmes, and"—pointing at Paul—"he's not Australia, he's Paul Boyd. Can't you see what I'm trying to say? There's good and bad, but you can't pull them away from when they happened, and you shouldn't drag them into the present, however unjust that leaves it all. Why risk wrecking your future because of the past? How can anyone make up now for what might have been done a century ago, by different individuals? You can't kill me just because my grandfather killed yours, assuming he did. Or at least, you *can*; because you have the gun now. But you can't make it *moral* to kill me *now* if you say it wasn't moral *then* for my grandfather—"

He stopped, breathless. Then, breathing deeply, unevenly, Calm down, Stephen, calm down. Speak slowly, quietly. Joseph was silent, so he went on "Surely it would be best if we all learn to work together as the world gets smaller—as its population gets bigger and bigger and our space, your space and my space, gets smaller. We have to work together, work harder and harder, to understand each other and each other's cultures and languages and religions—we have to improve the world for everybody—because if we don't—"

"We have to work together with our murderers? Is that what you think, England? Is it? A brave new world, an international Commonwealth, a new Colonialism—no, not a new Colonialism, a continuing and expanding Colonialism. All in the name of progress and co-operation and anti-Apartheid marches, and improving the world for everybody? Meaning for the rich West. So you can go on squeezing our balls. So you can keep our land. When you say 'the world,' you mean the rich West, England. Hypocrites! Hypocrites! Hypocrites! Hypocrites!" He hissed the last four words.

"But who's the murderer? You're holding your AK and I have no weapon, but you're not a murderer, are you? —I'm still alive, you're still alive. And we're talking to each other. An Indaba. But history is history. Why let it poison the present and the future? Improvements for your people will come through change, and—connection with other nations— And the White farmers will sell their farms if they are treated fairly—if there are honest negotiations—and the land—"

"So you think history does not matter? You think it can be folded up and packed away in little boxes?"

"That's not what I'm trying to say. You have to—outwit history, you have to know it and understand it and learn from it, and then you have to have the imagination to find a positive way beyond it." —*fly by those nets*— "You have to use history to defeat history. You have to control the fury you feel whenever you remember the—all the suffering and exploitation of the past; you have to work so it doesn't happen again. You can't change what has already happened. One of my grandfathers was a miner, he died at thirty-eight of what I suppose was lung-cancer; he died in his tiny drab terrace-house, in a drab town in the North of England, he died very slowly, in a tiny drab room, with only my father, who was a little boy eleven years old, to hold his hand; and I can't begin to imagine—" He stopped; cleared his throat.

"I thought we were discussing history, England, not your family, the callous way you English treat even your own people."

"All right. You're right. Irrelevant. Who cares about my grandfather. Even his wife didn't. So then— What about that weapon you're holding on your knees? Where was it manufactured? Did your people make it?"

Joseph smiled broadly. "Oh yes, I had completely forgotten! I had forgotten that Soviet Russia is a member of the Commonwealth, the great British Commonwealth. That England invented the alphabet, and writing, and paper, and law and order, and—"

"All right. Your point. But if we must talk about the past, your people's past, the Colonial past, why not let's be a bit more precise about that? I've done some reading about it, you know. Why not have *all* the facts out in the open. You say my grandfather was a murderer. All right: then he was a murderer. But what about *your* grandfather? Your father's people—you said so yourself—came here only about ten years before the Whites did. They were a warrior tribe, fleeing the Zulus. They attacked the local people, the Shona tribes. They killed, they raped, they took cattle, they took land—didn't they? They conquered. They called their capital Gubuluwayo, meaning 'the place of slaughter,' and they settled the land around it. They drove away the Shona tribes, to the north and the west and the east and the south, and, even after that, they raided them and killed them and took them as slaves. You see, I've read some of your history. And I ask myself, does that history have anything to do with what you say is going on now, the Fifth Brigade slaughtering your people, today, in the present, a few miles away, only a few miles away, you said—does it, perhaps? What do you think? And if it does, what does that do to your argument? Either we are both murderers—or neither of us is a murderer."

Joseph had been gazing above Stephen at the boulders surrounding them. He looked down. "I am not only Ndebele. I told you. My mother is Kalanga. They speak Shona, the Kalanga. My father is Ndebele. I am Ndebele and Kalanga, both. And both my peoples suffered under your people for nearly a century."

"And that gives you cause to kill me now? What good would it do? What change could it bring? How would it improve anyone's life in your country? Will it stop the Fifth Brigade? Will it save any lives, stop any suffering? Will it have any influence at all on Mugabe—?"

"Kill? Who said I am going to kill you?"

"But you have abducted us. We are your prisoners. Is that the freedom your people fought for? Do you want us to be grateful because you have taken our freedom from us, when your forefathers fought to regain theirs? How can you expect us to understand that? We are under threat of your weapons every minute of the day and night."

"Not only our forefathers. Not only Mugabe and ZANU-PF and those who rule in Harare today—whatever they tell the world, whatever they say in their little imitation Parliament in Harare. I fought for freedom; my people fought for freedom; the men who were with me, they fought for freedom, under my command."

"And now you have abducted us. Strangers, tourists. Why? Can you explain? Surely it can't make any difference to what is happening in Matabeleland? So why? Tell me."

Joseph meditated. Shadows were lengthening across the amphitheatre. The air was cooling.

Stephen tried again. "What are you going to do with us? Tell us. Please, tell us. Do you think it's fair, to keep us in ignorance as well as keeping us your prisoners? That's mental cruelty as well as physical cruelty. How can that be just?"

"Fair? Cruelty?" Joseph stroked his nose, then spoke rapidly, angrily. "You do not know what those words mean. You are a child. When you have fought in the bush for four years, when your friends have died screaming right next to you, when your families have been tortured and burnt in their huts, when you have had to kill even those you love because they are your enemies—when, after all that, your so-called Comrades betray you, turn against you—because you are from a different tribe—" He paused. "Then tell me about cruelty and injustice."

"Four years?" Stephen said slowly. "You fought for four years in the Bush War?"

"In the Bush War, yes. And then I worked in Harare, in the Government, for more than two years. Until I came back to my people. But we will not talk about these matters. They do not concern you."

"Why not? I want to understand. You said you killed people you loved because they were also your enemies?"

"I said we will not talk about such matters."

"But this is an Indaba. You said so."

"To discuss your situation. Only that. That is what you asked for, England."

"So then tell me what our situation is. Why won't you tell me that? Are we hostages?" Joseph looked into the distance. "Are we going to be killed if some condition or other isn't met? What condition? Who has to accept it? What do you want? Money?"

"We did not want *you*, England. But you gave me no choice."

"'No choice'!" Stephen laughed angrily. His voice rose. "Excuse me, but it seemed very much the other way round. We were just waiting for a lift to Bulawayo, actually. Or didn't we explain that clearly enough?" Control yourself, Stephen. Don't get hysterical.

"You came to *me*, I did not go to *you*."

"So—it was some sort of mistake?"

"Yes. If you like, some sort of mistake."

"But then—why were you roaming around the countryside with an AK and seven armed men? Was that also a mistake?"

Joseph's head swung round sharply. The sunglasses held steady as Stephen gazed upwards. "You are being impertinent now, England. Be careful."

"Well?"

"We were waiting."

"For what? Who?"

"That is not your concern."

"But—they didn't come. Or they got away. Which?"

"You say they got away. But we got you. Because, instead of getting your lift to Bulawayo and leaving our lives, you walked along the path right up to me, as if you were—'Hullo' you said, and you held out your hand. As if you were Livingstone."

"Stanley. 'Doctor Livingstone, I presume?'"

"So you gave me no choice. It would have been better to take just you, but of course the other two came to us too. They came along the path, shouting for you. Like children"—contemptuously.

Stephen looked round at Paul, who lay sprawled asleep on the sand. He was puzzled. "But—you mean, you'd already seen us? Before? You were watching us from the moment we were dropped off and started trying to hitch another lift?"

"We did not want to kill you."

"*Didn't* want to kill us? And that's why you abducted us? You expect me to believe that?"

After a short silence, "Well, do you have any more questions, or is the Indaba over?"

"But we still don't know what you want to do with us now, why you don't let us go. You say we're here by mistake, but still you go on keeping us prisoner. Except for Susanna, but that's only because she needed a doctor. And you wouldn't let Paul get away. Why? Why not just take us to a road and release us? You let Susanna go, why not let Paul and me go? If you want, we'll promise never to tell anyone about it—we won't even say we ever saw you."

"No."

"Then why? Is it—political? Only that? Or is there some other reason?" Joseph was silent. "Say that—" Stephen hesitated. "Say that Susanna tells the Police, they might force her to do that, and then they come and look for us— Wouldn't it be better to let us go now, and we can tell them we just got lost in the bush? Or we could say we weren't abducted at all, it was just a misunderstanding, we followed you because we were confused, didn't understand the language—we thought you were offering us food and a place to sleep, it was getting dark, we were frightened of being in the bush and not having any shelter for the night— We could say whatever you like, whatever you think is best. We would take an oath to say whatever you tell us to say."

Joseph brooded. "No."

Sunset was near. Joseph had again lit a small fire, and cooked the rest of the venison. He and one of the men squatted near the fire, eating.

Stephen took his chunks of meat to the entrance of the shallow cave, wondering if Paul was awake; but he was lying flat on his back, deeply asleep, snoring slightly, mouth open. Stephen put on his sweater, glad to find that his arms were slightly less painful; then ate his meat leaning against the side of the cave, at its entrance. Tender, though bloody—very rare. Yet, for an ex-vegetarian, I relish this meat disgracefully. Necessity is the mother of digestion.

After swallowing some water from the flask, he wandered across the amphitheatre to gaze at yet another melodramatic flaming and flaunting of massed cumulus. Surely the rains will begin soon? I must ask Joseph. Didn't one of the guide books say the rainy season begins around mid-October? But someone at the Victoria Falls hotel had said that for two years there had been a severe widespread drought.

Evening flows in. The air cools. *Each slow dusk—* He went back to the amphitheatre.

Joseph had again smothered the fire as soon as he had finished the cooking. He's worried, I think, that even a thin plume of smoke might be seen—otherwise, presumably he and the two men would have enjoyed squatting longer around its warmth.

The men. As he approached them, Stephen looked at Joseph and the squatted figure eating opposite him. The other one now—a changing of the guard. Tweedledee or Tweedledum? This is the one with the axe—which was lying in the sand beside him. Could I communicate with this man? Would Joseph allow it? We've all been together for—can it really be less than three days?—it seems so much longer. The men must be tired too, especially after today's hard tracking, walking, and capturing Paul. I don't know their names, where they came from, what their normal work is—any of the basic facts one might exchange with neighbours in England, say in a bus queue.

He squatted near Joseph, opposite the man. After a moment, he asked Joseph, "What's he eating? Doesn't look like meat."

"No, we have finished that. It was only a small buck. They will hunt for another one tomorrow. He is eating fruit and bulbs and roots."

"How does he know they aren't poisonous?"

"He knows."

"Can I try one?"

Joseph reached sideways and handed Stephen what looked like a large rough-skinned brown bean. "You can start with this. Chew it."

Stephen turned it over in his hand, smelled it: a seed-pod, warm husky scent. He started chewing, warily. "It's—tasty, quite tasty" he reported with surprise. "Tastes a bit like bread actually."

Joseph smiled sardonically. "Perhaps that's why the Whites call it monkey-bread. They saw us Black monkeys eating it."

"What's his name?"

"This man?" Joseph hesitated. "Ndlovu. Welcome Ndlovu. He is my cousin."

The man looked up when he heard his name, and blinked at Stephen. His eyes are yellow around the brown irises. Wide high cheekbones. Ragged yellow teeth—one missing; at least one. Shallow wrinkles—he must be middle-aged, say about forty-five? No, perhaps older—the stubble of his hair is peppered with white.

"And the other man? The one who's on guard duty?"

"Why? Surely, England, you are not interested in knowing anything about your subjects, lesser breeds without your law, hewers of your wood and drawers of your water."

"Were you educated on a Mission?"

The sunglasses flashed at Stephen, flinging a final glow of sunlight into his eyes. "Oh yes, I see. My quotations give me away. You are quite observant for an Englishman—Mr Holmes."

"But what's his name—the other one? The younger one?"

"Does it matter?"

"I'd like to know. Research. I'm a Modern Historian—or rather studying to become one."

"His name can make no difference."

"Yes. It does. To me."

"Gabriel Mpofu. Another one of my cousins."

"Gabriel Mpofu." Why does that seem such a beautiful name to me? It does. "What's it mean—Mpofu?"

Reluctantly: "Poor. And he is poor, he has no job. And Ndlovu means Elephant."

"Can I talk to him? Welcome Ndlovu?"

"You can try. I will introduce you." He spoke to the man, who smiled and nodded, "Aie."

Joseph turned to Stephen. "But you must do it correctly, England. Not like a Rhodesian. Stand up." They both stood, faced one another in the dusk. Welcome Ndlovu looked up at them.

"Now— First you must learn how to shake hands. He clasped Stephen's right hand firmly, then grasped the thumb, and again clasped his entire hand. "You see? You shake; you take each other's thumbs, one, two—yes, like that; you shake. Do it again. Yes."

"What does it mean? Is it just the usual greeting?"

"When two men shake like this, it means Freedom. It means 'You are my friend, I am glad to know you, I have confidence in you.'"

"Oh."

"At the same time, you say *'Kanjani!'* and then *'Sakubona!'* Say it."

"Kanjani! Sakubona!"

"Yes. That is our way of greeting, like your Hullo, how are you, I'm fine, how are you, I'm fine. There's more, the greeting is more elaborate than yours, but this is enough. Now you can meet and greet Mr Ndlovu."

The man stood up, smiling shyly. He was thin—skinny, almost emaciated; pale washed-out shirt with a grey-and-green checked pattern, patched khaki trousers held up by a red cord. A pungent unfamiliar body-odour—Stephen had noticed this before, fleetingly, when near Joseph or one of the men. Can't be any stronger than my smell, though—especially now—wish I could change my clothes— They shook hands, exchanged greetings, stood smiling and nodding at each other for a few moments. Then Joseph spoke in Sindebele and Welcome Ndlovu squatted down again.

"Does he"—Stephen turned to Joseph—"understand English?"

"No. He has no education. He has lived all his life in the bush. You could say he is a subsistence farmer. He has seen only a few Whites and he speaks only Sindebele. Gabriel Mpofu also, he grew up here, but he went to Bulawayo and got a job as a mechanic, but he lost it when the garage closed down—the owner went to South Africa, many Whites did that, even before Independence, 1980, what they called 'The Chicken Run.' So he came back to live in his kraal—he was living on mealies like Mr Ndlovu, if you can call that living, in our great nation Zimbabwe. He understands a few words of English—like 'Fuck off, *kaffir.'* Is that enough information for you, England?"

"And you? How did you - ?"

"I said, Is that enough information?"

"Yes, thank you. For now."

"There will be no more time for research in Modern History after this, England. We must all get some sleep, a few hours at least. We have a long march ahead of us tonight."

"A long march?" Stephen couldn't keep the dismay out of his voice. "But— Paul isn't— And my feet— Where to?" Joseph was silent. "Back east to the main road? Or west, or south?"

"A long march. You will see. You ask too many questions, England. About things that do not concern you. Now it is time to stop asking questions and go to sleep."

"I need some water."

"Mr Ndlovu will get it for you." Joseph was climbing up to his perch on the boulder. He spoke out of the near-darkness, "Welcome Ndlovu, your drawer of water. Give him your flask."

VII

"Paul, wake up." Stephen pushed gently at Paul's shoulder. "Wake up. We've got to go."

Paul groaned, "Wha' the fuck", thrashed on the sand, then sat up abruptly, pale shadow in the darkness. But it does seem just a bit lighter each night, the moonlight strengthening by a barely perceptible degree.

"I've got some water here, in the flask. Want some in your hands? Splashing some on my face helps me wake up. And you must be thirsty? Finish it if you like—I've had as much as I need."

"Yeah." Paul reached out for the flask. Stephen heard him splash water on his face and draw in his breath sharply—that gash across his forehead can't be closed yet.

The flask was pushed back against Stephen's arm. He whispered "Are you all right?"

"Yeah, I'll survive. Gotta take a leak." A spattering against rock and sand. A groaning yawn. "Tha's better. What's the time?"

"Don't know. Probably about ten—I don't feel I've slept more than three hours—if that. Sure you're all right?"

Paul was silent for a moment. Then a rapid half-whisper, "I bloody near made it. They got me at the railway line. A train was coming. Goods train. Did you tell him?"—suspicion distorted his voice.

"No. They didn't know you'd gone till we got here, to this kopje, at dawn. But then they realised you must have gone during the time we stopped for a rest—they must have worked out that you were with me up to then."

"Yeah, that fuckin' bloody Boss bugger listening again. Sure you didn't tell him?"

Stephen rubbed his right hand down his left arm. Still stiff and sore, but getting better. My feet are much worse. "No. I didn't tell them, Paul. Of course I didn't. So—what happened?"

"Kept going fast as I could. In the dark. Walked into lotta thorn-trees, how I got so many fuckin' bloody scratches. Kept right away from the path, of course. Heard some animal sounds, but kept going and it got light before long. Think I musta been heading a bit in the wrong direction in the dark—when the sun came up it was right in front of me, so I had to change direction. Then I just went on and on, heading north, and trying not to make too much noise—but enough to let animals know I was around in case they didn't smell me—they don't attack if they know you're coming, someone told me that. I saw buck, and zebras, and giraffes, and once a lioness I think it was, in the distance—no wild dogs, they're the ones you really gotta worry about. Then I heard a whistle—train whistle. So I knew the railway line was close. When I got to it, there was the engine coming towards me. Started waving, but then I saw those two, fuckin' Mutt and Jeff, coming out of the bush between me and the train—woulda reached me before the train did, so I ran over the railway line into the bush on the other side, heading for the road, thought it must be near. But they got me, I was too tired, couldn't run fast enough."

"I'm sorry, Paul." Inadequate response, but how can I do better? Doesn't want my friendship, he's made that clear enough—and certainly not my sympathy. Only admiration for his heroism.

"Yeah, well I bloody gave them a run for their money. And if it hadn't been *two* fuckin' nignogs—I'm not finished yet. I'm not fuckin' bloody finished, not by a long shot. That fuckin' bloody big Boss bugger. I'll get him tomorrow, you'll see."

"But, Paul—"

"And *you* can shut your face, Steve. You can fuckin' keep your whiny Pommy advice to yourself. You do what you like and I'll do what *I* like. Get it? *I'm* not Queer, just you remember that. You'll see what happens tomorrow. Just you make fuckin' sure you don't interfere or I'll fuckin' do you too." His breathing fast and ragged.

After a moment, Stephen: "Did the train-driver see you?"

"How do I bloody know? He was probably jerking himself off, or dead drunk, what they say about these new nignog train-drivers, having so many accidents, wrecking all those fuckin' shiny new engines donated by the Commonwealth. It's a fuckin' bloody wonder any of them are fuckin' bloody running at all."

"Ready? I can hear him coming."

The treks were long and tiring; four of them, as on the first night; each for perhaps ten kilometres.

Stephen was behind Gabriel Mpofu; Welcome Ndlovu was always close behind Paul; and during rests the two guards sat or lay in silence a few yards away, one on each side—obviously there would be no further chance of escape. Joseph they didn't see. Did he go ahead to reconnoitre? Or did his conception of leadership imply apartness? Perhaps a result of his four years of fighting as a guerrilla in the bush?

Stephen's ears were, he thought, sharper now. As he walked through the darkness, he was aware of a flurry of small sounds around him—cheeps of disturbed birds in their nests; an owl calling gloomily and monotonously; a crackling hiss of grass that surely signalled a small animal moving quickly away from them; coughs and snorts of larger animals; and, occasionally, the reverberant distant roar of a lion.

Both he and Paul slept more easily, firmly apart but within three feet of each other; they were less nervous of the wild, and also much more fatigued now. Stephen's feet, though still very painful—scratched and swollen—were now hardier. Thanks partly to my cross-country running at school? Arms less painful too. Stiffness in my lower back and thighs wearing off. All in all, I'm adjusting quite well to severe and unfamiliar physical demands, he encouraged himself.

As they walked again, he thought about Susanna, tried to visualise her. How quickly details become hazy to the memory. Beautiful grey eyes, freckles on her small nose, short brown hair—yes, but her humorous level gaze, the distinctive sweet open expression of her face in repose—that is so difficult for the memory to recreate; and the quizzical lift of eyebrows, the sideways tilt of chin, when she was teasing him; the narrowed eyes, pursed lips and slight frown as she listed her favourite Whatevers—that game she so enjoyed playing; which could be irritating but was so charmingly naïve; he smiled affectionately as he remembered. Is she playing it at this moment with the patient in the bed beside hers? "What's your favourite disease?" What has she been able to tell the Police or Army—how effectively direct them towards five tiny shadows threading this huge darkness?

Suddenly it occurred to Stephen that their plane would be leaving Harare for London in—how many days?—but I'm losing all sense of time. Soon, anyway. Will she be on it, even if I haven't been rescued by then? For a moment he was swept by a cold pang of fear, panic; then forced his mind back to the actual, to the rhythmic scissoring of his legs, the cold sand or stone pushing up firmly against soles and heels, the occasional brush of grass or thorn-bush against his trousers— At any moment, I may feel the sharp jab of a thorn. Strange that I stepped over the one that pierced Susanna's foot, when she was just behind me. If only it could have been me— Do I really mean that? At least she'll soon be cured now—and she's out of this nightmare.

He strode on behind Gabriel Mpofu. The path, or paths, they were following meandered, rose and fell, during the first two treks of the night; but he had the impression of a general descent.

Soon after their third trek began, they were walking, to Stephen's surprise, not on a path but on the edge of a dirt road that stretched ahead, pale in the semi-darkness. They continued on it for—an hour?—then were led some distance from it for their rest. Was it running south or west? Hard even to guess but, either way, they must surely be close to the Botswana border, perhaps somewhere near the Hwange National Park? He tried to recall salient details of the map that Joseph had confiscated. And then what? Where?

At the beginning of the fourth trek, they were led back to the road again. After they had been trudging along it for a while, more and more slowly, wearily, Gabriel Mpofu suddenly stopped, and Stephen, coming up to him, could hear Joseph talking softly a short way ahead. In Sindebele or Shona? An equally soft voice responded.

The four of them stood in silence, waiting. In the grey pre-dawn, Stephen could now see, over Gabriel's shoulder, about a dozen figures. Who were they? Dissidents? Kalanga villagers fleeing the Fifth Brigade? Was this the moment to call for help? But—that could result in the deaths of innocent people—and our own deaths? Better wait for a safer opportunity. Let's hope Paul keeps quiet too.

After a few moments, the travellers came silently past, ghosts drifting along the centre of the road. Dark inhabitants of my dream, my nightmare. Gabriel started forward.

Now light was thickening, very slowly drawing out of silvery darkness the sentinel shapes of trees on either side of the road. Suddenly two very bright lights, followed by two more, and then more, jerked over the horizon some way ahead and bounced towards them.

A sharp command from Joseph, and they were led hurriedly off the road and into the bush. As they went on, winding their way between trees, occasionally struck by thorny branches, the whine and roar of several trucks— Army trucks?—dwindled behind them. On, on; until, in the dull pinking light, a big kopje loomed.

Gabriel stopped. Stephen found a boulder, sat down against it. Paul leaned against a tree nearby. Welcome talked quietly with Gabriel, who then disappeared into the greyness. There was no sign of Joseph.

They would presumably remain here for the rest of the day? Stephen walked across to Paul. "All right?"

"Yeah, of course." Always resentment in his voice, as if the query, intended as friendly, implied a negative critique of his manhood.

"How are your legs? Did you get scratched a lot?"

"Think one or two more scratches would make any diff?"

"Well—I have to relieve myself." Stephen went a short way in amongst the trees. When he turned to come back, he found that Welcome had quietly followed him. "You needn't worry, Mr Ndlovu, I'm too tired even to think of running away," he said with a thin smile, passing the silent man. "All I want to do now is have a good long sleep. You must be tired too. Since you spend half your day on guard-duty, I wonder if you and Mr Mpofu manage to get much sleep at all?"

Welcome bobbed his head, turned away. He was holding his axe, as usual, across his chest. Must be tiring to carry that with you everywhere, Stephen thought; I suppose when he's walking he can swing it and move it from one hand to the other; but it must be quite a weight. In a way, I'm glad I don't have even my knapsack to carry—though I'd certainly like a change of clothing before I'm so totally disgusting that my own smell almost makes me puke; and, oh, how I'd like a toothbrush, and toothpaste—my mouth is foul, foul.

But what's the use of thinking about such things? Just concentrate on what is immediate, actual. That's how prisoners, incarcerated alone in dungeons, retain their sanity. My voices seem to have deserted me. If this goes on much longer, I'll have to develop some definite projects to occupy my brain, to hold madness at arm's length—I could keep a count of the number of birds I see or hear, the number of times we stop, the number of days and nights— But where are my voices when I need them? Oh God-if-there-is-a-God, please let this end soon, please let them rescue us, without violence, without bloodshed—just rescue us, please, please. Please.

As the sun rose, Joseph approached them from far ahead. When he reached Stephen, he lifted the AK from his shoulder and stood it against a nearby tree. What a strange shape it is, almost charming, almost unmilitary, Stephen meditated: its magazine like a banana, or like the new moon—curving so inoffensively, sweetly, towards the calm pellucid morning sky.

"Soon we will rest and eat."

"If Mr Mpofu has any luck hunting—what if he doesn't?"

"He will. And if not, there are many roots and bulbs and fruits everywhere—remember your tasty monkey-bread? Africa is always generous. Even when it is drought for several years, like now, there is food for all if you know where to look for it. Are you feeling well?"

"Yes. Some stiffness, some pain. But surprisingly fit, actually."

"The English did not establish an empire and rule us for a century by being weak, I give them that at least. Even if they also had rifles and machine guns to provide them with courage against savages who had only spears and axes. And how is Australia?"—he jerked his head in the direction of Paul; who, leaning against his tree, faced the sun with head thrown back and eyes closed, savouring the warmth.

"Oh I think Paul's all right too, in spite of all the exertion yesterday. He's tough." Mustn't let him think we are weakening. But I am, oh I am. How much longer can I hope to hold on?

"'Tough.' Is he? And you are a 'very impressive specimen of young man-hood,' are you, England? —I was once called that, at about your age, in your country. Follow me."

Stephen called across to Paul, who clambered to his feet as Welcome came towards them. Joseph led them up the big kopje. At first it seemed to have no sand on it at all. A tumble of ragged boulders at its base. A sweep of grey granite to the crown, at the far end of which several rounded boulders balanced, looking as precarious as giant balls on a smooth slope—surely a slight push could send them rolling down to crush us? And there were small trees and bushes in the miniature valleys that rived the kopje at almost regular intervals.

As he reached the top, Stephen caught his breath. They were looking out, through the upper branches of trees, at a great plain tilting into pale blue distance. *Mine eyes dazzle*— He closed his left eye, but his right eye was incapable of picking out distant detail—is it deteriorating now that it carries the burden of far sight alone? The question reminded him that he still had the left lens of his defunct glasses, so he took it out of his pocket and held it carefully between left thumb and forefinger, close to his left eye. Yes, he could see further this way; though with a sense of strain that made him feel dizzy.

The horizon quivering; nearer, to the right, a scattering of hills. Golden grass, surging over stony soil, flowing round occasional stipples of tree and bush, then sweeping on and away like a vast wave: *orient and immortal wheat —immortal sea—unplumbed, salt, estranging sea—The wrinkled sea beneath him crawls—across the floors of silent seas—alone on a wide, wide sea—serpent-haunted sea—multitudinous seas incarnadine*—Rosenberg, where are you? Where are you, Rosenberg? *That way madness lies—No more of that—* His head ached, he swayed, dizzy; his lips moved. "'*None saw their spirits'* *shadow shake the grass, Or stood aside for their half-used life to pass Out of those doomed nostrils and the doomed mouth—'''*Yes. Yes. Yes. Rosenberg.

Joseph touched him on the shoulder. "Look, can you see him?"

"See? Him?" He followed the finger's pointing. "Oh—yes." A small figure, dark brown head and arms, pale green-and-brown shirt and khaki trousers; with a soft dun shape laid across a thin black one over his shoulders. Gabriel had hunted successfully again.

Welcome came up the kopje, carrying a bundle of dead branches. Joseph spoke to him, pointing, and he went on to their left. In among several boulders he laid down the branches, then quickly made a low fireplace with stones, and gathered twigs and leaves to form a pile inside it. He selected two sticks and began to rub the smaller and harder one vigorously against the larger softer one. Stephen went over to see, and noticed that Paul, leaning against a boulder some yards away, was watching Joseph closely; and knew simultaneously that Joseph was aware of Paul's scrutiny.

Soon Joseph came towards him, still carrying his AK. "And so you are interested, England, in how the hewers of wood start a fire to cook your food? It is simple now, when everything is so dry."

Stephen glanced up at the glittering sun. Already the day was heating up—it would be another of those breathlessly heavy days that, he had begun to sense, were piling relentlessly towards some climax, some urgent fulfilment. Now there are only a few fluffy frivolous clouds high in the sky; but by mid-afternoon big cumulus clouds will cluster ominously, as they did yesterday, and advance stealthily towards us, surround us like a dense distant forest. —*from Birnam Wood to Dunsiname*— And at last, at last—*consummation comes*—

He took off his sweater and tied it round his waist; flapped a hand at flies circling his head. Thank goodness for this hat—Susanna's hat. He put his hand on top of it and for a moment saw himself as Paul must see him, ridiculously feminine, a parody of girlhood—this wide-brimmed straw hat my emblem. Too bad, Paul—it's practical, protects me, I need it, I want it. You're the macho one, and he looked across at bare-headed Paul, now sitting against the boulder with his eyes closed.

When he looked back at Welcome's fire-making, he became aware of the sunglasses: Joseph was watching him. He said "I'm so thirsty. Can we have some more water?"

"When he has finished, give him your flask."

A trickle of smoke was rising from the friction of Welcome's rapidly moving stick. I once tried to do that, while camping in a muddy field, during my long-ago scouting days; in vain. But I wonder if my lens would work, in the glare of this fierce sunlight? Might be quicker.

He looked around. To his right, at the kopje's higher end, the sweep of solid granite culminated in a gallery of boulders and rocks. Along the crest, to his left, a short way beyond where he was standing, the solid granite obviously ended, since a big tree stood there, isolated; it must be growing in soil accumulated in a fissure, Stephen thought, noting its pale rough bark covered with large knobby thorns, its fresh foliage—small shiny round leaves, vividly green—and it was in blossom, a multitude of radiant white spikes. Beyond it was a sweep of sand open to the sky and dotted with low clumps of grass.

A crackling of twigs, heavy breathing, and Gabriel was making his way steadily up the kopje. He plodded up to them, and set down a small buck, and the spear that had killed it, on the granite floor near Joseph; who nodded curtly.

"What is it?" Stephen asked, gazing at its tawny bloodied coat, the black markings on tail and forelegs. Beautiful harmless defenceless creature. How can I eat it? But I will. Compassion, squeamishness—emotions irrelevant to Neanderthals.

"*Impunzi* we call it. One of the smallest buck. It is shy and runs very fast, and goes alone, not in pairs or groups like other buck. Killing it is not easy. But Mr Mpofu is a good hunter. Whites call it a duiker."

Stephen moved closer, and bent to scrutinise it. Dead eyes stared at him out of their darkness. Expressionless, extinct. *Put out the light, and then put out—the light—*

"Now Mr Mpofu will cut it up." The small corpse was pulled a few yards away from them. Gabriel drew out three tin plates from the small bundle that Welcome carried over his shoulder while they journeyed; then a graceful slim-bladed knife, from the sheath attached to his belt; and began to hack off the buck's small legs. Meanwhile the fire was crackling quietly. Joseph gauged the smoke as it drifted past him. At his order, Welcome pulled some burning twigs away from the fire's centre, then went silently away with his axe and Stephen's flask. By the time they sat eating the lightly-cooked meat—so tender and succulent—Stephen was almost sick with hunger. They all ate fast, blood and fat running down their chins and hands. Neanderthals.

Joseph was sitting on a boulder, leaning over the AK, which rested across his thighs; Stephen and Paul sat opposite him. Gabriel had vanished down the left side of the kopje, with his spear and two chunks of meat. Welcome, after delivering Stephen's flask, presumably re-filled with water, had also vanished—he's on guard again, of course. Joseph had put out the fire as soon as its function was done. "You can go and sleep in the shade behind that rock" he said, when they had finished eating.

As they went in the direction he had indicated, Stephen saw that they would be able to emerge only into Joseph's unimpeded view, on one side or the other of the very large boulder, behind which the highest and widest of the boulders rose like a wall.

Stephen stood up. "Can you—?" hesitantly. "What will happen tonight? Can you tell us now? Will we be going on still further?"

Joseph smiled. "Persistent, England. You are very persistent. You will see. Sleep now. We all need rest."

Stephen awoke with Paul's hand clamped over his mouth. "Listen to me, Steve" whispered in his ear.

He sat up cautiously. How long had he been asleep? The foul gummy state of his eyes and mouth, his befuddled brain, suggested several hours; his back was stiff and sore, from the uneven granite he'd been lying on. He reached for the flask, took a sip of acrid water and then pushed it back under the shade of the big boulder.

The sun was still high, but westering; cumulus clouds had gathered on the wavering horizon glimpsed through tree tops: it must be early afternoon, say two o'clock. A heavy silence humped round them—no, not quite silence: there was a high monotonous distant rattle of cicadas. He looked questioningly into Paul's eyes.

"Listen," Paul whispered again, as he removed his hand from Stephen's mouth. "I just been to take a leak, he sent Tweedledum with me. He's been sleeping, now he's sitting there, in the shade of the tree, and the AK is leaning against it, about four feet behind him. Gotta take this chance."

"Paul—"

"Don't you"—hissing—"fuckin' mess this up, Steve. Could be our last chance. You think he's ever gonna let us go? Think so? He'll fuckin' kill us first, you know he will. He *will*. When he wants to, when he's ready, when he's finished playing his games with us. You wanna die that way? If you don't care about yourself, you fuckin' bloody think about me. *I* don't wanna die like a rat in a trap."

"Why would he—? We're hostages, he needs us alive."

"Are you gonna help me? Or not?"

"What do you want me to do?"

"You go to him and say you need to take a leak. Do it slowly, stand in front of him so he can't see past you. Keep him talking and looking up at you. Then he'll look down the hill to call Tweedledum. I'll come out the other side of this rock, he won't see me—and by the time he looks back at you, I'll have his AK. I'll be covering them both, and I'll have my back against the rock."

"Where's the other one?"

"On guard somewhere or other. But he'll be too late to do anything, even if he hears what's happening. Now go. We gotta do it quickly—*now*. He's still buggered from sleeping."

"So am I."

"*Do* it."

Stephen got up stiffly and, without his hat, slowly walked out towards Joseph. Who was sitting cross-legged in the shade of the hook-thorn tree, sunglasses turned away from them towards the far panorama. The AK was where Paul had said it was—about four feet to Joseph's right and slightly behind him, propped against the tree-trunk. Don't look at it. Don't look at it.

A knot rose in Stephen's throat. Relax, he told himself—relax, relax. He was almost there.

Joseph looked up at him.

"I'm—" Stephen coughed. "I'm feeling a bit constipated. And I need to—have a piss—I need to—you know, urinate and defecate. Could I, please—?" He forced himself not to glance to his left, smiled into the sunglasses. "Have you been resting? It's so hot I hardly slept at all but— Is it going to rain soon, do you think?"

"The clouds are not heavy enough, you can see that." Joseph looked down the kopje, to his left, and at the same moment Stephen saw the flash of Paul's arm reaching towards the AK.

Joseph whipped round, flinging himself upward in one lithe movement—and looked into the barrel of the AK. Paul's finger was on its trigger.

"Don't shoot!" Stephen hissed.

"Stand up"—Paul, softly, to Joseph, stepping back against the boulder. "Put your hands on your head." As Joseph obeyed, he looked at Stephen. *Corrode, consume*—

Paul: "He has some flex in his right pocket. Take it out and tie his arms together behind his back. Tight."

Hands trembling, Stephen moved behind Joseph and pulled the flex from his pocket.

Paul nodded at Joseph. "Put your arms behind your back."

Stephen tied Joseph's arms together above the wrists as firmly as he could, then moved back opposite him.

"Now call the man who's down there" Paul ordered Joseph softly. "Make it sound normal. Remember, I could shoot you, I could kill you all, I would too. I want to."

Joseph called out.

"Now look at Stephen. Don't speak again."

Soon Gabriel was coming up towards them, spear held loosely.

Stephen glanced at him. As he looked back at Joseph, his left eye caught a slight movement on the boulder behind and above Paul. Welcome stood poised to leap.

Joseph's sunglasses grappled with Stephen's eyes. Stephen saw a tiny mouth opening. He turned to Paul. The knot in his throat rose. He gasped.

Paul saw the shock in Stephen's eyes. He began to turn. At that moment Welcome's body struck him.

They were sprawled on the granite, thrashing against each other. Paul screamed "Steve."

Joseph was moving, throwing himself forward and down like a hammer. Stephen seized his shoulders, tried to yank him back.

Gabriel ran past them and dragged the AK beyond the reach of Paul's flailing hands while Welcome slammed Paul's head against the granite. Then Gabriel placed the tip of his spear against Paul's throat.

Joseph was pulling the flex tight around Stephen's crossed wrists. Stephen gasped in pain. The sunglasses aimed a tiny twisted face at his eyes.

Paul lay inert on the granite. Gabriel and Welcome stood one on each side of him. Spear and axe. The afternoon towered in a breathless heat.

Joseph turned from Stephen and looked down at Paul. He murmured an order. Gabriel put down his spear and dragged Paul's flaccid body towards the big tree

Joseph murmured again. Gabriel lifted Paul's torso and pulled off his torn red T-shirt; then lifted his trunk and legs and pulled off his shorts and underpants.

The four of them stood silent beside Paul's naked motionless body. After a few moments, he began to writhe and moan. A few more moments and his eyes flickered.

Joseph murmured. Gabriel grasped Paul under the armpits and pulled him to his feet. Paul twisted his bleeding head from side to side, gasping harshly; swaying in Gabriel's arms. When he spoke, his voice was thick and slurred: "Headache. Gotta headache."

For the fourth time, Joseph murmured. Gabriel pulled Paul against the tree; drew his arms back round the trunk and tied them together at the wrist with flex drawn from one of his pockets; then tied his legs to the tree just below the knees.

Paul groaned, twisting. He cried out dully with pain as the flex and the thorns cut into his flesh. He lifted his head, and his eyes opened wide, blood-shot, staring up unseeing at the tree's pale blossoms. He began to weep silently, spasmodically, tears furrowing the dust and dirt on his cheeks and ploughing on through blond stubble. Blood ran slowly around his left ear and down to his chest. He writhed against the thorns of the tree's pale trunk.

Stephen, trembling, gulping, spoke through the knot of phlegm in his throat. "Joseph. Please. Let him go. Please. He didn't mean— We didn't mean—" He fell back against the boulder. "Please—"

The sunglasses shone above a wide pleasant smile. "Don't worry, England. I will teach him to be gentle, friendly, kind. Civilised. That is all. I know that is what you want, too."

He went up to Paul and kissed him.

When he stepped back, Paul's head swung down and his scream reverberated around the kopje. "Fuck you. Fuck you, you fuckin' bloody nignog."

Joseph spoke to him very quietly. "You are uptight, Australia. That is your problem. Relax. I will teach you how to relax." The tips of his fingers caressed Paul's chest; ran down his flanks, and up over his stomach to his nipples.

Paul shrieked again, his voice cracking. "Leave me alone. You bloody Queer, you fuckin' nignog Queer. Just leave me alone."

"Joseph. Please. Joseph." Stephen looked desperately round at Gabriel and Welcome. They were squatted, watching impassively.

Joseph stood in front of Paul. "Now. Kiss me."

Paul's eyes opened. He spat in Joseph's face.

They stood, both breathing deeply. Spots of spit glittered on the sunglasses.

Gently, Joseph spoke again, to Gabriel and Welcome. They went to Paul, one on each side. They dragged him away from the tree, out to the glare of the sand. He began to struggle, digging his heels into the sand, lurching from one side to the other, grunting angrily.

They forced him down, onto his knees, and then spreadeagled him on his stomach, holding his arms and legs. Sweat and blood gleamed through the dirt on his back. He lifted his head and moved it from side to side, then laid it on the sand and closed his eyes. His arms and legs struggled weakly, futilely, against the hold of the two men. He was muttering. "Fuck you. Fuckin' bloody nignog. Fuckin' bloody Queer. Fuck you."

None of them had heard the plane. It was right above them, a small plane, white and blue, sparkling in the sunlight.

Joseph heard the plane and stopped moving. Paul heard it, raised his head for a moment, and muttered "Oh God. Help me." Gabriel and Welcome heard it and moved back into the shadow of the big tree. Stephen heard it and looked up and was dazzled by the blare of the sun.

Three times the plane circled over them; then swung away, its buzz sinking slowly into the distance.

Silence shrieked—shrieked louder than Paul had shrieked.

Joseph stood up, walked over to Welcome, took the axe from him.

Stephen, horror flowering blackly in his brain, stumbled towards Joseph gasping "No. No. No."

Gabriel caught Stephen by the shoulders, pulled him backwards. As he fell, he saw the axe hang glittering against pale sky for a brief moment, then flash downward. *—a deed without a name—*

Paul's final scream was crushed into bellowing gurgles by a crunching thump—and another; and another; and another.

VIII

Stephen lay on stone, his mind stammering. *Men must endure their going hence—Oh God-if-there-is-a-God—There's nothing serious in mortality—My heart is turned to stone—Oh God-if-there-is-a-God, oh God—To have seen what I have seen—a deed without a name—*

A sour smell, wetness at the side of his mouth and on the stone below his head. He became aware that he had vomited. He lifted his hands and tried to wipe his mouth; but they fell back on his stomach; he was still pinioned. Eyes blind under the heavy brightness. He writhed, flung his whole body onto its right side, looked into the blackness under a boulder. If now it would roll down upon me, crush me, obliterate me. *Out, out, brief candle—Out, out—* When hands touched him, he screamed in silence. But was pulled back to face the sun. *Memorise another Golgotha—*

Joseph was dressed. The sunglasses searched Stephen's face. "Get up," urgently.

Stephen stared blankly up at him. *There's no art to find the mind's construction in the face—a mind diseas'd—corrode, consume—*Joseph seized his shirt collar and yanked him upwards. *—brief candle—Out, out—*

Joseph unfastened the flex around Stephen's wrists. "Get up."

—to die, to sleep—After life's fitful fever— Stephen began to laugh weakly. His laugh collapsed into an agony of retching. He fell sideways back against stone.

"Get up. Get up." *I have seen such things—*

Between Joseph's legs Stephen could see, six or seven yards away, a gaudy lizard—blue head, red and yellow body and tail; it had emerged from under a boulder. With a brilliant beady eye it scrutinised them, motionless except for the pulse in its neck, and a tongue that slashed out to taste the air. Then it scurried up the boulder and flattened itself soporifically near the top to take the sun.

"Get up." Again he was pulled upwards. He slumped forward. The back of

Joseph's hand struck his cheek. His head struck the boulder. Pain. "Get up. Get up." Pain.

Slowly he pulled himself up, clawing the boulder. I feel sick, I *am* sick. Feverish. I have a headache; my head, oh my head, pounding— He swayed, nearly fell. —*life's fitful fever—Out, out—too, too solid flesh—Out, out—*

Joseph pushed the hat—Susanna's hat—onto Stephen's head, the sweater into his hands. Then he pushed Stephen ahead of him to stumble down the kopje. *—a walking shadow—*

Where the axe had flashed, where Paul— Nothing. *—will come of nothing—There's nothing serious in mortality—* The sand had been brushed into innocence. *—clears us of this deed—* There's not even—to be seen, not even a drop—to be seen— *O blood, blood, blood—Blood will have blood—* Nothing.

They were sitting near where they had sat when the sun, now dropping westward, had risen that morning: in a grove of mukwa trees near the big kopje. Stephen leaned back against rough ribbed grey bark, breathing erratically. He fingered one of the strange frilled seed-pods shed by the tree. Joseph, watching him, was again sitting on a rock, AK slung at his back. Over his shoulder hung the bundle Welcome Ndlovu had carried; across his thighs rested Gabriel Mpofu's spear. Stephen, eyes closed, his voice toneless— "Where are the men? Gabriel and"—his mind stuttered—"Welcome—Welcome."

"They have returned to their homes. I sent them. It was time for them to go."

"So. We're on our own now."

"So we are on our own now. Only two of us, you and me. Surrounded by Africa."

Stephen ran the fingers of his right hand through tussocks of pale brown grass, laid the hand flat on dry soil. A black ant scurried over his wrist. "Why? Why didn't we go with them?"

Joseph didn't answer, didn't move. The sunlight, striking through the trees, falling in stripes across Stephen's dirty trousers, was reddening towards sunset. Blood. *—will have blood—* Blood. Another ant scurried down his arm and over his fingers, frantically about its food-gathering, its survival.

What is the point of talking to him, trying to communicate with him. Now, after— He may look human, he may talk like a human, but he is a monster. *—a most delicate monster—* A hideously vicious monster. Vile. Vile. *There's no art to find the mind's construction—* And he will kill me too. *Blood* *will have—* No escape. I am at his mercy. He will kill me. *Who would have thought there was so much—* Monster. Monster. *—so much—blood—*

"We must go" peremptorily.

"No. Wait. I must, I have to—I have to defecate." Suddenly he was shaking violently and screaming. "Shit. Fuck you, Joseph. Shit. I have to shit. That's how we met. Remember? Shit. I have to shit." Then he was weeping, gobs of grief bursting up, excruciatingly, through the knot in his throat; he was sobbing, gasping, sobbing, gasping; but tearless—I have no tears to shed, Paul.

At last he stood up, shakily. "You wait. I have to shit." He dropped the filthy sweater and tottered a short distance, yanked down his trousers and underpants, squatted. Unexpectedly he recalled telling Joseph, an hour or so ago, a century, aeons, ago, that he was constipated. His giggle was a sob. Don't get hysterical, his mind instructed coldly, that can only make things worse. His head still pounding fiercely, swelling and deflating, swelling and deflating.

As he stood up, he smelled, and then saw, how badly soiled his underpants were. Carefully he leaned against a tree, pulled off his trousers, then the underpants, which he dropped on the sand before jerkily pulling his trousers back on.

Joseph had been watching. He came over; in silence dug a shallow hole with the spear; in silence pushed the discarded garment into it; in silence covered it carefully with sandy soil. "Now we will go. Take this and follow me." He held out the spear to Stephen.

"What—?"

"It is *your* weapon now. Mr Mpofu left it for you."

"For me?" suspiciously. Yet another lie?

"Yes. He has his knife for the journey to his home, and he is travelling with Mr Ndlovu."

"But—I don't know how to use it."

"You will learn. It is easy. You will see."

"'You will see, you will see,' that's what you say over and over again. 'You will see, you will see.' But how can I see anything if you don't *tell* me anything?" He bit hysteria back.

"I will tell you, England. We will talk." Joseph proffered the spear, handle touching Stephen's arm.

"I don't want to talk. To you— You're— You—" beginning to sob again. "You are—" He choked.

"It is time to go."

Trembling, Stephen tied the sweater round his waist, so that it hung down behind him like a pelt. Then he grasped the spear. It was surprisingly light. He held it cautiously across his body, as he had seen Gabriel holding it, the razor-sharp point well in front of his chest.

Joseph struck out in a westerly direction. For a while they walked on flattish grass-tussocked sandy soil, often threading their way among flat-topped mopane trees. Then there were more kopjes ahead. Joseph picked their way along small valleys between kopjes; only rarely did they have to clamber up rocks to hold to the direction. They seemed to be skirting the edge of a great sandy plain, Stephen realised, keeping along its northeastern perimeter.

It was nearly evening. Joseph led Stephen up a low kopje, and from its smooth crown, fringed with trees, they again looked down towards the great plain glowing like honey in the low sunlight. "We will sit here until the sun is setting." He settled himself on a rock.

"And then what? 'You will see'?"

"And then we will walk."

"In which direction?" Stephen stood in front of Joseph. Who pointed southwest. "Over that plain? Is that Botswana, or still Zimbabwe? Are we going into Botswana?"

"You will see" mockingly.

"Why? Why are we going there? Do you know that country?"

"You will see. No. I have never been there. If we are going there. But my people have. And my mother's people, the Kalanga, they live there as well as in Zimbabwe. It is not very different from here."

"When were your father's people there?"

"Questions, always questions, England. If you want me to stop saying 'You will see', you must stop asking me so many questions."

"There's something *you* must stop saying to *me*. I am *not* England. You are not Zimbabwe. I am Stephen. You are Joseph. Joseph who? I don't even know your surname."

"You are not Baas now, England. That time is gone. We have already discussed these things. The British Empire is gone. You must remember that, if you want me to call you Stephen. But do you really believe geography and history, language and culture, have nothing to do with what we are, who we are? We have already discussed these things. England made you. So I call you England."

"That's simplistic. You know that. We are—" Stephen stopped. Why am I even talking to him. Polite conversation with a monster. Mesmerise your murderer with cheerful chitchat. It's love that makes the world go round. And round. And round. And round.

"What is the matter, England? Is it because I am Black and you are White that you adopt that arrogant tone when you address me? 'That is simplistic,'" mimicking Stephen. "'You ignorant niggah'—why don't you say that, why don't you say it openly instead of sneering behind your so-called liberalism?"

"Don't be silly." He's clever. Playing with me. Probing for weaknesses. But why does he bother? Because it gives him pleasure? Yes. There are manipulative monsters. In fact, to *be* a monster, you must be clever, no doubt—strong and cunning, always defeating your opponent, always humiliating him. Triumphing in his pain. Select your weapon—rapier first, then, if necessary, a club. Or AK. Spear, axe. Axe. Oh God-if-there-is-a-God— Still standing opposite Joseph as the light faded slowly from orange to pink to grey, he looked away. "Aren't you afraid, as you walk, Joseph, that I have this spear? Just behind you? I could stab you in the back—that would be easy."

"Easy for some people, but not for you. You are sensitive, cultured, civilised, England. Aren't you?"

"Don't be too sure. And do you really think that no sensitive, cultured, civilised man has ever killed? Didn't the most sensitive, cultured, civilised nation in all of Europe rape and torture and murder Jews and gypsies and homosexuals?"

"Not to mention what the sensitive, cultured, civilised nations of Europe did to Africa. But I was referring to individuals—you asked me to acknowledge your individuality."

"Oh. You mean like Hitler, Stalin, Idi Amin, Mugabe? And what about *you?* As an individual of course. So sensitive, cultured, civilised. And a torturer. And a rapist. And a bugger. And a murderer."

Joseph stiffened. The sunglasses, catching the sun's last rays, swung away, swung back. "You do not understand. We will talk."

"Oh, we will talk? 'We will talk'? A sensitive, cultured, civilised conversation about torture and rape and buggery and murder." Careful, Stephen, careful. Enrage him and you die. But what's it matter, he will kill me anyway, why not get it over with. Why is he waiting? The axe, glittering for an eternal moment, began to fall— Oh God-if-there-is-a-God— Monster, monster. Yes, but he did save Susanna, remember that. Raped her—horrible, *O, horrible! most horrible!* —But then took her to the road so she could have her foot healed in a hospital. Remember that. All human beings are complex individuals, isn't that what I have been preaching? Cling to that. The liberal tradition of my tribe, Joseph, asserts that no human can be entirely evil, that there is some good in all of us. So I must continue to look for the good in you, Joseph.

My tribe has condemned me to that. Casually, "You said your people lived in Botswana. Did they settle there when they fled north from the Zulus in South Africa during the nineteenth-century?"

"Later. More questions! I told you—"

"Later? They settled there later? When?"

"No, I will *tell* you later. We will talk later. We must go on now. Soon it will be sunset. We must walk as far as possible tonight. Can you do that?"

"You think I'm weaker than you? Remember, the English conquered your people. You said yourself they were strong."

"Inconsistent, England, inconsistent and unpredictable"—with irritation, exasperation. Is his self-control slipping? "You say 'Call me Stephen, do not call me England, I am an individual,' then you say you are strong because you are English."

"No, I'm strong because I'm inconsistent and unpredictable. Shall we go?"

Silence. My eyesight is fading badly—I squint, and struggle increasingly to make out details. I'm also losing any sense of time, any sense of reality—days and nights bleed into each other—in this dream landscape, in this interminable nightmare. Maybe I'm actually dead, a dead man walking? I am dead. But I walk, I walk. My throat, my mouth, are parched. My feet ache, my eyes ache, my entire body aches and aches. He stops, I stumble into him, I stop. We sit. Cross-legged I sit in the middle of vast darkling Africa. And each night takes me closer to—what? Each night is continuity, repetition; but also change. The moon, no longer new, sheds a pale blue light over the ghostly earth. *Slowly, silently, now the moon Walks the night—The moving moon went up the sky—* And each day moves this parched land closer to the rains? Maybe. The cycle of nature—parturition, repetition, change. *Ripeness is—*

"What about food?" Stephen asked. "I'm hungry. Aren't you? And water. I'm—" As he said "thirsty", he saw the flask in the shadow of the rock, and his heart jumped, but immediately fell. The pilot of that plane must have seen all of us on that kopje; the flask could add nothing but confirmation that we were there—and it is a serious loss.

Joseph: "Where did you leave it?"

"The flask? *You* left it. It was under the rock, the one we slept behind, Paul and I."

Stephen imagined the impassive face he could barely see, the swift movement of Joseph's mind in pursuit of his to the same conclusion. Then "You must wait for water," Joseph said. "Down in the plain we will find water.

I will show you how to suck moisture from the earth. I have some meat still. We will eat after our next walking. Follow me." He set off, Stephen stumbling behind him. Now they were in a grassy vlei running downward between two kopjes.

And Turner was there, with him, ahead of him. Where had he come from, leaping into life so suddenly? Stephen was following him, as so often he had done in the distant past. "Come on, Holmes, buck up now, Boy, *tempus fugit!*" Dr G.R.O. Turner, nickname 'The Grot' or 'Grotty,' Housemaster and Senior English Master at a minor public school, would-be actor, dictatorial director of annual Shakespeare plays, vain egotist and— I remember the first midnight when he came to my bed in the dorm and circled my sleepy penis with his cold hand, only my fourth night in his House, and whispered in my ear "It's all right, Holmes, keep quiet and don't move, Boy; just relax"—first of how many midnight visits? But during the day, no sign of that secret connection, unless severity was a sign. In Form One he made us learn verses from long poems like "The Ancient Mariner" and recite them in sequence so we could "appreciate the aural genius of Coleridge, Boys"; then, in higher forms, we had to learn and recite whole poems. Shy, reedy-voiced, 'weedy,' I hated the prominence of performing to a gallery of suppressed mirth; but I owe to that torture my love of poetry. Yes. I do. And he introduced me to the English poets of the Great War: Owen, Sassoon, Gurney, Thomas, Blunden, and of course my beloved Rosenberg. He gave me so many of my voices. I should not forget that. Yes, I owe much to that man, who also—

Movement ahead, beyond Turner, beyond Joseph. He stopped.

Guttural barks. "Baboons"—Joseph, quietly. "If we walk slowly towards them, they will go. They will only attack us if we seem to threaten them." He walked on.

In the grass, up small thorn-trees, on an ant-hill poking up out of the grass, a troop of dark figures; their long-muzzled faces, fringed with rough hair, turned towards Joseph and Stephen; faces almost human, almost canine; sharp pale eyes. Some were already moving, forming a tight group. Females with their offspring riding on their backs like minuscule jockeys; and several males busily shepherding, supervising, protecting.

Joseph stopped again, some fifty yards from the troop, which numbered about forty, excluding the very young on their mothers' backs. Meanwhile the quick but orderly—almost military—activity had continued, in response to barked commands by one very big male, who was patrolling between the two humans and the baboons.

Joseph again began to move forward slowly. The baboons loped off unhurriedly, at a tangent, towards the kopje on the left. With their pink rubbed-bare buttocks, long tails raised sharply from haunches, their clumsy four-legged gait, reminiscent of a human baby's just before it rises on two legs to discover that it can balance and walk—these creatures were almost comical. The leader, as he herded the troop, glared, intermittently but balefully, over his shoulder at the two human interlopers, his barks now directed at them— warnings or complaints?

"Are they dangerous?" Stephen asked.

"They can tear a leopard apart," Joseph answered, still watching the steady retreat. With a soft laugh: "I remember once—I was a small boy, about eight years old. It was sunset, I was hurrying home to the kraal. I did not even notice the baboons until I was so near that I was almost surrounded by them. I have never run so fast in all my life."

"What did they do? Did they follow you?"

"I thought they did. Perhaps they did. I climbed a tree and stayed there for a long time, until it was dark. Then I ran home, by a long way round. I thought I was seeing them, all the way, running after me—I was crying with terror. When I got home I could not explain at first what had happened. My father wanted to beat me—I should not have been out in the bush so late. But my mother would not let him. She took me in her arms, she was crying too, and she held my head between her breasts—I can still smell them, the milk in them for my baby sister, I can still feel the warmth of them pulsing in my ears."

They came out onto the plain: a grey sandy sea spreading out and out to meet the onrush of darkness. "Now we will eat. And I will show you how to get water from dry land." They squatted under a marula tree surrounded by hard black pitted cores, remnants of its last fruiting. Joseph propped the AK against its trunk, opened the bundle he had been carrying. Several pieces of the cooked duiker were wrapped in a cloth. He handed one to Stephen. They ate in silence. There were three pieces each.

Afterwards Joseph stood up and pissed into the darkness.

Stephen got up stiffly, walked a few paces away, and gazed up at the sparkling blue-blackness. When the moon rose, as it would soon, there would be a ghostly diffused glow which would restore shadows to the trees as pools of thicker darkness. He listened to the sounds of the young night. Distant coughs. A faint scream—bird or animal?—must be an animal, for he knew that birds fall silent at night. Nearer, a yelp, answered in a few moments by a second one. A crickling in the grass—small creatures, mice, rats, about their nocturnal struggle to survive. *Provide, provide—*

He pissed. A comforting activity, really; links one to the primal cycle. Why is there so much pain in life when the natural functions are so pleasurable? Well, not all natural functions are pleasurable—what about birth? And why is that so painful? Shockingly so, after being set in motion by the most intensely pleasurable of all natural functions—for men, anyway. Here you go, Stephen—Q and A, Q and no A—and anyway, that answer's obvious enough: the pain is to ensure the survival of the species, QED— Survival again, survival, survival, all is survival— *Ripeness is all—* The sugar of sex ensures procreation, but then the mother must be bound tight to what has cost her so much pain to deliver; to ensure protection, survival. Obvious, Stephen—banal. "You don't value what you haven't paid for, Mother," as Dad used to say, and Mum's inevitable reply, "Yes, dear, but I still value *you.*"

Joseph spoke from just behind him. "I thought you were thirsty, Mr Stephen. Come with me. Here is your spear." After a few yards, he stopped. With the spear, he had already dug a deep hole in the sandy soil. "Push your hand in deep, right to the bottom."

Stephen knelt and reached down. "Yes, I can feel wetness."

"Cup your hand, and water will begin to gather in it. Then, if you are careful, you can raise the water up to your mouth. The Bushmen suck it up with straws—dry grass."

"Yes." Stephen raised his hand carefully and sucked moisture into his mouth. "Yes."

"With a little more practice you will be able to do that proficiently. Try again. Are you still thirsty? Have you had enough?"

"Well—perhaps for now."

"Then pull up some grass near you. Put the bottom of the stem in your mouth. Chew and suck it. You can do that while you are walking. In the morning there will also be some dew to lick off grass and plants. Now we must walk."

The land was flat, almost level. Trees were few now and scattered—thorn-trees, acacia. Desert-like savanna, Stephen decided, even drier than the savanna behind them. They walked over grass—tussocks of short rough dry grass, expanses of drooping tresses. The moon was up now. Joseph was a shadow swaying ahead. *Life's but a walking—* Walking, walking.

And here is Turner again, 'Grotty'—I don't know what his first name was—George, Geoffrey, Gordon?—just as I don't know Joseph's surname. I was too shy even to audition to act in his annual play-production; so he made me his Prompt and later, in Form Four, promoted me to Stage-manager. So I got to know, painlessly and with almost perfect recall, the text of the annual Shakespeare plays he directed during my time there. He acted the main role in *Macbeth,* blacked himself up as Othello, finally rampaged as a long-white-bearded King Lear—claiming there was no one else who could act those all-important roles, schoolboys being much too *gauche,* a favourite word of his, you needed *maturity* to enact a hero—you needed to be Turner. Yes, and maybe that's why we didn't do *Hamlet*—he was too old to be Hamlet, and no doubt he didn't want one of his younger colleagues to star. My one role, he forced me into it, was the Fool to his Lear, in my last year—"No, don't argue, you are just right for it, Holmes, your size, your voice, you *are* the Fool," and I was. And a success, to my joyful surprise! But what a *prima donna* Turner was! A closet homosexual, of course—and a pedophile who was eventually caught, just after my time—I was told this at Oxford by Myers when I happened to meet him in the High—and died soon after that, in disgrace.

Stephen almost bumped into Joseph. "Now we will rest."

Then another trek. Easier walking now, much easier. Walking, walking. My sore feet, oh my feet!

But I remember with most pleasure those Sunday afternoons in The Grot's study, in my final two years. He would read poems to me, in his rich baritone, and tell me about the poets—and then a glass of sherry, while we sat companionably side by side on the leather couch in front of a fire. That was the epitome of pleasure for me, my weekly epiphany. What came after was *his* epiphany. The nocturnal visits to my bed had stopped when I reached Form Three. But in his study, the door into the passage carefully locked, he would very slowly strip me to my underpants, with caresses, kisses and murmurs; then I would stand before him, my back to the fire, and he would pull down my underpants, tell me that naked I was "a young god," and suck me off. That was the Sunday afternoon ritual, and I can't say that it was unpleasant; in fact, it was guiltily *enjoyable,* made me feel attractive and significant, and I think I would have accepted it without complaint even if it had been mildly painful, as payment for what he gave me. I never saw *him* naked, although he was a tall handsome florid man, and vain about his appearance; he just didn't seem to want or need anything more, or perhaps he had that in relationships with other Masters—or masturbated after I left his study, who knows? Did he turn me into a homosexual? No, I would have become one anyway, *was* already one surely? I think he merely recognised in me similar personal qualities, proclivities, to his own, and fostered them. Was that wrong? Questions, questions, England! But no answers.

Stephen was sitting against a tree. He dozed, drifted into a light sleep. When he jerked awake, he knew immediately that Joseph was gone. The AK was there, leaning against the tree under which he had been sitting— A surge of excitement, quickly extinguished. How could I survive on my own in this wilderness? Even now, a leopard may be sliding towards me through the night—

And then Joseph was back, standing beside him. Have I been asleep again? Joseph holding the spear. Hanging from it was a small furry body.

It was almost dawn. This is like sleepwalking. The moon holding the world around me in a deep blue mystery. Dream landscape. Does it exist? But we are walking deeper and deeper into it. Into its heart of darkness? Or— The closer one comes to the core, the utter centre, blackness, the closer to a blinding blaze of light? Ultimate paradox. But reality rests in paradox, doesn't it? Cold needs hot, high needs low, hatred needs love: opposites bound together at the root, immitigable. Ultimate impossibility of Apartheid! *Too deep for me, Steve—Mind's the fucker—*

And Turner turns towards me. Soon he will be gone, perhaps for good. He never smiled at me, and now he simply stares. Yes, Myers told me there was some gossip that he committed suicide. A boy two forms below us had complained to HM, Myers said; and, when nothing happened, the father, a prominent MP, visited the school. Faced by the threat of scandal, of police involvement, they hushed it all up of course: Turner 'retired.' But what troubled me most in my brief conversation with Myers was his comment that my relationship with The Grot was known, surreptitiously—the other boys used to joke and speculate about it backstage, he said, and apparently they found it hilarious when I called him "Nuncle"; and when he took my hand in the mad scene—"Come on, my boy. How dost, my boy? Art cold?"—they would fall around in stifled laughter. Why was I so discomforted to learn this? Then Myers said "But you're not gay, are you, Holmes? Do you have a girlfriend?" and I said "Not yet" and quickly changed the subject. But I think that was when I began to decide I must 'come out'. And now here I am— *Out—Out, out—Out, out—brief candle—*

I sense more than see Joseph walking smoothly, alertly, ahead of me, the dead dark body over his shoulder lifting and falling to the rhythm of his stride. His mind flowing sinuously ahead, watching, searching. It circles, then advances again. Probes constantly, flicking like the lizard's tongue, sniffing the air that caresses us as we pass steadily through it.

Turner? Going. Gone.

Now there were portents of dawn high in the sky. The stars fading, glimmering to hazy pinpricks. The moon sinking gracefully, ineluctably, towards a horizon that rises slowly to greet it. Sunglow. Stephen heard the air soughing, barely soughing, past his ears. *Be not afeard—sounds and sweet airs—* But what do these sounds, as they wax and wane, say to me? What do my voices mean? Where do they come from? Merely figments of myself, ultimately—an elaborate dance of self-communing? He gazed part-seeing at grey movement ahead. His legs scissored, scissored; his hands grasped the spear, now lifted against his left shoulder like a rifle. His head throbbed. His throat ached. My whole body aches, aches. Am I going mad? I came to Africa to find myself—I told Susanna that. But I am losing myself. I am fragmenting. Rosenberg, can you save me? *Sombre the night is. And though we have our lives, we know What sinister threat lurks there—* Joseph's mind curls round trees, touches the grass, runs along the earth ahead of him, probing, probing, probing— *Dragging these anguished limbs, we only know This poison-blasted track opens on our camp—On a little safe sleep—*

Joseph stopped. Stephen stopped. Another tree. Another rest.

Dawn rose like a lily. Why did he think that? It flamed, it seethed, it leaped, it warmed, it melted, it spread gold and silver across the vast land. Yet the voice in his mind stubbornly repeats: It is like a lily. I must be going mad. *But hark! Joy—joy—strange joy—* A great chorus of birds. They flit across the rising sun, leap from warm nests into their new day of unremitting toil—what is there for them to rejoice about? I have never paid much attention to birds; I should have; if I survive, I will. *Music showering on our upturned list'ning faces—* He sat down, stiffly; leaning against the tree to gaze sleepily, glassily. My head aches still, my eyes ache still, my sight is deteriorating fast. The flies torment me. I'm hungry, I'm thirsty. He looked up into the deep blue dome that rested against the tree's bare branches.

Joseph came into focus. He was speaking; standing beside Stephen, looking down at him. Stephen grimaced. "What did you say?"

"I say that when the sun is higher, I will cook the meat. Now I will look for roots and bulbs."

"What is the animal you killed?"

"A young tsessebe. We call it *inkolimi*. It was with a herd of females, all with young."

Stephen went across to where Joseph had lifted it from his shoulders: it lay in a soft absence, its red coat, glossed with purple, unmarked except for the spear-gash in its gut from which a skein of blood still oozed. Oh impossibly beautiful. Impenetrably sombre eyes. *Death could drop from the dark As easily as song—* The animal spoke to him in the silence of the grass's whisper. *But song only dropped, Like a blind man's dreams on the sand By dangerous tides, Like a girl's dark hair for she dreams no ruin lies there, Or her kisses where a serpent hides—* Oh voices, voices, my voices. They comfort me, but also confuse me? Many voices can madden. *—and we drown—* But one voice can enslave. Is that a crucial difference between Joseph and me? But still I long for unity, simplicity, integrity. As we all do, must do? Even though that can destroy us.

He gazed out over the great plain. *The grass is singing—* A dawn breeze; it will die away soon. Sere. A sere landscape, pale brown, colour of drought, colour of death; pale brown grass, brown earth, occasional dark brown trees. Only the blue sky speaks of release. But when will the thunder speak? Above the horizon he thought he saw low cloud, a dark plume. To the left of it, the hills that he had noticed earlier—closer now, of course, but still far—ten, twenty, thirty miles away? They were beginning to quiver already in the day's heat-haze. Are those baobabs—a cluster of baobabs—in the middle distance? A movement, still further to the left, drew his attention to Joseph's approach— he was walking through a sparse copse of thorn-trees.

When Joseph reached Stephen, "I have brought roots and other food for us to eat. That bush fire may come this way."

"Fire?" He followed Joseph's pointing to the distant smudge. "Oh. Yes." Now he became aware of a faint acrid smell.

"But it will move very slowly unless a wind comes."

"So where are we going? In the direction of those hills?"

"Yes. Now we will eat. You gather twigs and branches for the fire while I skin and cut up our meat." He had taken a small knife from the sheath attached to his belt.

Stephen's task was simple. He soon had a pile of dry wood laid between two stones. As he was about to pick out two pieces for his attempt at flame-by-friction, he remembered the lens; and was soon squatting over the wood, with the lens focussing a fierce ray on dead leaves. Blue smoke twisted out of them; then a tiny flame. The fire was blazing before Joseph came over with chunks of venison to cook. "You made the fire quickly" Joseph complimented him.

"I used this lens"—displaying it, with the gratification of a schoolboy whose invention has proved useful.

Joseph was looking at him closely. "But you are trembling and flushed, Mr Stephen. Are you sick?"

"I'll be all right. I think I was a bit feverish during the night. That's all."

"Where is your sweater? Put that on until you feel better."

Stephen put his hands to his waist. "Oh," foolishly, "it's gone." When did it slip off? He had no idea. "Well, it won't be really cold again now, will it, so close to your summer? Not in this low country, surely? Last night it was warmer, I didn't even think of putting on my sweater when we stopped to rest."

The sunglasses reflected a stiff guileless expression. He thinks I did it on purpose—marking our trail for the Police or Army. Well, let him think so. Even if it didn't happen like that, I should be doing what he thinks I did, I should be leaving signs whenever I can.

Joseph reached down into his bundle. "Here are some roots for you to eat while I am cooking the meat." Stephen stood near him, trying to avoid the smoke. The roots tasted strangely like suet, but succulent.

"Did you love your father, Joseph?"

"Yes. Of course. Why do you ask that?"

"I wondered. You said he wanted to beat you, but your mother stopped him. Were you closer to her?"

Joseph looked into the smoke. "When I was a small boy, I was taken from her."

"Why?"

"My father went to work on a farm. He took me with him. He had a woman there; she did not like me but I could not go back to my mother. I started work on the farm when I was eight—soon after those baboons—"

"Eight?"

"That was not unusual. And I was strong."

"What did you do?"

"I was a herd-boy, driving the cattle in the bush, and I also helped my father in his work. He was the cook on the farm. And—" He hesitated.

"Cook? But I thought he was a warrior?"

Joseph smiled bitterly. "Who could be a warrior then? The Whites would not allow that. And how could you earn money as a warrior? The Whites made us pay taxes. My father had to make money to pay taxes. The farmer's wife taught him to cook. She wanted a nice clean responsible servant who would be polite to Madam. *I* was the warrior. Later."

"You mean in the Bush War?"

"Yes. And after that."

"Can you tell me about it?"

"Here is your meat," handing Stephen the knife with a piece of meat skewered on it. They were squatting side by side. "It is not pleasant to talk about it, or even think about it, most of it. Better to forget. So I do not talk about it."

"But you do think about it? How can you forget it?"

"Yes, I think about it sometimes. That I cannot control."

"Well—I can understand. My father said my grandfather—he was at the Somme—he would never talk about his experiences in the First World War. No matter how often you asked. Even when he was dying of cancer."

"You think anyone can understand if they were not there, in the fighting? No. How could they? Of course not. It was—like the end of the world some-times. We had to kill. We had to follow orders. Sometimes the orders— You wished you were not there, you even wished you had never been born. But— Once—" He stopped; chewed the soft succulent meat for a few minutes.

"Yes?"

"This was not long ago. Will you tell anyone?"

Stephen's heart leaped. Then he doesn't intend to kill me! He is going to let me live. I'll see Susanna again. Or is this a trap, a lie, to lull me till the time comes? "No. I promise."

Joseph spoke rapidly, the words rattling up his throat, piling against tongue and teeth. "It was at a Mission. But it was not a true Mission. It was called a Mission, but how could they believe in Jesus Christ and do such things? They behaved like Boer farmers, they told our people to get off the land because they said it belonged to the Mission, the Mission had bought the land. The people begged them, but they said No, no, you must go, all of you, it is *our* land. Where? Where could the people go? They had been on that land for many many years. Those White bastards came just—yesterday. But they said it was *theirs*, they owned it all. So—" He paused; passed Stephen another piece of meat; gazed into the smoke.

"So?" Stephen prompted.

"I— The leader of those people came to us. He knew us. He was the uncle of one of us. He told us that the Mission was evil, it was taking the people's land from the people. He asked me to deal with the matter."

"You were—?"

"I was—I am—of some authority. The people knew that. I told you I fought for four years in the Bush War; then I was in Harare, in the govern-ment, until the trouble began between the Ndebele, my people, and Mugabe, until I saw that nothing had really changed, that the Black bosses who had replaced the White bosses—ZANU-PF, Mugabe, and others, the Shona bosses—they were abusing their power and attacking my people. They accused our top commanders in the Bush War of being traitors—traitors!—and put them in prison, only because they were ZAPU not ZANU—and they would not respect the leader of my people, Joshua Nkomo. I had warnings to leave Harare and Mugabe's government, and I could see what was happening anyway. So—I returned to Bulawayo first. Then—the Mission. I took a risk. I went myself, at night, to see the leader of the Mission, an old man with white hair who should have been wise. I spoke to him, calmly, respectfully, begging him not to send our people off their land, but he refused to listen to me, he told me it was not my business, I was wasting his time. This Missionary, this servant of God, he called his servants and ordered them to throw me off the Mission's property."

"And did they?"

"They pretended to—they knew who I was. They were frightened of the Missionary, but they were more frightened of me."

"Then?"

"I led a group of our men to the Mission. We killed all the Whites."

"Killed? All the Whites? How many were there? How did—?"

"With axes. We killed them with axes. And spears. To get our land. The people's land."

"Oh God." *A deed without a name—* Oh God-if-there-is-a-God.

"Seven were there that night. And four children."

"Oh God." *Blood will have blood—*

"They had done evil to my people. They took our land. We followed our orders. *I* followed my orders. They—begged, they promised to give us back the land, they cried out, they prayed to God to save them. But it was too late. God did not save them." He passed another piece of meat to Stephen. "So—Now you know. You always ask questions, Stephen, you always want to *know.* Now you know."

"I can't eat this." Stephen handed the meat back. "And— Were all the men, Gabriel and Welcome and the others, all those seven men, were they with you then?"

"Yes. They were with me. Did you look closely at Welcome's axe?" Stephen stared mutely at Joseph. "You should have. It is a battle-axe of my people."

Stephen swallowed. "It was with you for a purpose."

"Yes. For a purpose. To execute."

"But then— Why him? Paul. Why?"

"He tried to escape. He attacked us. You saw that. He—behaved like the Missionary, proud, scornful. He was—racist. He would not even look at me. I did not intend to kill him. If he— But he would not—co-operate. He spat in my face. He made me kill him."

I will not respond, I will not comment. What can I say? *I have supp'd full with horrors—*

"One of them looked like you, Stephen—at the Mission. He was young, a boy. With glasses. He was the old man's son, I think so. The Missionary's son. He tried to protect a girl. Sister or—girlfriend. He was the last to die. I did not want to kill him. When the girl was taken away by my men, he looked at me. The way you are looking at me now, Stephen. With accusation in his eyes."

Joseph did not put out the fire as soon as the cooking was done. Perhaps he doesn't feel it'll be noticed in this wide wilderness, especially with the big bush fire not far away—or perhaps he is growing careless. "We must sleep," he said. "You can sleep first. Then it will be your turn to watch. There will be more animals now, especially in the evening. We must be watchful. I will wake you."

Curled in the shade, between the fire and the tall mukwa tree, Stephen slipped almost immediately into deep sleep. When he awoke to the gentle pressure of Joseph's hand on his shoulder, it was with the knowledge that he had dreamed vividly; and with relief that the dream had not risen to consciousness with him.

Joseph lay down on the other side of the gently flickering fire, in the shade of the tree. Yes, I didn't think of that: the fire as deterrent to predatory animals—of course that's why he didn't put it out. Stephen sat against the tree, gazing towards the smudge of smoke in the distance—wondering if it was widening, darkening?

Now Joseph lay flat on his back, his head on the bundle, his breathing regular in the rhythm of sleep. I could kill him. With his own AK. The murderer murdered. Why don't I? But he knew he couldn't. Joseph was right. Pacifist or coward—what's the difference? Stephen Coward. Stephen Coward.

Yet Joseph, lying there, looked innocent, incapable of violence. We all do, Stephen thought bitterly. We all look so—human. A man somewhere in America inveigles gay man after gay man into his bed, tortures them as he destroys them. A smiling respectable man in Yorkshire gives lifts to a six-year-old girl, mangles her before allowing her to die. Eichmann, a gentle old man's smile in a glass booth. Stalin, cuddly grandfather. There is no mark of

Cain. Who is in fact more attractive—more beautiful, more intelligent, charming—than clumsy shifty Abel. Puerile, Stephen! Don't we all know this? We just have trouble accepting it, remembering it. So very human.

And you, Joseph. Beautiful, powerful, intelligent, sensitive, charming. And vicious, mysterious, impenetrable. *I love you, great new Titan! Am I not you?—Love! you love me—your eyes Have looked through death at mine— When you sleep you remind me of the dead— I love you, great new Titan! Am I not you?—Let us sleep now—*

Voices. Voices, too many voices. Yet I need them now, their wisdom, their companionship, their consolation. But do they deafen me? Conceal me from my self. So I must—I should try to close my mind to them. Let them converse with each other in the void. Simplicity, I must seek simplicity. Can one achieve simplicity without sacrificing reality—the diversity and complexity of reality? Are the voices real? But I must seek the simplicity of my self. Joan trusted her voices, they became her reality. Bound to the stake, screaming as her blood bubbled, did she think that she had been misled? For a moment, he saw a girl maddened, trembling, her shaven head, vacantly staring eyes—the flames crackling, the screams—Oh God-if-there-is-a-God— Why? Why create a world of such suffering? *Corrode, consume—* Or is it the pain of birth, again—a necessary ugly ritual to force us to learn love? Dare one think that? And to open our eyes to beauty—the blinding beauty of your crazy creation? Can we ever make sense of what we are, who we are, where we are, what we do day after day, night after night? What does it all *mean?* God-if-there-is-a-God— Gradually his mind drifted into a trance.

Whether it was the movement that roused him, or the mind's slow return— He couldn't focus at first on what was moving, but was aware of movement. It was late afternoon; that now-familiar golden treacle spreading over the brown landscape. Then the skin on his neck crawled. He swallowed, painfully. Several animals were approaching, cautiously, silently, from his right; a pack of them. For a moment he couldn't speak. Then he heard his hoarse voice—"Joseph."

As Joseph sat up abruptly, one of the animals came up to him; stopped two yards from him, pale eyes fixed below its large rounded ears. Speckled fur—black, yellow, white. Like a dog in appearance, size— Yes; Stephen swallowed again: wild dogs; which hunt in packs, tearing their prey into shreds, into running skeletons. Have been known to attack humans when famished. One of the books he'd read described them in fascinated detail. Rare now, their survival threatened, but 'the most vicious of all African predators.' Joseph and the leading wild dog stared at each other, both motionless. The other wild dogs, ten of them, were slowly creeping closer.

"Stephen"—very softly. "Get my AK and hand it to me. Move very slowly."

Stephen leaned across, grasped the AK for the first time, and then gradually pushed himself, on his haunches, to his left, until he could extend the heavy weapon towards Joseph's extended right hand; which grasped the butt of the AK, while his left hand closed on the stock; and then, very slowly, his right hand slid up towards the trigger and the barrel drifted down level with the wild dog's chest.

Stephen's eyes were seized by swift movement beyond Joseph. The troop of wild dogs was running, scattering—and at that moment the one opposite Joseph flared into movement too—was hanging on the end of the AK, was gone— Joseph turned towards Stephen, his mouth opening. Stephen's head swung right to follow his gaze—

The lion was charging, it was barely five yards away— Its body lifted as the world filled with a vast roar—

Joseph's AK exploded in Stephen's ear, once, twice, and the huge tawny body was falling sideways, blood spewing from its neck and chest, blood pumping scarlet onto the sand, blood spurting sizzling onto the fire—

The roar heaped reverberating into silence. Stephen couldn't move. The lion's legs sawed air and sand, its great maned head tossed and lifted, its eyes flamed at him, its bared teeth sought his throat— Then it fell back to shuddering death.

Joseph was shaking his shoulder urgently. "We must go, we must go."

While Stephen got shakily to his feet, Joseph seized a burning stick and pushed it into his left hand. Then "Your spear" and Stephen grasped it in his right hand. Joseph took another burning stick from the fire. "Follow me, quick, quick, quick." The wild dogs were creeping back towards them.

Half-walking, half-running, Stephen followed Joseph. They were heading towards the bush fire. The sun had fallen close to the horizon. Behind them, the lion's corpse had disappeared below a frenzy of feeding and whimpering and growling.

Baobabs enlarging ahead of them, on a slight rise. Blood-red in the sunset glow. The bush fire's black plume of smoke rose beyond, like a fist. Joseph was heading for the baobabs. He was already some way ahead.

When Stephen stumbled breathlessly up to the nearest of the baobabs— there were twelve in all—he found Joseph feverishly gathering twigs and dead branches. "There"—he pointed to where the AK leaned against one of the giant trees. Near it were some big boulders, and beside one of them a small fire was alight, started with Joseph's brand. "Make another fire between the rock and the tree, on the other side, quickly, quickly."

By the time evening had thickened into night, they had accumulated a large pile of dry wood against the boulder. In each of the two wide openings between their boulder and their baobab, a fire burned strongly. The space within, about eight feet square, was their refuge. Exhausted, they sat in silence.

IX

The twin fires, fed frequently from a pile of wood, burned vigorously. Neither Stephen nor Joseph felt able to sleep, but they dozed from time to time. There were sounds in the semi-darkness, some close, most distant. Growls, coughs, shrieks, hisses, scuffles, rustles. Green eyes occasionally glowed briefly—the wild dogs? Stephen worried that an animal might leap up onto the boulder opposite them; but Joseph seemed unconcerned about that, so he said nothing.

The smooth bark of the baobab behind them had been pitted and hollowed. Stephen shifted, trying to find a smooth surface for his back. "What caused these holes?" he asked after a while.

"Elephants. They dig out the soft bark with their tusks when they are very thirsty. The tree-trunk holds water. Elephants like the baobabs' fruit also. My people too—they eat the fruit. Baobabs are holy trees, my people believe they have good spirits."

"I believe that too. This one is protecting us right now. Our guardian spirit."

Later Stephen spoke again. "I thought it was lionesses that did the hunting, not lions. At least, I remember seeing a TV nature film about them, and that's what it showed—a pair of lionesses hunting, the lion just waited till they provided his food. Nature's male chauvinist."

"There may be lionesses around here, we must be very careful tomorrow. His mates. But more likely he was alone, an old rogue lion. We call the lion *shumba.* They attack humans when they are old and alone and also very hungry, famished—then they are desperate, like the wild dogs, because of the drought. Did you notice how thin he was, how you could see his ribs? He must have noticed the wild dogs circling round us, or maybe they were following him, waiting for him to tire so they could kill him. But we nearly fed them all."

"If your shot had missed the old *shumba*— So instead he fed them, and saved us."

Stephen leaned forward to pull some wood from the pile and push it into his fire. "And I suppose the big bush fire might have driven them from their usual hunting areas, and they got separated from the animals scattering in all directions, and so they came—"

"They were desperate. I should have been more careful."

The first time I have heard him utter self-criticism. Perhaps his self-confidence is waning now he is out of the countryside he knows? But would that be a good thing? "How much further are we going, Joseph? Is there any point in marching on and on?"

Joseph's lips twisted. He turned his face away from Stephen. "Listen. You said I am a murderer. What do you think will happen to me if I am caught? Even before you came to me and shook my hand—long before—I could not have gone back. That is why I was there, where you met me and shook my hand. Partly."

"You mean—because of the Mission, because of what you did there?"

"Yes. But not that only. The Police are looking for me. And the Army are looking for me. Mugabe wants me. They took away my wife—where is she, what did they do to her, is she even alive? The Fifth Brigade are all round Bulawayo looking for me, and others like me—and they are beating and raping and murdering my people. So am I any worse than them—worse than Mugabe and his wild dogs? The Whites, some of them, still think he is a good man, they believe him when he says he wants peace—but I know Mugabe, I know him well, he hates the Whites—even his own people he does not love. He loves only himself. You will see, we will all see. But you do not know anything, Stephen. I told you, if you do not fight in a war, you know nothing about it. If I go back now, I will be captured, I will be tortured, I will be killed." He turned away to put wood on his fire.

"So you will go on and on? Running away? Is that a better way to die?"

"Yes," fiercely. "It is better to die a free man, Stephen."

"But you don't *have* to die, surely it's better to—live." Yet surely he's right. I don't know what I think now. Now that we're down to the most basic facts of our situation: life, or death. "And what about me, Joseph? Do *I* have to die because of what you have done?"

"Do you wish to leave me, Stephen? You can go if you like. I will even give you the AK if you would like to take it. I will exchange it for the spear."

"Do you mean that?"

"Yes, of course I mean that. Think about it. You are a free man also. Tell me what you want to do in the morning. But tonight"—he looked up into the darkness—"I would like to talk to you, to know more about you. I have answered *your* questions—"

"Some of them. And I haven't had a chance to ask many."

"You can ask more questions later—if you decide to stay with me. You will see—I will answer them all. But I have not asked *you* questions, so it is my turn. Is that fair?"

Stephen pondered. Can I trust him? Does he really mean it when he says I can leave? "You will see"—always, "You will see." But if I am to have any chance of survival, I should try to keep him in a good mood at least—try to make him understand me, perhaps even like me, sympathise with my situation. Clearly he wants to talk, needs to talk. "Yes. Fair enough. Fire away."

"Are you a university student?"

"I thought you knew that. Yes, I'm reading—studying—Modern History."

"Where?"

"Oxford. Oxford University."

"Oxford. I was there once. I visited someone, I met him when I was studying, in London— He was a tutor, is that the right word?—at Christ Church College, the one with the Cathedral inside, and—what do they call it— the Tom Tower?"

"Yes."

"It is in *Tom Brown's Schooldays*, he told me that—he read me some parts of it, the story."

Stephen smiled. "That English classic of puerile snobbery."

"Oh, I thought it made England a great nation. That and 'Rule Britannia' and 'Land of Hope and Glory' and of course the Empire."

"All the same thing. All gone now."

"And which college do you study in?"

"Corpus Christi. The smallest one. Under the backside of the one you visited—I don't suppose you would even have noticed it."

"My friend the tutor took me to see the college where the great Cecil Rhodes studied. It was nearby. I wanted to see where he learned to be so evil."

"Oriel. Then you were very close to my college."

"And what is your life like there?"

"Oh. It seems to be very far away—from here, from now." He paused. When is the day of our flight back to London, Susanna and I? Soon she will be surging above the darkness of Africa, leaving far behind her two tiny shadows. "Sorry; you want to know what undergraduate life's like in Oxford? Tutorials; reading—heaps of reading, books, articles; writing an essay every week for your tutor to criticise; lectures; in the afternoons, walking or cycling in the countryside; and sport—rowing, I'm cox of our second boat—and cross-country running, squash—"

"That is why you are so fit."

"Fit? I just like to keep the old arms and legs in motion. Then—in the evenings I sing in a choir or go to concerts and plays and films—pubs, late-night coffee with friends, the occasional party—"

"A busy life. Was it the same before—at your school? Did you go to a private school, what you English call a public school?"

"I didn't want that, in fact I rebelled against it—I was a socialist, and a pacifist too, by the time I left school—or I tried to be a pacifist, just as I tried to be a vegetarian. I used to wish that my parents hadn't sent me to a public school. I'm an only child, you see—they scrimped and saved to give me what they thought was the best education—so I could claw my way up to a higher rung than my father's - you know, the ghastly class system that permeates the whole of English life."

"But I thought it was dead and gone, like the British Empire."

"No, you didn't, Joseph. Why lie? You were in England, you said so. When we were talking earlier"—I can't even recall how long ago—"you made negative comments about English society. So how can you expect me to believe—?"

"You are right, Stephen. It was insulting to be sarcastic about England when you are answering my questions. Go on."

"Well, when my turn comes, I'll ask you about those experiences you mentioned—when *you* were in England. But— My schooldays. Not quite the same as Tom Brown's—I was at what they call a minor public school, meaning not as posh as Eton."

"Only boys? In—what are they called, dormitories?"

"Yes. Even today, some of the public schools don't admit girls. At Oxford, most colleges, including my one, are mixed now, women as well as men undergraduates. But my school still hasn't changed, and I don't think it ever will."

"How can you grow up without knowing girls? Without having sex with them? No wonder the English— No, I will tell you later, if you ask the right questions. The Whites made the education system in our country—Southern Rhodesia it was then, before the Bush War, before Independence—they imitated your English public schools as much as they could, especially for White schools—there were separate schools for White and Black children. Of course. Did you like your school?"

"Sometimes. My English Master did a Shakespeare play every year—I mean, he directed it, and usually acted the main part as well. And I was the Prompt, and then Stage-manager, and once I acted a part. The Fool—in *King Lear*, you must know it."

"No. At my school we had to study *Hamlet* for the Cambridge school-certificate, 'To be or not to be'—rubbish like that. But Hamlet got his revenge on them all, he killed them all. And I passed English."

"*Hamlet* was the only Shakespeare tragedy we *didn't* do. But our Master had a thing about Shakespeare, 'The whole of life and death—all of human experience'"—declaiming in imitation of Turner at his most hortatory—"'is in those plays, Holmes; if you know Shakespeare, you know everything you need to know about life.'"

"Do you think he was right? Was he a good teacher?"

"I did then, I thought he was wise, and— Oh, he did some bad things, but I don't think he was *evil*. And he taught me—well, a love of poetry—" My beloved Rosenberg. My absent voices. "Once he mentioned that his father had been killed in the trenches, so his mother had to bring him up on her own, by working as a charwoman—you know, a domestic servant, doing hard dirty work."

"As if she was Black, working for Whites, in Africa? Like my father. She must have had much suffering."

"I found that I could memorise poems easily, almost without trying. My best marks were always in English. The English Master said I should study English at university, but by then I'd decided to read History, to try to find out how and why things have come out the way they have, how and why the world wars started, how and why human beings allow so much suffering to happen."

"It is life, Stephen. We can change many things, we must try to change many things, but we cannot change that. Life is suffering."

"No, Joseph, I will not accept that. Life is not suffering—or at least"—remembering his own meditation on the pain of childbirth—"we cause so much more suffering than would ever exist otherwise. Violence, so much violence. Just to hurt others, make them suffer, and maim them, kill them. Surely you accept that?"

"Death is part of life, Stephen. Our lives are short. We come from death, we go to death. What is between? It is a dream."

Stephen looked at him, surprised. "An Anglo-Saxon writer said something like that, a long time ago. He said life is like a hall in winter, with a big fire in the centre, and a little bird flits through the hall, in at one door and out the other—and that is life. A flash of firelight in the darkness."

"Yes. He said it well. It is like us now, here—'firelight in the darkness.' Put more pieces of wood on your fire, Stephen," as he added some to his fire.

"But it's not true! I don't believe it. That's only one way of thinking about life—the tragic way. And I don't believe what you believe—that death is part of life. Death is death. Life is life. And when you are dead"—the axe glinted, lay on the air, slipped downward, Paul, Paul—"then—you are dead, life is utterly gone. I don't believe in an afterlife. Death is just death." *—an empty pail, a slate rubbed clean, A merciful putting-away of what has been—* And only a short while ago, Stephen, you were arguing that human experience, the universe itself, is composed of opposites—that low needs high, cold needs hot—life needs death? Do you even know what you think? Muddle, muddle— you're befuddled by fear, pain—and your voices. Stop listening to them. Simplicity, unity. Close your ears, your mind. Seek simplicity, seek within. Go naked. *—unaccommodated man—* And there I go again. *O fool! I shall go mad—* Or am I already mad? A figment in Joseph's dream, my nightmare, unreality? *—till human voices wake us, and we drown—Out, out—To be, or not to be—To be or—* He smiled bitterly. Has it come to that? Most banal of Shakespearean quotations, thrown at me by this man who is my enemy. This monster. His monster's voice.

Joseph was talking. "—then you will see why it is so. You will know why none of us can be responsible for what happens."

Stephen closed his eyes. "So you're a Communist? Dialectical materialism, end justifies the means, all that stuff?"

"No, I am not a Communist, England—I am Joseph."

"All right. All right. But nothing will make me accept what you've been saying, Joseph. We're each of us responsible for what we do. And even if we aren't, we must still believe we are. Otherwise how can there be morality? Nothing would have meaning, life would be just—nothing. Nihilism is— What's that? I thought I heard rumbling."

"In the far distance? Thunder, it is thunder, very far away. And if we could see the horizon to the north, we would see faint flashes of lightning. The rains will come soon, maybe tomorrow, maybe in a few days. If we are fortunate. Then the drought will end. Maybe it will end. There is a breeze now too, can you feel it?"

"Will it put out the bush fire?" The acrid smell, now familiar, seemed to have intensified.

"I do not think so. But the wind may shift the fire's direction, maybe put out the fire by blowing it back on itself, or maybe it will drive it where we are going, across our path. We must start walking as soon as the sun rises, and go fast. Now we will walk during the day and sleep at night. Your fire needs more wood."

When they were again leaning back, side by side, against the baobab, Stephen: "Any more questions? When you're finished, then it's my turn."

"You have had many turns, Stephen. You asked me about my father, remember? Tell me about *your* father. Do you like him?"

"He's a civil servant. Very—rigid, distant; likes order in all things. I used to think his life was very narrow—well, I still do, but I'm less critical now. He likes it that way, perhaps that's the only way he can live, and my mother seems to accept it."

"Is *she* happy?"

"I think she would have liked more adventure, more romance. I think she's bored with housekeeping, cooking, shopping, all of that. Why she started working as a dental receptionist."

"You do not have servants?"

"Oh no. Only the rich have servants these days in England. Didn't you notice that?"

"You are close to her—closer than to your father?"

"Yes. Actually, she made me her confidant when I was small—I'm an only child, as I said. She gave up work—she was a secretary—when she married. That's what my father wanted. So she was lonely in the house, and that's why she talked to me, I think, and read stories to me. She's very religious—my father isn't, he's an atheist—and so she read to me from the Bible, every night at bedtime. And church and Sunday School every Sunday. My father was in the War, the Second World War, he fought against Rommel in North Africa, though he would never talk about that. He didn't marry until he was in his forties. He finds it hard to express his feelings, I think because—well, I told you, didn't I, he had to look after his dying father when he was eleven, he was the eldest child. My grandfather was in the First World War, he lost his job during the Depression, my poor grandmother had a dreadful struggle to survive, with five children, and then my grandfather got cancer— My father could never forget those early experiences, poverty and worry and pain, it's why he goes on about security, getting a good education, a good profession, saving for the future, and so on."

"Do you admire him?"

"In a way, I suppose. He never gives up. But, to be honest, I don't *like* him. He doesn't have a sense of humour. Quintessential civil servant. But my mother—she enjoys reading and music and art and she's not above a bit of frivolity now and again. She's more—loving."

"So you are more like your mother than your father?"

"Yes. No, I think I'm probably a bit like both of them."

"But Stephen, we are all individuals, we are not formed by our parents and our countries and our language and culture."

"Oh all right." Stephen smiled wryly. "Have a go at me, if you like. You win—again. But now I've given you a potted history of my family, and answered your questions. That's enough! I'm sleepy. And thirsty."

"Yes, we must sleep. Thirst we must endure till morning, then we will find more moisture. Make sure you put enough wood on your fire. I will wake up and check on both of the fires during the night."

Stephen, while tending his fire— "I wonder what our fathers would make of each other if they could ever meet? In some ways they are almost similar: your father had to be a cook when he wanted to be a warrior, my father had to be a warrior when he wanted to live a quiet life in England— But they wouldn't be able to communicate, would they? Couldn't understand each other. At least we can do that."

Joseph, firelight flickering over his face, eyes and teeth glinting: "An English tourist studying Modern History at Oxford; and a Zimbabwean—what did you call me?—rapist, torturer, bugger, murderer? —We communicate?"

"Why, Joseph? Why?"

"Why what? You will ask your questions later, Stephen, if you decide to remain with me; and I will answer them. That was our agreement. Let us sleep now."

Stephen was beginning to recognise the subtle stages of dawn's unfolding. Not just the gradual increase of light, but the swelling sounds—cheeps and trills accumulating into a birds' chorus, even here, even during the drought. And he could sense swift nervous movements and tense silences of animals as, hunter and hunted, they sought necessary sustenance. A vibrating anticipation in the still-cool air.

"It is time to go," Joseph said, putting on the sunglasses and rising. He pissed on his fire to put it out; Stephen imitated him. "Are you hungry? How thirsty?"

"I can wait"—but not for too long, please. "Let's move on."

"We will find a place to rest later." Joseph shrugged the bundle over his shoulders, picked up his AK.

As both fires fizzled out, Stephen: "Oh, I need to have a shit."

"Do it here, next to the tree, and cover it with sand. You can use leaves from there": pointing at the remnants of the wood. "I will go and watch outside. Do not forget your spear. They would be able to follow our trail without that help, you know."

Soon they were walking swiftly away from the cluster of baobabs, which stood at the edge of a dry pan, its grey cracked clay trailing to the south. They were going west-northwest now, across bushveld, towards hills that rose in the distance like stubby fingers—beckoning, warning? Just to the right of the hills, smoke hung, thick and grey, blown sideways by the breeze. Below the smoke, spurts of flame, glitter of burning bushes and thorn-trees. Stephen could no longer see these clearly by closing his left eye, but he was relieved that he could see them at all. How much longer will I be able to see? He feared the rapidly-increasing glare.

After stopping in a donga to find moisture, they walked for five or six miles. The dry-tussocked ground was generally flat, with occasional low valleys, and seemed to be tilting slowly downwards. Another group of baobabs lifting slowly in the distance. By mid-morning a heat-haze was shaking and bouncing the horizon. Flies circled their heads, bit their sweaty necks. There was game to be seen, though not in abundance. A warthog tripped past, just ahead of them, on its absurdly tiny legs, with its absurdly tiny tail poking the air; it glared at them, tossing absurdly ferocious tusks which reminded Stephen of the moustache of an elderly retired colonel his father had once brought home for dinner. Two wildebeest—so threatening in appearance, with their huge torsos, so shy and submissive in actuality—gazed at them in comical alarm, then suddenly wheeled into flight. No lions or lionesses so far—they would be anything but comic, Stephen thought, holding the spear firmly across his chest.

They were coming close to the bush fire now; could hear its constant gnawing and crackling; could see its restless tongue licking at the dead grass, see the newly-burnt blue-black smoking stubble, and the silhouettes of trees and bushes behind the flames. Joseph was right: the fire was being fanned across their path by the breeze. But, fortunately, not fast enough to cut them off, if they hurried—and Joseph was walking very fast now towards the fire's leading edge.

He stopped, waiting impatiently for Stephen to catch him up. "We must go faster, or we will be trapped. The wind can shift or get stronger suddenly, then we will be surrounded by fire." Stephen nodded, struggling forward on his calloused swollen feet. "As soon as we are past the fire, we will stop and eat."

Their route took them towards the baobabs, which now seemed themselves to be threatened by the fire. As they approached, a flurry of movement beyond the first of the great trees; and a few minutes later they could hear, above the fire's crackling, a cacophony of croaking, hissing, squawking.

"We must go as close to the fire as possible"—Joseph, over his shoulder.

"What's happening?" Stephen gasped, breathing unevenly.

"They are fighting over a kill, I think a young wildebeest. Vultures and hyenas": jerkily—he was breathing heavily, too. "Hyenas usually look for food only at night. These must be very hungry. Also there can be lionesses nearby. If they killed the wildebeest."

Joseph walked as near to the flames as he could. Stephen followed closely. The heat seared up at them, smoke assaulted their eyes, noses, mouths. Stephen gasped painfully, tried to run as he saw he was falling behind Joseph. The baobabs were joggling past on his left. The fire seemed to be lapping his ankles. He was stumbling. His feet, though considerably toughened now, were aching from the heat, and from his inability, in the smoke and anxiety, to avoid stones and thick clumps of grass. Throat burning, eyes weeping. Heart lurching.

Then they were past. Through the smoke, he could see a placid yellow landscape quivering rhythmically ahead. They found low rocks to sit on, under a large marula tree, and were grateful for its shade. Stephen slumped back against its trunk and reached down to rub his feet. He gazed back at the smoke and flames. "I'm knackered" he croaked. "Can we rest now?"

"Yes. But not for long. We must reach the hills before evening." Joseph handed Stephen a piece of tsessebe meat. "I forgot to warn you to look out for snakes."

"Snakes!"—shuddering at his memory of the puff-adder.

"Fleeing the fire. But we were close to it, and they would have gone further away than where we were. So maybe you were not in great danger."

"You also forgot to ask me whether I wanted to leave you. I think you're determined to kill me, one way or another."

Joseph smiled faintly. "You want to go, Stephen? Go. Go now." He held out the AK.

"Oh fuck off, Joseph" smiling back wanly. "You remind me of a Master at my school, when I was in Form Two. He grinned while he twisted your ears. Making promises he had always forgotten next day. A bully and liar. How about more meat? And I'm bloody thirsty."

"Here." After Stephen had consumed the chunk of meat, Joseph held out a yellow corm. "This has water inside it. You will see. It is delicious too." Stephen bit sharply into it, and grimaced. "I am like a father to you, Stephen," Joseph continued, "so why would you leave me? You are my son. I watch over you. How old are you?"

"Nearly twenty-two. My birthday is—soon."

"I am thirty-three. You see, I am old enough to be your father."

"At eleven? That's impossible."

"I was very potent in my youth. I started fucking at ten."

"I don't believe you, Joseph. That's not physically possible, as far as I know. Anyway, if I'm the Son and you're the Father, Susanna was the Virgin Mary. Is that why you raped her? And Paul was the Holy Ghost?" Joseph turned away, his lips tightening. "On second thought, if we have to be allegorical about it, I think Paul was your Son, not me. That's why you crucified him."

Joseph was silent, his jaws slowly opening and closing. Then "It is time to go, England. Follow me."

Slowly the hills swelled and lifted on the horizon. Even Stephen's eyes, battered by the glare, could now define their ragged silhouetted forms. His throat ached with thirst. Sweat ran down his face, back, stomach, arms, legs. His feet almost unbearably tender and painful: not only stones and grass continued to afflict them, but the increasing heat of the sandy soil. I can't go much further. I can't, I'm knackered, knackered. But, aware of the anger expressed by Joseph's silence and rigid back swaying ahead of him, Stephen stumbled on—silently, except for his wretched erratic breathing.

In the distance, at what was probably, he thought, another pan, he noticed movement—and Joseph pointed to three giraffes nibbling at tree tops, zebras in flight from some unseen predator, a throng of buffaloes. Birds occasionally flickered nearby, calling out strangely. One that settled in a thorn-tree just to Stephen's right, was, apart from the dark red in its eyes, glossily black from beak to forked tail—beautiful, sinister. Still no lionesses, however; or wild dogs. Indeed, in the somnolence of midday, it seemed sometimes that they had the veld almost to themselves as they hurried towards the hills.

Joseph stopped. He pointed ahead in silence when Stephen came up and looked at him enquiringly. "Can't you see them?"

"No." He strained against the glare, the dancing horizon. "Oh—yes. I think— But surely those aren't people?"

"Bushmen. They have been hunting, they have bows and arrows." Joseph walked on.

As they approached, the three Bushmen watched and waited impassively. There was an animal lying at their feet. "They shoot poison arrows into a buck," Joseph explained. "Then they come back the next day to find it and finish it off and take it back to their people to eat. That one is nearly dead, I think—a kudu, can you see the white stripes on its back?"

"Do you speak their language?"

"No. I have never seen a Bushman before, only heard about them from my uncle in Bulawayo, he works for the Museum."

The Bushmen looked up at them from the other side of the dying kudu. Small slim yellowish men with wrinkled high-cheeked faces, keen black eyes under heavy lids, short dark hair thickly whorled. Barefoot of course, and dressed only in mottled brown animal-skin loin-pouches. Each with a bow in his right hand and, looped from the left shoulder, a small animal-skin bag and a cylinder of bark holding arrows. One of them held a spear.

Stephen had read a little about Bushmen—San, as the book said they called themselves. He felt a pang of excitement. These are the original human inhabitants of Africa—or, at least, they were here long before Joseph's people, and mine. He scrutinised them covertly. They looked almost Asiatic; yet one knows immediately that they belong here, are utterly at home here; the most authentic of all Africans? It is we who must look like Martians as we loom over them—me with my filthy smelly clothes and girl's straw hat and ragged sketchy beard; and Joseph with his sunglasses and green shirt and military cap and camouflage trousers and AK. Why don't they burst out laughing at us?

The three hunters talked softly to each other, in their language of many clicks. The one with the spear came forward to the kudu, now barely breathing; raised his spear and plunged it into the kudu's chest. The big animal reared up, snorting, legs kicking wildly; its liquid eyes, separated by a white bar beneath the twisting razor-sharp horns, widening; then its head fell back to the sand. The other two Bushmen came forward. They pulled the spear and two arrowheads out of the animal's chest and flank. Then one of the men squatted down and, with a knife, began to cut away skin and flesh from around the wounds. The other sat on his haunches at a pile of dry leaves and sticks, and began to twirl a thin hard stick above a softer one held steady by his left foot.

Joseph walked round the dead kudu. The standing Bushman looked impassively up at him while he gestured to the hills, to Stephen and himself, to the distance beyond the hills, and finally to his mouth and stomach. The small man nodded and spoke softly in response.

Stephen watched while the squatting man cut open the kudu's stomach and pulled out its liver and intestines. Soon these were cooking over the newly-made fire, with all three Bushmen squatted round it. Joseph and, after a moment, Stephen, joined them; accepted, with smiled gratitude, small pieces of proffered half-cooked intestine, but refused larger pieces and waited in silence while the Bushmen, obviously hungry, ate the rest unhurriedly.

After scattering and extinguishing their fire, the hunters went back to the kudu corpse and, with their sharp knives, skinned it and hacked it apart. It was mid-afternoon by the time the meat had been wrapped in pieces of the cut-up skin. Loading their burdens on their shoulders, the three men set off towards the hills at an easy walk, Joseph and Stephen following.

"Do they live here?"—Stephen.

"They must have a camp. They are hunters and gatherers, these Bushmen. The men hunt. The women gather food—fruit and roots, melons, nuts, birds, snakes, insects. They do not remain in one place, they go where the hunting and food are good."

"And they don't have any leaders or rulers, do they? I think I read that. Everyone has the same power and status as everyone else. They live in groups and share everything and live in peace and in harmony with nature. A true natural Communism, you could say?"

"Yes—" There was a note of doubt in Joseph's response. "But they are not—progressive. It is a very simple way of life. Like an animal's. Surely you would not like that? No literature, no history, just living always from day to day, season to season, always in the present. And because they did not fight and organise and defend themselves at all, they were conquered by all the others who came—my people, your people—they could not control their destiny. That is why there are so few now, why they live only where no other people can live."

Stephen sighed, cleared his throat. "I don't know. I'm so glad to be able to see how they live. They've kept something that almost all other human beings have lost. Can't we learn from them where we have gone wrong? They have kept innocence. Or am I just being romantic?"

"So you are glad you did not leave me, Stephen? Yet you attack me, always, when I am helping you and protecting you."

He wants me to apologise. Should I? After what he did, the vile enormities? How can I? How is it possible to be friends? He hasn't shown one sign of remorse. "I hope we get to their camp soon. My feet are so sore—I'll soon be hobbling. And I'm so thirsty."

The hills were close now. Red rock towered sheer above the brown and green of thick vegetation. Yes—green: must be water there, running down from the hills, conserved somehow.

And then at last they were walking into a sandy cleared space surrounded by trees and bushes, under the shadow of the nearest hill. There was a central fire-area, and among the trees several—nine—huts that looked like unkempt yellow igloos: straw bundled over saplings that had been bent to form domes. Near the huts, in the shade of a big mukwa tree, five men sat on their haunches, apparently gossiping. Six children, some naked and others wearing white necklaces and aprons, came running from behind the huts towards the three hunters, shouting happily. Three women came forward at a leisurely stroll, holding what looked like large pale-brown speckled eggs. When they neared, they stopped shyly, gazing; but were soon in lively conversation with the hunters, casting curious glances at the two strangers, who stood waiting patiently.

One of the women came over and held out her two eggs, her eyes turned away. A necklace of what seemed to be small white beans hung from her throat; round her legs, just below the knees, were ornamented animal-skin bands. "It is water in the ostrich eggs," Joseph explained. He took one, threw his head back, and held the egg to his lips. Reaching for the other egg with a grateful smile, Stephen saw that it had a small hole at the upper end, above a jagged design of triangles. He imitated Joseph, lifting the hole to his mouth. A flow of sweet cool water trickled down his throat.

Meanwhile the kudu meat had been laid down and, when the other men came over, it was shared out among them in an amicable and leisurely ritual. The meat was taken to where piles of embers indicated that small fires had burnt in front of each of the huts; and, as sunset came with a brilliant sweep of red and pink across the cloudy western sky, new fires were quickly set and lit.

Joseph and Stephen were motioned to join one of the nine family groups, and sat down on the sand opposite two women, a young man, an old man, and three children, round their low crackling fire. The women wore two aprons, made of the skins of small animals, to cover their vaginas and strikingly large buttocks. Slung over their shoulders and tied at the waist were cloaks, each made of a single large animal-skin. One of the women had a sleeping baby slung from her left shoulder; it rested on her hip, one cheek against a bare breast.

When the meat was lightly cooked, the man of the family distributed it, and they all ate in a companionable silence disturbed only by the sounds of chewing and gulping, and the children's murmurs. Then ostrich eggs of water were passed round. As the meal ended and the youngest children were led off to the huts, Stephen noticed that the big central fire had been lit.

Night came. The stars were piercingly brilliant. As he looked up at them, even though he was without his glasses, he thought he had never before seen a night sky pulsating with so many vivid stars. A vast celestial conversation, an assembly of silent voices calling to us from the swirling darkness of space.

Soon all the adults and some of the older children had gone across to the big fire. The women and girls sat down in a tight circle to one side of the fire, facing inwards. The men and boys squatted around the fire. Joseph and Stephen joined them. For a while there was silence; except for conversational murmurs among the women, a child laughing sleepily in one of the huts, and familiar rustles and distant noises of the African night.

Then a woman's voice rose softly into a chant. Other voices joined in. And rhythmic clapping twined contrapuntally into a monotonous hypnotic melody rising, falling, rising; louder, ever louder. Some of the women began to sing above the melody in falsetto; others ululated shrilly. The clapping grew more emphatic, gathering speed.

Suddenly one of the men lifted his head and called out fiercely, throat trembling below his gaping mouth. His voice reached up, higher and higher, penetrating the dark air, challenging the rising moon. Abruptly he stood, began to sway and stamp, leaning forward with his knees bent, shuffling towards the circle of chanting clapping women. Stephen recognised him: the hunter who had speared the kudu. All the other men, and all the boys, rose and joined him. Stamping, twisting, they dance clockwise around the women. Are they imitating animals? They push their heads forward and jerk their buttocks, stamping, stamping, stamping. Some of them grasp the man ahead round his waist.

Sound and movement melding; slowly, steadily, inexorably lifting towards a climax. Stephen, watching rapt from across the leaping sinuous flames, feels a new tension crawling up his back as the rhythm beats, beats, beats into him.

On the men dance, while the chanting, ululating, clapping radiate into the star-crowned darkness. On and on the men dance, sweat coursing like blood down their skin. The firelight flickers over their glistening bodies, licking bronze to gold as they stamp round and round their women. On and on and on—

A wailing shriek, and the hunter bends down, lays his hands on one of the women; collapses towards the fire. Several men break from the ring to pull his jerking body away from the flaming logs. He lies on his back in the sand, legs thrashing, arms flailing, chest pumping; eyes wildly open on the circling universe.

The dancing, chanting, ululating, clapping subside slowly. Deep uneven breathing; sweat glinting in the firelight. Women murmur to each other again. A subdued laugh. The men squat again around the fire. One puts more logs on it. The tranced man moans, closes his eyes, opens them wide, sits up, looks about. He stands up, walks round the fire, squats beside Stephen. The acrid scent of his sweat. And soon all have gone to their huts, except for seven young men; who lie down quietly on the sand, curled on their sides, close to the fire.

Joseph stood up. He walked to the far edge of the circle, facing away from the huts. Stephen followed him. They pissed together into the darkness. Neither spoke. How could one speak, Stephen thought, after that?

They lay down near the fire, joining the seven young men.

Stephen turned onto his back to gaze blindly up at the stars, the moon, the universe. I am happy. My feet are sore, very sore; my eyes are weak, dry and strained—I am almost blind. But I am happy. Have I ever been so happy? Is *this* why I am here? Why I came to Africa?

Susanna, I wish you were here. But I'll tell you all about it. You'll be filled with wonder. A melody swayed into his mind. *She shows you where to look / Among the garbage and the flowers—* The last time I felt such intense happiness, I was lying beside you in the darkness, on the first night of this endless journey. —Yes, we'll talk about it, Susanna. We'll meet and talk about it.

I am here.

I am happy.

I hear your voice.

Susanna, Susanna, Susanna.

He slept.

Waking to children's voices, he smiled into new sunlight. *There are children in the morning—*

No. No more voices. No more quotations; no more words; no more songs. Now face reality, Stephen. Yourself. Simplicity. He sat up.

Dawn. The fire still burning softly, but beyond it the sun's greater fire setting mopane trees alight. The sky a rich clear blue above tufts of golden cirrus. And the last stars, the ghostly moon, will soon be sucked into the obscurity of light. Already heat is flowing across vast Kalahari, the Matobo hills that I will never see. Across Zimbabwe, across Botswana, across the whole of Africa. Across this small encampment, these little people drawing brave life from a parched land; dancing, singing—the Song and Dance of Life. Did it really happen? Or did I imagine it? Have I truly crossed the border from reality to dream?

He looked across at the children chasing each other round the huts, and smiled again in the memory of his intense happiness under the bright darkness of the moon and stars. He looked around him. The seven young Bushmen were gone—on a hunting expedition? Or preparing their weapons, gossiping in a circle while they smeared poison on the tips of their arrows? And where was Joseph? Then Stephen saw him, with one of the men, near a hut. He seemed to be pointing up towards the hills. My eyesight is blurring so badly now. Stephen reached into his trouser pocket, then held the lens in front of his left eye—yes, now I see him more clearly. A woman is coming up to him. But I can hardly walk along holding a lens in front of one eye. He put it back in his pocket.

Joseph came over to him. "Good morning, England. I have some food for you"—holding out a soft bag made of animal-skin. "And one of the Bushmen will lead us up into the hills when we are ready. I showed him that we would like to clean ourselves. It is surprising how you can communicate without even using your voice—by pointing."

"But perhaps your stink helped you communicate that message. I'm surprised they can tolerate being anywhere near us." He sat down and opened the bag. Dark lumpy roots, red berries, a small spiny cucumber, pieces of what looked like white meat. "What do you think this is?" and he held up one of the pieces.

Joseph shrugged. "The women catch lizards, snakes, birds, small animals like mice. And they do not cook all their food, only the big meat. Try. I have eaten it and you see I am still alive."

Ridiculous to be cautious after all I've eaten in the last while. He bit into the meat. Dry, but sweet, chewy, almost like cold chicken—like crocodile. Then moist bitter roots and sweet berries. Better by a long shot than breakfast at school or college—he grimaced at the memory of slimy beans, coagulated sauce, cold burnt toast. One of the women brought across an ostrich egg and Stephen rejoiced again when cool water channelled down his throat. As he handed the egg to Joseph, "How do you think they get the water into the egg? The hole is small."

"Oh Stephen! That is how we know there is a good water supply here, up in the hills. They would need to hold the egg under water to fill it." He handed the egg to Stephen, who passed it on to the woman, bobbing his head in thanks. "Are you ready, Stephen?"

"I will be, in a few minutes—after the usual offices." He walked a little way among the trees and bushes; beyond which the savanna was a golden glare. *And the sun pours down like honey—* No. No, no. Leonard Cohen, Isaac Rosenberg, William Shakespeare, all of you—let me be. Let me face this world, this phantasmagoria, alone, by myself. Free me to try to make sense of it. Before it's too late. Let me find unity in the crazy diversity of this world, while I still have time. —And you too, Graves. Let me be. *Facing the wide glare of the children's day.* Yes. I hear you, yes, in spite of myself. Yes. But I am mad already, and will *surely* die that way. *And the fire and the rose are one—* He had almost collided with Joseph, who put a hand on his shoulder. "Are you all right, Stephen?"

"Yes. Yes, why?"

"Bcause you did not even see me. Are you—?"

"No, I'm all right. I was just thinking, that's all. And my eyes are—" *Mine eyes dazzle—* They're aching and I can't see clearly any more. You remember—my glasses—you broke them. And it's the glare too." He looked into the sunglasses and flinched from a bright flash that, as Joseph moved slightly, sprang at him from the minuscule face set in darkness.

Joseph hesitated. "Do you—do you want the sunglasses?"

But Stephen did not hesitate. "No. They're Paul's, anyway. Are we going now?"

"Yes, if you are ready. Where is your spear?"

"But we're coming back afterwards, aren't we?"

"No."

"But— Can't we stay here, for another night at least? We're both exhausted. And we don't have to get anywhere else quickly, do we? In fact, we don't have anywhere to get to at all, do we? And my feet are swollen and purple and still painful—"

"No."

Anger took Stephen by the throat; shook him into fury. He gulped. His breath spurted. "Why not? Why the fucking hell not? *Why?* I want to stay longer. I need to stay longer. Why can't you consider *me* for once? *My* feelings. Not just yours. Whatever feelings you have." Calm down, Stephen— you're hysterical. Then, quietly tense, "Why *not?* Perhaps they *want* us to stay longer, too."

"Eating their food? Do you think it is like a hotel in the rich West? Do you think they just pick up the telephone, 'Send me a steak, the most expensive dinner on your menu, charge it to the account of Mr Stephen Holmes, the world-famous wealthy Oxford undergraduate who represents the Old Commonwealth.' These people have to struggle to survive, every day they must struggle to survive. Sometimes, my uncle told me, they are forced to leave an old man to die, because there is no food and they have to move on and look for a new place. And the old man sits in the sun waiting for a lion or wild dogs or hyenas—"

"All right, all right, I get your point" Stephen muttered sullenly. "You don't have to lose your temper and shout in my face. And I still think you're wrong. But *you've* got the AK, haven't you? *You're* the Baas. So why don't you just leave me sitting here in the sun, waiting to die? Why don't you put me out of my misery." But I'm not miserable; not really; how could I be after last night? Pull yourself together, Stephen. You wanted simplicity, simple reality. No voices. Then why can't you deal with yourself, control yourself? Simplicity.

He went stiffly across to the tree against which the spear was leaning. Joseph waited in silence. Then they walked together over to the Bushman, who had been watching them impassively.

They were climbing up a steep rocky path. All around them were trees, bushes. Vivid variety of foliage subduing the browns and greys of trunks and branches, linking earth to the fiery air above. Blossoms. Birds, in song. "The African Garden of Eden, at last!" Stephen mocked himself. *Did I say that? Was that my voice?*

The Bushman moved with swift grace, his feet, pale yellow underneath, lifting from rock to rock with easy certainty. Joseph, clumsier in his climbing, fell further and further behind, sweat beading his neck and arms. Stephen, even clumsier, stumbled upwards, losing his balance at times, stubbing his toes more frequently as he tried to protect his tender feet. Sweat dripped off the end of his nose, oozed under his shirt and down his chest and back. He looked up at the two men ahead of him. *We husband the ancient glory In these bared necks and hands—*

When the noises ahead of him stopped and he looked up again, the little coppery man was standing on an immense boulder and Joseph was scrambling up to join him. As Stephen followed, laboriously, Joseph reached down; he grasped the damp hand, and was hauled up to stand beside the other two. They were high enough to be able to see into a valley running to the north and, beyond it, several more hills—soft purple, brown, grey, green; and, beyond those, a yellow and brown expanse lifting to the blue horizon, against which the pale sky lay asleep. *Perhaps it's the more beautiful to me,* Stephen wondered, *because it's blurred?*

They climbed down from the boulder, and he and Joseph followed the Bushman across shallow domes of granite crowned by tall shady trees. He stopped. Stephen reached him, looked down over his shoulder, and gasped. Water! It shone up at them, a circle of serene green, and beyond it was a dark green glisten descending over smooth stone. *A spring? Or a sinkhole, is that what it's called?* All the water, the rain and dew, sucked in by this great stony hill whenever rain had fallen; draining slowly down, through secret cracks and channels, into a great cavern open only here, at this small circle, a moist green eye gazing at the sky; and then seeping onward, over the stone lip, to ferment the wave of vegetation cascading into the valley.

He looked at Joseph, grinning with delight. "Can we wash?" He put the spear down at his feet. The Bushman looked at him steadily.

"Yes, but we must try not to dirty or disturb the water. Obviously this is where they fill their ostrich eggs. My uncle told me that Bushmen do not reveal to strangers their water sources, in case they get polluted or run dry because of over-use."

"So it's a big favour, a great privilege."

"Yes. Maybe because we are travellers, maybe for you, Stephen—do you see how he is looking at you?"

"How can we thank them? I have nothing to give him. Nothing. The spear?" No, we need that, for our survival.

Joseph was taking off his watch—Stephen's watch. Funny, Stephen thought, I haven't even noticed it for days, let alone asked him the time. I have stopped thinking about time, I am living by the movements of the sun and moon now, the swing of the seasons. As the Bushmen do. "You can't give him that"—impulsively, putting his hand on Joseph's arm. "What would they do with that? What use is it to them?" But Joseph was holding the watch out. The Bushman took it, held it glittering in the sunlight. Joseph took it from him, fastened it over his left wrist. The Bushman lifted the watch towards his eyes, staring intently at it.

"I—think it's wrong to give him that. I don't think he needs it, it's not part of their lives."

"Why, Stephen? Because you think it might change their lives? Because he is uncivilised, a *kaffir*? What harm could it do to him? He doesn't even know how to tell the time, so how could it change his life?"

Stephen took off his hat—Susanna's straw hat. He held it out to the Bushman.

"You cannot give him that, Stephen. You need it." The Bushman took it. He looked intently at Stephen, put it on his head, took it off again; stood holding it. "You think he needs that? What will he do with it? His head has been naked in the sun all his life"—scornfully.

"No. He doesn't need it. Perhaps he'll throw it away. It's filthy anyway. Or perhaps he'll give it to his wife or one of his children. I just want to give him *something*. Something I value, the only thing I have now that I can give him. Not only for leading us here and showing us this water, but for their hospitality—food and water, and—last night. Anyway, I've done it now. Can you ask him a question for me?"

"I can try. But you will regret giving the hat when we are walking in the sun. Whites get sunstroke easily. What is the question?"

"Ask him if there are Bushman-paintings here. There must be caves."

"You can ask him yourself."

Stephen looked across at the small slim wrinkled man, in his brown loin-pouch, in his simple patience; wearing Joseph-Stephen's watch, holding Stephen-Susanna's hat. Then he raised his left hand, and with his right index-finger made swirling patterns against the palm. After a moment, the Bushman pointed upwards to their left. Stephen squinted into the glare. But, yes, there was a sheer purple sweep of shadowed granite. The man pointed again, twice, slightly lower, to right and left. "Thank you," Stephen said, smiling and nodding.

The Bushman looked steadily, unsmilingly, at them. Then he came forward, walked between them and on over the low rocks. They turned to watch his unhurried departure.

Then Stephen: "Let's go," excitedly. Joseph took a pace in the direction of the sinkhole. "No, I mean to the paintings. We can wash later. It'll be hot sweaty work getting up there. When I wash I want to enjoy it, every moment of it, I want to cleanse my body and then lie in the sun to dry, and then stay clean for hours and just—oh, relish every moment of it. I can wait a bit longer for that, and enjoy anticipating it while I'm looking at the rock-paintings. You wash now if you want to. I am going to find those paintings." He set off, almost jauntily, up the smooth slope to his left.

"What about your spear?" Joseph stooped for it. "There may be leopards up there." But Stephen was striding up the slope; he scrambled over stones, between boulders, slipping on sand, reaching for branches to pull himself upwards. Joseph followed.

When they reached the huge boulders, Stephen was panting harshly. He looked up, squinting. Animals! Firm ochre outlines, with ochre stippling over lithe bodies— "And look at those hands!" He pulled out his lens so he could see the paintings more clearly. A giraffe stood in eternal anxious stillness, head high, listening. A buck—"What is it, Joseph?" "Impala"—was about to leap towards a crack running down the centre of the smoothed rock. There were several other animals lower down—buck, buffalo—and in their midst the two small hands like a child's: the artist's hands, they must be, laid ochre-saturated against the rock, his signature—expressing now, aeons later, a dignified pride and pathos, "I have done this"—with pigment mixed from, what, blood and mud and tree-gum?—on this sheltered expanse of granite. "It will last longer than me, I made it to honour the spirits of the animals whom I have killed to feed my people, I give it to the sun and the moon, I give it to you, my brother." How ancient are these images—representations so accurate, so convincingly realistic, so direct, unselfconscious?

But the most beautiful and moving of all the animals was at the centre: an elephant; in delicate outline; one forefoot lifted, tail swinging, trunk raised against the crack; blending with the stone it inhabited. Art breathing into nature. Metempsychosis. Yes. *Every discoloration of the stone, Every accidental crack or dent—* The elephant shifted, probed; in an eternal stillness, moving constantly into the stone, out of the stone. I could gaze at it for ever; it's perfect; miraculous. *Consume my heart away; sick with desire And fas-*

tened to a dying animal, It knows not what it is; and gather me Into the arti-fice of eternity—Oh, the voices, my voices! But how otherwise can I respond? I am puny. My own words, my thoughts, inadequate. I need a poet's words—as Susanna did at the Victoria Falls. We all do. He realised that he had been holding his breath, and now let it out in a long wavering sigh. Of rapture? Rapture. *Beauty is truth*—Rapture.

"Are you ready to go?"—Joseph, impatient.

"I want to see the other paintings. The Bushman pointed to the right and to the left." Stephen made his way around the boulders to the far end of the granite wall. "I thought Bushmen always did their paintings in caves. I suppose these ones have been preserved because the rock face leans out enough to protect them from the direct rays of the sun. I bet the other paintings will be in caves. Isn't that a cave?" He was clambering downwards.

The cave was not deep. Its inner surface was covered with brown, grey and purple figures, some of them human. Many had been superimposed so that one could not always decipher the earlier shapes. But there was also a simple unitary scene: a great rhinoceros stood at bay, tusk raised; round it were stick-like Bushmen, their bows raised; arrows flew at the rhino; and near its feet one of the hunters lay prone. Stephen moved to stand at the centre of the cave. Here one saw a melange of figures, mostly human; some very faint, barely perceptible. One big figure loomed over them—*was* it human? Obese—with long ears, a snout and lashing tail—is it a god or a devil?—caricature of some enemy of the hunters?—the spirit of a fiercely dangerous animal? Evil—a shape expressing evil? Stephen turned to ask Joseph's opinion; but Joseph was sitting on a boulder at the entrance of the cave, looking outwards.

What else? Moving to his left, Stephen was surprised to notice, beside the pale giraffe, several strange oval designs in white and purple—they look like huge pupae, the centre of each divided into irregular rhomboids. What could these possibly signify? After scrutinising them for a while, Stephen rejoined Joseph.

"The other cave is there—behind those trees." Joseph pointed below the granite wall. "While you go there, I will find food so we can eat after we have washed. Here is your spear."

While Joseph went quickly downward, Stephen carefully made his way to the opening Joseph had indicated. It was a narrower but much deeper cave. Apart from ancient, now indistinct paintings, it held one insistent scene. Eleven Bushmen were dancing, close beside each other, their penises erect or semi-erect. Through the tip of each penis the artist had painted a short straight line. Stephen stared, fascinated, through the lens. The scene looked naturalistic—but was it? Did those lines represent sticks infibulated, surely very painfully, through the hunters' penises? If so, why? An initiatory ritual of pain? Sexual prohibition while hunting? If it was naturalistic, did this scene define some intense collective emotion? Or was it symbolic? Stephen stood staring at the leaping male figures, his mind troubled. A dance of life? Or a dance of death?

At last he turned away, climbed carefully down the boulders to the dome above the sinkhole; and sat cross-legged under a tree in brilliant flower, a mass of tiny yellow blossoms. He gazed out at the soft panorama of hill and bush. So here are my hieroglyphics, prepared for me, waiting for me. Ultimate revelation—if I can crack the code. An oracle, no less. Let me ask my question: What is the source of violence, of evil? I ask and ask, compulsively. And what do these people say to me? Their voices speak to me in these ancient paintings. What can I hear? Their lives, lived in the plains and valleys below their paintings, lives unchanged through the millennia. A people of peace, their only violence the necessary slaughter of animals for food, their world a wide wilderness. The paintings tell me that the people respect the animals they kill, know them intimately through close observation, perhaps love them. They are egalitarian, hospitable; their strictly ordained social duties defined by gender, age, tradition; at night they rejoice in dance and singing; and surely that Bushman's trance, even the dance itself, expressed an intensely religious spirit?

And so—what do they signify, ultimately, for me, for us? Can the hordes of a Europe saturated, beyond any possibility of absorption, with technological invention, living day by day detached even from the sustaining earth; terminally confused, values and standards hijacked by complexity, relativism; deafened by the cacophony of a million commercial voices—television, radio, films, telephones, photocopiers, faxes, books, magazines, newspapers— Can we learn anything at all from a heartbreakingly harmless people who patiently repeat the immemorial patterns of an existence bounded by the cycles of nature and tradition; who enter and leave their lives with a humble dignity that sinks to silence under swinging stars, leaving only dwindling echoes in succeeding generations, and the reticent beauty and mystery of images that they probably did not conceive to be art? I seem to remember trying to face such questions near the beginning of this journey, my unintended pilgrimage—and failing, as I fail again now. I am confused! But they have, some of these people, survived our violence. Will we?

After a while, Stephen shook his head; looked around; looked at the tree shading him. Smooth pale roots, under a wide canopy of leaves, snaking over the stone surface in search of sustenance. Then he knew: I sat under just such a tree on just such a shelf of rock that first morning as the sun rose, while Susanna sat beside me and Joseph walked towards us. But no, not the same species of tree—this one has no figs fattening on it. A thick smooth trunk, green bark peeling away in yellow papery sheets. Stephen pulled at a sheet, which tore off in his hand; and at another, and another, until there was a pile of them around the trunk. You could write on these. Words, words, words. But the tree had already written itself into them. One could imagine peeling the whole tree into a heap of drifting pages—*Fool, I shall go mad—*

He wandered out into the sun's blare. There were small dark plants in the sand, like those he had noticed— He shuddered. *—memorise another Golgotha—-* The axe hovered, lay on the bright air, slid— Oh God-if-there-is-a-God— He squatted to pull up one of the plants, held it close to his left eye. It was black—merely a pithless black stem with tiny bumps running along it.

As he stood up, he heard the sound of splashing at the sinkhole. He walked slowly towards it, down the granite slope, the dead plant in his hand. Joseph, at the edge of the pool, was naked. His face and arms glistened. He was scooping up water with both hands, and throwing it back over his face, torso, shoulders. As it cascaded to the stone, rainbow colours flashed in a myriad droplets. Stephen walked slowly to him. "What's this plant, do you know?" holding it out.

Joseph took it; drops of water rolled glinting down his smooth skin. "Whites call it the Resurrection Plant. When the rains come, it will burst into bright green. It will come back to life." He stooped and placed the plant carefully at the edge of the pool, stem in the water. "Come. Wash yourself."

Stephen took off his bush-jacket and trousers; stood awkwardly, aware again of his dirty smelly skinniness. To his surprise, he also felt shy, as if on display; as if, on this high shelf of granite in this wilderness, he was the focus of a thousand eyes. Ridiculous! He glanced at Joseph, before gazing past him, out over the panorama now wriggling in the late-morning heat-haze. He had noticed, as his eyes brushed over Joseph's lithe burnished body, that the leopard's claw-marks on the left side of his torso were now almost healed, were smooth striations. And he had suppressed a sudden urge to reach out and touch them.

"You are slow. I will wash you." Joseph scooped up water and cast it, deliciously cool, over Stephen. Then he came close, took Stephen by the shoulders, turned him to his left, rubbed his back; then scooped up more water and did it again. He rubbed Stephen's flanks, buttocks, legs. Stephen giggled—"Pity we don't have soap. Then I could get really clean and sweet-smelling."

"Turn round." Joseph scooped water over Stephen's head, and rubbed dirt from his hair, from his face and scraggy beard, his chest and arms, his stomach. Stephen flushed, aware that his penis was rising, swelling. Joseph seemed to ignore that—he knelt and his hands moved to Stephen's thighs, legs and feet. Then "You must finish your washing yourself," he said abruptly, and walked round Stephen to the slope above the pool. There he lay down on his back and closed his eyes.

Stephen knelt, trying to wash away, with water and much rubbing, all the dirt that had accumulated in the crannies of his body. I want to be clean, clean, clean. Then he went to lie near Joseph.

The sun beat down; a small breeze played over their quickly drying skin. He felt as if he were sliding interminably off the edge of the world. Drowsy, he was drifting towards sleep. I mustn't lie too long in the sun, he warned himself; and knew at the same moment that Joseph was leaning towards him. He did not open his eyes. Joseph took the tip of his flaccid penis between thumb and rounded forefinger, pumped it slowly to erection, and on to orgasm. Stephen gasped and jerked as he ejaculated. Then sleep closed over him.

When he drifted back to awareness, just as simply and smoothly, he raised himself on his elbow and looked across at Joseph. Who opened his eyes, turned his head towards Stephen, and smiled. Without the sunglasses, he is so handsome, his eyes calm, gentle. Stephen crawled to him, across the short space of warm granite. Joseph opened his legs. Kneeling between them, Stephen leaned forward and took the dark phallus into his mouth. Lips, tongue. It's like sucking at your mother's breast. Milk surged into his mouth and down his throat.

He lay down beside Joseph, pressing against him. I have waited for this, without knowing it. Have always wanted it. When I stood in front of you, at the beginning, and you were sitting on the rock with your AK across your thighs, and you looked into my eyes. As you are looking at me now. When I offered you my hand, and you took it, and we shook hands; and the evening sun was all around you, a golden aureole. Yes—and long before, when I was at Oxford, I wanted it; when I was at school, I wanted it; when my mother kissed me goodnight and shut the nursery door and the fearful darkness enfolded me again, I wanted it. I wanted it. I wanted it. And now it has happened, simply and inevitably, and I can never be the same, I am renewed. *I love you—Titan lover, My own storm-days' Titan—* He put his hand gently on Joseph's chest, moved it slowly down over smooth hairless skin, over the shapely breasts and nipples, the flat stomach. Joseph smiled again. *Love! you love me—your eyes Have looked through death at mine—*

Stephen slept.

When he awoke, Joseph was gone. Stephen got stiffly to his feet and instantly realised that his skin, especially the skin of his back and stomach, was very tender, sore. He had been lying too long in the midday sun—*Mad dogs and Englishmen*—and the areas of skin normally protected by his shirt and trousers had been exposed. His neck and ears were maddeningly itchy where flies had bitten. He hobbled to the tree under which he had sat earlier. Afternoon shade stippled his cross-legged body.

Joseph came up over the rocks. He had put on the sunglasses and his clothes again; his bundle swayed swollen against the AK; under his left arm were Stephen's bush-jacket and trousers—like Joseph's clothes, rinsed clean and dried in the sun; under his right arm was the spear; and he was carrying two melons, bright yellow with green stripes, one in each hand. "I am hungry. You too, Stephen? There is good food in the valley below this hill, and after sunset I will also hunt." He set a melon in front of Stephen, together with the spear and clothes; then placed the AK against the tree trunk and sat down, opening the bundle.

"I don't want to dress yet" Stephen murmured. "But yes, I'm ravenous."

Joseph cut a hole in the top of his melon, then leaned across and did the same for Stephen. Playfully Stephen reached out and snatched off the sunglasses. "Give them back"—Joseph's voice was curt, humourless. Stephen held the glasses teasingly out of reach for a few moments; then handed them over and Joseph put them on again.

"But you do look much better without them, Joseph."

Joseph didn't answer. He lifted his melon, and with his fingertips began to scrape its succulent flesh into his mouth.

As Stephen finished his melon, Joseph announced "We will sleep in the small cave tonight. While I am hunting, you gather wood for a fire."

"All right. But why that one? Have you seen it?"

"Yes, I went there. It is deep and narrow. One fire will block the entrance."

"Are you worried about leopards?"

"This is the type of country they like."

Stephen was trying to enjoy the watery but sweet green flesh of a wild cucumber, tearing away, with some difficulty, its spiny yellow-striped brown skin. "Did you notice the Bushman-painting in that cave? The men dancing?"

"No."

"They had— It looked as if there were sticks through their cocks. What does that mean? Do Bushmen actually do that?"

"I do not know."

"Couldn't they die? Of an infection? And it looks so painful. Is it an initiation test? Or do you think the artist was trying to show that they weren't allowed to have sex while they were hunting?"

"But they hunt all the time. They must, or they could die."

"Yes, but perhaps when they were new hunters, young men learning how to hunt? Until they become good hunters?"

"The Zulus did not allow their men to marry until they were about thirty years old. Because they were warriors, and they must keep their strength for fighting. Also, in old days, I have been told, the men of my people were forbidden even to go into their huts with a woman if they would be going on a raid to take cattle or women from the Shona."

"And did it work? Did the men obey?"

"You would be killed if you disobeyed. But it is hard to stop men fucking."

"What about you? Have you fucked a lot?"

"Of course. In the War, the chiefs of the villages would send women to us."

"What if the women were unwilling—if they didn't want that?"

"They wanted it. They knew we were fighting for the people's freedom. There must be many children in the bush in Zimbabwe called Chimurenga."

"But"—Stephen swallowed—"what if they *really* didn't want it?"

"Then we still fucked them. Men must fuck."

I should stop, now. Why do I provoke him with my questions? I must stop. "And men?"

"Men?"

"You must have fucked men too?"

"Not in Zimbabwe, that is not allowed in Zimbabwe. In England, yes."

"Did you—?"

"I told you I know all about the English, what English gentlemen are really like. Only a few months after I was there—I was your age, Stephen, I was twenty-two—I was raped."

"Raped? By?"

"You ask questions, Stephen—questions, questions, questions. This is not a game— life is not a game, question and answer, that is not how you find out about life, Stephen, how you live life. Why should I answer your questions?"

"Because you promised to, Joseph."

"Yes—but not just *any* questions, I do not have to answer whatever stupid questions you ask me." He turned away, looking out at the wavering panorama; sun and shade flickering over him. "All right. So you want to know everything, Stephen. So I will tell you. It was in London, that glorious capital of the Old Commonwealth. I was a student at London University, I wanted to be a lawyer, I had a scholarship from the British Government. One night I was in a pub, in Earl's Court, drinking that sour piss you English call 'bitter,' trying to make friends with the English; I was eager to do that. A man, a nice middle-aged man, was very friendly, he invited me to his house, to meet some of his friends, he said—a small party. So I went."

Joseph paused for so long that Stephen began to think he had decided not to continue. Then his account rushed to its conclusion. "He came to my hostel for me, the next night, in a car. I should have noticed where he was driving. They were all men there, at the house, eleven of them, in masks, I thought for the party. They gave me wine, they laughed and joked, then they blindfolded me, I thought it was a game at first, but then I started to fight, because then I knew. They stripped me, and after, they held me down, two of them, and—I don't know how many, four, they fucked me, raped me. It hurt, I didn't heal for many days, they laughed and joked, and— Then afterwards, they dressed me, and gagged me, I was still blindfolded, and they drove me in the car and pushed me out onto the street in the dark, I didn't know where I was, but—I found my way back to the hostel eventually." He stopped abruptly.

"And did you—? Surely you told the Police? Surely you—?"

"Nothing. What was the point? I did not know the address, the real names of any of the men—and I was Black, who would believe me? Do you think they would have believed a nigger? A *kaffir?* And also I felt—stupid, I was humiliated. So I did nothing." *Nothing will come of nothing—* No, *much* came of this nothing, I think, Joseph; much. "But I decided that nobody would ever be able to do that to me again. And revenge, I wanted to make the English suffer for what they did to me, make them know what it is like to suffer in the way they made me suffer." Stephen saw that Joseph's hands were trembling.

"Paul. You were going to do that to Paul, just what those men did to you— But he wasn't English, he was like you, he disliked the English."

"I could never be happy in London after that happened. And it was always grey and cold, the streets were grey and cold, the people were grey and cold. Also I was not succeeding in my studies. And Whites were always wanting sex with me—women and also men. Because I am Black. Because they thought

I have a big cock. At the University I got involved in political meetings, anti-Apartheid, anti-UDI, anti-Ian Smith. I would stand up and wave my fist and scream 'Down with Smith! Down with the Whites!' and they loved that—they loved *me*. So they invited me to their parties, to their rich houses, and into their bedrooms—even to Oxford, I told you—and some of them were very rich and powerful. So—"

"So?"

"So I went. So I fucked them and they gave me money and I fucked them again. I was angry, violent, I hurt them, but still they asked for more. Men and women. It made me happy to hurt them, to feel so much contempt for them. But then I began to feel contempt for myself too. My marks were lower and lower, I missed more and more lectures. I was going to fail. So I decided to leave. I went to the Canadian Embassy, and soon I got a bursary—it was easy at that time if you were Black, African—I went to Toronto. And I tried to work hard."

"Where were you studying?"

"At the University. To get an undergraduate degree so I could go to Law School. But—I got to know Yonge Street better."

"What's that?"

"Like Soho in London. You know Soho? Sex for sale. Strip joints, whore-houses, blue movies. Well, it makes money, lots of money—most of the money is taken by the bosses, of course—you get what is left over, just enough to keep you interested—no Communism on Yonge Street! But they liked me, I was popular with the clients—'Black men are *so* sexy!' And it was easy work. Dancing, loud music."

"How long did you do that? What did you do with the money?"

"About a year. But I also got into drugs, selling drugs. And I was caught by the Police. But I was beaten up and robbed before that, four men on a dark night outside my apartment. And"—he held out his right wrist to Stephen. "Did you notice this? Or are your eyes too weak?" A small pale cicatrice. "But they got me to a hospital in time. I always wanted to live, in the end."

"So what happened?" And there is another question I must ask.

"As I said, I got caught, someone informed on me. They were lenient with me. I had met a Minister in the Ontario Government after an anti-Apartheid protest outside the Ontario Parliament, at Queen's Park. He became a client, he liked being whipped by me. So I told him I was being blackmailed by South African agents, and he spoke to the Police and so I was not charged, but my university career was finished anyway, I failed two courses because I had not attended many lectures or written any essays. So I decided to come home. I was still doing political work—big meetings on the campus and at Queen's Park—I had contacts in both ZANU and ZAPU, both the freedom movements, so I knew what was happening at home. It was 1976—about seven years ago—I was twenty-six. ZANU and ZAPU were just forming the Patriotic Front, to try to unite politically, and, the year before, their two armies, ZANLA and ZIPRA, had combined into the Zimbabwe People's Army. The Whites were losing the War. But a lot of our men were still being killed. I was ashamed, inside I was ashamed, that I had failed academically, it seemed the right time to be back in my own country to join the fight for freedom. But the political agreements soon broke down, there was too much bitterness between ZANU and ZAPU, and anger and jealousy between their leaders, and of course, between Shona and Ndebele. I didn't know about all of that till later, but it would not have changed my decision. It was a time of hope for my people."

"So you were back in Zimbabwe in 1976—a freedom-fighter?"

"It was still called Rhodesia then, Ian Smith was still Prime Minister. Before I came back, I travelled around the United States, I knew I might not ever get another chance, I wanted to see it, and I still had some money left. And I made more money as I travelled around, not from drugs, that would be too dangerous—from sex. It was so easy. Fucking men, fucking women. In the YMCAs there were always rich middle-aged homosexuals hanging about, looking for young men, I didn't even have to go out into the street; and if I sat for ten minutes in a hotel lobby, some rich woman would come up and sit next to me, 'Hi, my name's Sadie, you a stranger, how's about a drink?' So I travelled around, I went up to the top of the Empire State, and down into the Grand Canyon, talked with jazz trumpeters in New Orleans, and gambled in Las Vegas—"

"Why did you do it to her, Joseph? Why?"

Joseph turned a frowning face to him. Stephen swallowed. "Susanna. Why did you do that to her?"

"I had to. She would have told the Police and the Army, the Fifth Brigade, where we were, they would have made her tell them. Also she could not walk any further."

For a moment, the granite lay serene under the sun; for a moment light and shadow oscillated around him, chasing each other like happy children. Then the whole world was tilting, was collapsing into brittle fragments of shock. *Corrode, consume—*

Stephen got shakily to his feet. He walked—tottered, staggered—down the slope to where the pool shone silky green. He squatted beside it; gazed unseeing out over the hills now rising purple from their soft shadows; gazed unseeing out over the great plain bloodied by the fierce sun.

A voice spoke to him, much later. "But you always knew." That's me. That's *my* voice.

"No" I replied. "How could I?"

"You knew," I replied. "Somewhere in you, somewhere in some cranny of the subconscious. You knew. That's why you can't weep. You knew."

"No," I replied. "No."

Then it was even later. Nearly sunset. The hills quivered as rays poured angrily at them like arrows from a sky now cruelly bare. Trailing capes of shadow, they cowered from the sun.

Joseph spoke, from behind him. "I am going to hunt, Stephen. Go to the cave. I have made the fire and lit it." Stephen didn't answer; didn't even turn his head.

Then it was sunset. Again, again. He saw the sun contract, then slip like a corpse down the horizon's gullet. As it did on the Zambezi, a few days ago, just a few days ago, when Susanna was still alive—the three of us, before Joseph existed for us—drunken obscene Paul, gentle generous teasing Susanna, and me, whining pusillanimous Stephen, the effete Oxford undergraduate. And the crocodile rising towards us, inevitably, interminably, through the darkness. The crocodile rising.

Now darkness flows over the hills towards me like a river of death. Slowly he got up. Slowly, stiffly, stumbled up the sweep of granite, a slight breeze shuffling against his nakedness. *We shall go mad no doubt and die that way—* Die anyway. *Children are dumb to say how hot the day is, How hot the scent is of the summer rose, How dreadful the black wastes of evening sky—* And die that way.

I will not wear clothes again. *—you lendings—* I will not. *Off—*

As he clambered over rocks, fell sideways, backwards, reached for branches, pulled himself painfully up towards the cave, staggered towards it, he found that he was weeping at last. *When we are born we cry—I have supp'd full with horrors—The worst is not—On horror's head horrors accumulate—I have seen such things—*

*Thou'lt come no more—Her voice was ever soft—*Oh God if-there-is-a-God. *Lay her i' the earth—* Oh God—*A guiltless death I die—Cold, cold, my girl—Thou'lt come no more—* Oh God-if-there-is-a-God. *Are there no stones in Heaven—? Never, never, never, never, never—Out, out—brief candle—Out,*

out—Tomorrow and tomorrow—Out— Beyond the trees a fire was burning in the cave entrance. He eased round it; almost without thinking found Joseph's large pile of dead wood, and pushed several pieces into the crackling heat. He sat down on the sand, shivering. There was movement behind him, above him. When he turned and looked up— The eleven hunters. In the flickering light, they stamped their feet; their heavy burdened phalluses jerked and swayed.

Out of the darkness, Joseph came sidling round the edge of the fire. A small furry shape hung from the spear; another drooped from his left hand. He sat down in silence, drew out his knife, skinned the corpses, cut them up, put pieces on the fire. The smell made Stephen's gorge rise. He kept looking at the two skins, pink grease oozing from them, red blood matting the delicate brown fur. I will not eat. When Joseph held out a piece of bloody blackened meat, he shook his head. Then heard himself speaking. "Where did you go that night?"

Joseph, squatting near the fire, looked round at him in silence.

Stephen spoke again, hoarsely. "That night, after you killed her. Where did you go? You didn't come back till much later, in the early morning. Where did you go?"

Joseph turned away.

Stephen screamed at his back "Fuck you, Joseph, fuck you, Joseph, fuck you. Fucking bloody answer me. Where did you go?"

Joseph's face again: a dark blank, firelight haloing it. "I went to see my sons, and my mother and my sister. My mother soothed my wound. My sons were asleep."

"You knew it would make me think she was safely on the road, that she was alive, didn't you? Didn't you? If you stayed away long enough. Didn't you?" He swallowed painfully. "And did you find another woman to fuck? Surely one fuck wasn't enough. Did you fuck your sister too? Or your mother?"

Joseph turned back to the fire. He sat eating, with his back to Stephen.

Stephen lay down on the sand. He spoke dully. "You said we were Father and Son, Joseph. You were wrong. We are Brothers. You have made us Brothers. We can never be separated now. Like Cain and Abel. Marlow and Kurtz, Billy Budd and—I can't remember his name, Claggart, yes Claggart. Like Didi and Gogo, like Othello and Iago. Lear and the Fool. Even if you kill me, or I kill you, or we kill each other. We belong to each other."

He twisted onto his back; groaned at the pain from his tender swollen skin; looked up. As they stamped their feet, the men bled. Blood dripped and dripped from the sticks piercing their phalluses. Dance of death. The ululating, the chanting, the syncopated clapping rose higher and higher, beat faster and faster. The men dance. Their blood drips. Their phalluses jerk and sway. Dance of life, dance of death. Then one man falls; he is kicking, writhing, his face contorted, eyes glazing on blackness. He opens his legs and arms into the sign of the cross. Joseph comes swiftly to him out of the darkness, seizes the stick from his phallus, raises it, thrusts it— No, no, no, no. Paul's mouth opens and he shrieks twice. Blood fountained. His body, his face, waver. A pale pink pupa. Metempsychosis. Red fangs. And blood fountained from Susanna's mouth, from her vagina. *God's blood is shed.* Susanna weeps. And Joseph raised the stick. It is an axe. It sleeps on the darkness, on the silence. Then slowly, slowly, it sifts downward.

Stephen saw that there was a leopard on the other side of the fire. Restlessly it paced to the right, to the left. Its green eyes are black. They reflect the fire, they reflect Joseph's face, and my face, they reflect darkness. Restlessly the leopard paces to the left, to the right; restlessly paces, paces.

XI

His shoulder shaking; being shaken. He opened his eyes, was looking into Joseph's fixed gaze. And shivering; sweat beading his forehead. "Stephen. Are you all right?" Joseph continued to shake his shoulder. "Are you sick? Stephen."

He sat up. The fire was still burning, the cave still dark, but a thin grey light silhouetted the trees. He knew he must not look up again. Carefully he looked to his left. *—saw morning harden upon the wall—* Leave me, please leave me; and he lifted his arms to push the voices away. *You were weak and lame, So you never came, And I went alone, and I did not mind, Not thinking of you as left behind.* Oh God-if-there-is-a-God. Please. Leave me. Please leave me.

With a warm hand, Joseph clasped Stephen's cold one; pulled him to his feet. "Come and sit near the fire."

Stephen sat cross-legged, the heat beating at him. His teeth chattered.

"Here—eat. Stephen. Eat." He chewed desultorily. Meat. He spat it out.

"Here, Stephen. Eat." Joseph was holding something against his lips. "Open your mouth. Stephen." He opened his mouth. Melon. Chewed, swallowed, sweetish liquid. *The art of our necessities—* Chewed, swallowed.

Water. I need—I need— He took the ostrich egg from Joseph. He wanted to crush it, wanted to caress it. He lifted it to his lips and sucked from it. Milk— He wept, dropped the ostrich egg; fell sideways; gasping, gulping, moaning, shivering. Looked into the heart of the fire, its roaring darkness.

After a while, he sat up. Joseph was watching him. Stephen spoke. His voice was a stranger's. It boomed and rasped. "I'm all right now. Still a bit feverish, that's all. Caught the sun. I'll be all right."

Joseph was handing him his clothes. Stephen pushed them away. "No."

"You must wear your clothes, Stephen."

"No."

In silence, Joseph stuffed them into the bundle; tied the bundle to the AK.

Looks like my head dangling there. And Stephen shuddered as the reference fused into image: a film he had seen by chance one rainy day in Oxford— A bundled severed head touring dusty Mexico on a car seat, haloed by a wail of flies and no doubt a sweet foul smell. *Vile, vile—* He couldn't recall what had happened to the head, or why it was being transported through Mexico.

He got to his feet shakily. I must not look up at the dancers. "We will go on. And on and on and on. We will go. On. You will see." He passed Joseph, sidled through the narrow gap between the fire and the cave wall.

The sun was rising.

They were clambering down from the cave. They passed the green paper-tree, came to the green pool. A tiny slash of darker green caught Stephen's eye. He stooped to the Resurrection Plant, lifted it from the water marvelling. On each side of its green stem, frond after tiny fluted frond. Green. Totally green. Impossible, beautiful, hideous. He crushed the sprig in his hand, his fist; dropped it to the grey granite. Then led the way down the steep smooth slope.

As they reached the frothing fecund valley, Joseph tried to pass him, but Stephen caught at his shirt, yanked him back. "I will lead now. It is my turn to lead. I will lead."

"No, Stephen. You do not know the way. And you are sick."

"I will lead" stubbornly. "I know the way."

"How can you know the way? Stephen."

"I know the way." He turned, stared implacably into the strange familiar miniaturised face. I am blind, I will see. "I know the way. You will see."

The valley led them north-west. To their right and left the rounded grey kopjes swayed past. *Why did you give me no hint that night?*—But you did, Susanna—you did, and I refused to see it. You knew, it was in your eyes. And in your voice. But I refused to hear, refused to see. I sent you to your death. Because I wanted to be rescued, because I wanted to live—because I was a coward. But what else could I have done? No, Stephen, even if you couldn't have stopped him— To have let her go alone to her death. Alone to her death. Stephen Hero! Stephen Coward, Stephen Coward. To have abandoned you, Susanna, at the moment you needed me most— *All's past amend, unchange-able—*

A stir near the bushes to their right. He stopped, whispered over his shoulder to Joseph. "What are they?"

"Kudu" the whisper returned. Stephen strained to see them. Three, one taller than the others—mother with young. Three pairs of ears, ridiculously large and wide, above gleaming wide-set liquid eyes. Slim fragile necks. The honey of their fur, banded with delicate white stripes. I yearn towards them, their innocent stillness. They gaze at me, they linger. Then suddenly, in unison—yes, I am your enemy, for even in my nakedness I am all too human— they leap, they skitter away in a flash of grace. Sunlight inhabits their absence. Oh, Susanna. *Woman much missed, how you call to me, call to me—* God-if-there-is-a-God. *Thus I, faltering forward—*

The valley was steadily dropping, its vegetation thinning as the parched plain lifted again towards them. The last of the hills fell behind. They were walking along a sandy depression, a dead river—dead till rains resurrect it. If the rains ever come. Glare accumulated. Oh, Susanna. Lead me, you *are* leading me. *—faltering forward—*

"Look, Stephen." Joseph's arm came past Stephen's neck, forefinger pointing upwards.

"What is it?" Red and black, brown and white, jaunty crest above beady eyes, long narrow beak—the bird swooped off its high perch, and in a moment they heard its clear whooping call.

"Hoopoe, a shy bird. We call it *impupu*, you heard it make that sound? Hoopoe, impupu, almost the same word."

Stephen walked on. The sun pressed down on them. His arms, stomach, back, feet, almost his whole body, were sore; the swollen bites on his neck and ears itched; and his head ached, ached, a rhythmic pounding behind his eyes. All of me sore, sore.

Then— Streaks of sheer pain. He cried out, falling backwards. He had walked into a thorn-bush; long white thorns had raked his stomach and thighs. When he looked down, blood was welling out unevenly along slashes in his puffy red flesh.

"Stephen." Joseph put a hand on his shoulder. Stephen shrugged it off, staggered forward.

Joseph caught his arm, held him close, touched his stomach softly, brushing away blood. Stephen jerked away. "Leave me alone. Don't touch me."

"Let us sit here for a short time." Joseph sat on a rock in the shade of a big thorn-tree. "Please, Stephen. Sit." Stephen sat cross-legged on the hard red earth, a few yards away, in the sunlight. He did not look at his wounds, or touch them. Flies circled him, settled to bite.

"Put on your clothes, Stephen. Please. It is wrong to go naked like that."

"Why? Because I haven't got a stick through my cock? The animals go naked. I am an animal. I go naked."

"You did not see that thorn-bush. Your eyes—"

"Fuck my eyes, Joseph. Fuck *you*. Leave me alone."

"Please, Stephen—take the sunglasses." He held them out to Stephen; they glinted darkly.

"No." *I stumbled when I saw—* Stephen scrambled to his feet and began to walk again. A melody was infiltrating his mind. At first, he thought it was "Suzanne," but as it defined itself, more and more insistently, he knew what it was—a song from his distant past, from sing-songs around campfires during his brief scouting career, a marching song—his feet fell into its rhythmic regularity. *Oh! Susanna, Oh! don't you cry for me—* Leave me alone. *I thought I saw Susanna, A coming down de hill. The buckwheat cake was in her mouth, The tear was in her eye—* Leave me, lead me, leave me. He shook his head, trying to drive the banal words, the cheerful melody, the bouncing rhythm, from his mind. *Out, out—And when I'm dead and buried, Susanna, don't you cry—Out, out—*

They were sitting under a baobab, the first they had encountered since emerging from the narrow valley. It stood, aged, lonely, its gnarled pink-grey bulk rising high above the thin bush. Its spirit has summoned us. They sat side by side, Joseph looking out into the dancing heat waves, Stephen looking down at his stomach, its nest of livid blood-encrusted scratches and swollen bites.

They ate, in silence. Flies circled, more and more of them, attracted especially by the meat Joseph was eating. Flies and mopane-bees had become an intermittent painful nuisance after the descent to the low-veld; but now they were increasingly numerous, and Stephen's nakedness made him utterly vulnerable to their bites. He fluttered his hands to drive them off; but they were soon back, attacking him for the moisture they sought, needed. *I had a dream de odder night When ebry ting was still. Susanna, don't you cry—*

"Stephen." *But if I do not find her—* "Stephen. Listen to me." *Susanna, don't you cry—* "Listen. Listen to me, Stephen."

"No. We speak different languages, Joseph, how can I understand you?"

"You said we were Brothers."

"I was wrong. We are separating, all the time we are moving further and further apart. Like the end of *Passage to India*, do you know it, did you read it at school? I did. One of my favourite novels, once, long ago. Total separation, that's how it ends. I listened to you, Joseph. I tried to hear you, I thought I was beginning to hear you. In spite of our differences. But I was wrong." Flies circling, buzzing. "As you said—and how glad you must be to be proved right once again—we are not individuals, we are warring cultures, histories, nationalities, you are Black and I am White, you are Zimbabwean and I am English, so— How can we ever communicate?" Buzzing, circling. *My voice, your voice. Voices. Babble. Babel.* "You talk, I talk, we talk, but we can't hear each other."

"We can. You said we can. You ask questions, you always want to know."

"Know? No. Not any more." *Never, never, never, never, never—* "What do I know? There's nothing to know." *My banjo on my knee—*

Joseph leaned towards Stephen, caught his arm, held it. "You must listen, Stephen. You must. Please."

"Must? Why '*must*?'" He squinted into his own tiny frowning face. "Who says? You said you don't have to answer my questions. All right, I accept that. But I don't have to *ask* any questions. Why ask questions when there are no answers? Finis. The End. Finis."

"No. You must." The sunglasses twisted away. "You must. For me. I want you to know the truth."

"The truth, the *truth*"—jeering, giggling, choking. "The truth, oh the truth, the truth, the truth—" *That's what I told myself I was searching for, the truth the truth the truth, I told myself that it existed, that you could find it if you looked hard enough, read enough, thought enough, studied hard enough. Education. Answers to all those festering questions that have obsessed me—* 'What is the meaning of hahahaha life?', yes, we're all asking that one, a very popular question, even as we ooze out of our mothers' wombs, aren't we, and here's a good one, 'What is the source of hahahaha evil, why do we hurt and kill our fellow humans, not to mention our humble speechless companions on earth, and even the earth itself now that we've learnt how to wreck that too?' —now *that's* a good question! And above all, below all, 'Who am I, what am I?' It's all the biggest fuckin' bloody laugh, mate! —And how you *would* laugh, Paul, now, if you could see me sitting under this fuckin' bloody tree in the middle of this fuckin' bloody continent with this fuckin' bloody nignog, this monster, your murderer, Susanna's murderer—see me sitting here naked, cock dangling—fuckin' bloody Queer, naked fuckin' pusillanimous bloody Queer in the heart of his own darkness— How you would laugh— He sobbed. His chest heaved. *I've come from Alabama, Wid my banjo on my knee—* He scraped his fingers against the bare stony ground around him, grey stones, grey—*grey sunken cunt of the world—*

"Stephen"—putting his hand on my knee. "Stephen. Please. For me. Stephen."

Pain. Emptiness. "All right. All right, I'll try. But I can't see much and I can't hear at all. Well?"

"You never asked me about my childhood."

Stephen struggled with his lurching mind. *Oh! Susanna, Oh! don't you cry for me—* He spoke with difficulty out of his hurting throat; hoarsely. "You told me about it. You told me that your father took you away from your mother to work on a farm when you were small. You told me your father was a cook on the farm."

"Yes. Then ask your questions. Please."

"You don't need my questions"—wearily. "Talk. Just tell me."

"But ask."

"Oh—all right, whatever you want. Well— What happened then, were you happy?"

"Yes." Joseph ran his right hand along the AK resting across his thighs. "And no. I was happy to be with my father at first; and herding the cattle; until I saw how he was humiliated. The farmer and especially the farmer's wife—they humiliated him, every day, every day. They shouted at him, complained about his cooking, though he worked all day in the hot kitchen, sweating over the wood stove. Even in front of visitors they shouted and complained. One of the visitors was a priest, a Missionary, he would say grace, he would smile at my father when the Whites were not looking. But the farmer's wife would tell them all that my father was stupid, he could never remember a recipe no matter how many times she showed him, he was dirty, stole sugar from the pantry, all lies, lies— He had to listen to that, and it was hard also because she was a woman and he was a man, and yet he could not even reply, he could not say anything, only smile and 'Yes, Madam, yes, Madam.' But when he came to the hut at night, he would bang his head against the floor, he would groan, he would say 'We will go back to the kraal tomorrow', and I would long for that."

"But? So he never did? He stayed there?"

"Yes, he had no good choice, he had to earn money to pay taxes—I told you. He never beat me, even when she had been screaming at him that she was going to get rid of him because he was a stupid Kaffir, a dirty Munt, all those things. But when I grew older, I despised him, I despised him more and more. I thought I would run away to Bulawayo, to my uncle. But I would have been sent back. But then—it got better for me, because of Daniel."

"Daniel? Who was he?"

"The farmer's son. There were two sons, and three daughters. The youngest daughter was almost my age, Daniel was a year older, but he was smaller than me."

"And you became friends?"

"Yes. But we were not supposed to be friends. It started because his father thought Daniel should have physical activities, sport, to make him stronger, before he would be sent away to boarding school in Bulawayo, he said his wife was making a sissy out of Daniel, he blamed her for letting him read books instead of being outside working on the farm. So she said why didn't they make me be with him, because she saw me when I came to the kitchen to help my father sometimes at night, she said I could be Daniel's servant, go into the bush with him to shoot buck, play games with him. My father did not like it, he thought I would be unhappy, he thought Daniel would bully me. But that did not happen—because I was bigger than Daniel, and because of Daniel."

"What was he like?"

"You. You are the third one, Stephen."

"Third?"

"Daniel. And the Missionary's son. And you. You even look like him, except he had fair hair. He was clever, he could have gone to university if they had encouraged him, he was not interested in being a farmer, he liked reading and learning. He was kind and sensitive. I saw that he was nervous of me, not just because I was bigger, but—I don't know why, because I was Black maybe, but we became friends, real friends. We talked a lot, about many things—what he was reading, his ideas. We went for long walks in the bush, he was curious about birds and animals and trees, everything around him. He did not want to hunt, once he shot a kudu but never again, so I would shoot instead of him and his father thought he did it. And he was always asking questions—just like you, Stephen. I taught him Sindebele, and he taught me good English, how to write and speak good English. But we knew we had to be always careful, because of his father. His father wanted to see him getting strong, tough, only that—so we had two soccer teams, five on each side, with some of the other Black boys on the farm, that was my idea, and we used to play a game on Sunday afternoons. All of us knew that Daniel had to score goals when his father was looking, so we did not tackle him hard, we let him dribble past us. His father and mother would watch for a while, and his mother would say 'Just look at Daniel running, he's getting so strong and fast' and his father would say 'I'm bloody glad I had that idea—as long as he doesn't get too close to that Munt, he must always remember that he's *White*—it's all right if he talks

Kitchen-kaffir with them, that'll be useful on the farm, but he mustn't start *living* like a kaffir, he mustn't let them get familiar with him, he has to remember who's the Baas, hey.' Well, that's what I think he said—I didn't actually hear that, I was too far away." Joseph paused. "Then it went wrong."

"What happened?"

"It was not my fault, and it was not Daniel's fault. We were so happy being together, companions—we wanted to spend every minute of the day together. At night he had to go to his home, and I had to go to my father—he had a woman now, so I had to sleep in a hut nearby. Often Daniel and I would meet secretly at night, it was easy for me but he had to climb out of his bedroom window—but we were never caught. Sometimes we would just sit and talk, and always he asked his questions. And when he got to be eleven years old, I was ten, he liked to have debates with me, he called them that, about all kinds of things, like Apartheid or religion or predestination. Then the next year he was sent to boarding school. But even that didn't separate us—of course it did during term time, and I missed him and I did not like going back to the other jobs again, dipping the cattle and so on; but he lent me books and when he came home on school holidays we discussed them—we longed for the holidays to come, and then we tried to be together as much as we could. And that was when the trouble began. His father grumbled more and more, Daniel told me that eventually. 'Are you still spending time with that kaffir boy, haven't you made any friends at school that can come and stay, hey? I don't want to see you with that kaffir boy', like that—I was not needed to be with Daniel, now that he was at school. So we had to be extra careful. By now I was fifteen, he was sixteen. It was the year of UDI, but there was trouble even before that, even on the farm, between Blacks and Whites. My father warned me to be very quiet, say nothing about politics. He heard the Whites arguing at dinner, cursing all Blacks—the Missionary never came now, they said he was a Kaffir-boetie, a lover of the Blacks. Then UDI—you remember that, Ian Smith's Unilateral Declaration of Independence?"

"No, I don't, I was only a baby then. In 1965, wasn't it?"

"The 11th of November 1965. You are an Englishman, you should know why Ian Smith chose the eleventh hour of the eleventh day of the eleventh month? He was a pilot in the RAF in the Second World War, he crashed and nearly died. A hero! But he *should* have died. And yet he is still alive today, he is a free man in Zimbabwe, he is still farming on our land. We did not kill him, even though he and his Army killed many of us—many, many, many."

"So what happened?"

"I would go to Daniel's window, at night or very early in the morning, before sunrise. And sometimes we would meet during the day, but only if we were sure that was safe. His bedroom was at the back of the house, and there was a big tree and the water tank next to it, so you were protected from being seen if you were careful. That morning, Daniel and I had arranged to meet because his father and mother said they were going to Bulawayo to the bank and to buy provisions, and my father too to carry things for them. We had a special whistle, Daniel and I, like a bird's call, a dove's. So I whistled to say I was coming and then I went to the window and looked in and then— On Daniel's bed, but it wasn't Daniel, it was his father."

"And?"

"He was not alone. His trousers were down, he was fucking."

"His wife?"

"No."

Oh God. "Daniel?"

"One of his daughters. The one my age, the young one, I hardly knew her—she was never allowed to play with me. She was looking right at the window when I looked in. She screamed and he stopped and turned his head and saw me. I just looked at him and he just looked at me. Afterwards I knew what had happened. He had made Daniel go into town with his mother, so he could stay at home and fuck his daughter, I don't know why they were doing it on Daniel's bed. Maybe— But Daniel could not warn me, and of course he did not know about his father and his sister anyway. He never knew."

"You never told him?"

"I was sent away. After his father had beaten me with a sjambok. You know what that is?"

"No."

"An Afrikaans word, of course. A sjambok is a short whip made of hide— the best ones, the worst ones, are made of rhino or hippo hide. It cuts into you, it tears you apart. He pulled on his trousers and left the girl lying on the bed crying and came outside for me, I was just standing there, I was petrified, I was too terrified even to think about running away. He pulled me into the barn and made me take off all my clothes and pushed me down on the straw and he beat me with the sjambok—after a while I fainted. When I woke up, I was bleeding all down my back and legs, and he said if I told anyone what I had seen, anybody at all, my father would lose his job and I would be killed. You are the first person I have told."

"How could you keep it secret so long? And what did your father do?"

"My father did what he was told, of course. He sent me away, he was ashamed of me, the Baas told him I had been caught stealing sugar from the pantry. So my father sent me to Bulawayo, to my uncle, the one who works in the Museum. I was lucky. My uncle sent me to school, in Mpopoma first, the government school for Blacks, there were only a few schools like that before Independence, and he paid my school fees. He was older than my father, he only had grown-up daughters, I think he always wanted a son. He was a good man, and kind to me always—he is dead now. I did not see my parents after that, I thought they would never believe what I said, only what the White Baas said, that's how it was in those days. I had to pass an examination to be accepted at the school, but I worked hard, and Daniel had taught me well, and my uncle had a friend who was a teacher, and even the Headmaster at Mpopoma School, a White man, he was a friend of my uncle's, there were some White men like that, a few. And after UDI, there were more spaces in the school because some students ran away to train to be freedom-fighters, so I was accepted. There was a lot of—unrest in the Bulawayo Townships, that's what the Black suburbs were called, and one morning people were marching, a protest march, and they made me march with them, and the Police came and I was arrested—I did not run fast enough. They put me in the jail, in a big cell with men from the march, but somebody told my uncle and he came and argued with them, he said I was only a boy, and so in the end they let me go. After that, he sent me away from Bulawayo to a Mission school near Inyati, he knew one of the senior teachers there. I worked hard, I was a good student, I passed my School Certificate with good marks."

"So, in a way, you owed all that to the farmer—Daniel's father. What was his name?"

Joseph's hand ran along the AK. He was looking into the distance. "Owe him all that? Yes, I owed him—I owed him for beating me and lying about me, humiliating me, I owed him for separating me from my father and mother, and from Daniel. We were like brothers, Daniel and me— White boy and Black boy, yet we loved each other. His father separated us for ever. Yes, you are right—I owed him."

Stephen flapped at flies; picked up a small stone, rolled it in his palm. "And then—what happened to Daniel?"

"He is dead. I killed him. I think I killed him."

"When? How?" Stephen balanced the stone on his knee.

"In 1978, near the end of the Bush War. He was in Ian Smith's Army, he had no choice, he was conscripted. Poor Daniel, he must have been a very bad soldier. But of course he knew a lot about the bush, we learned that together, and he was intelligent. I wonder what he did all that time I was in London and Toronto and— I saw him once in the distance in Bulawayo, a long time ago, I think the year after UDI, when some of us at Mpopoma School were taken by the Headmaster to a concert of the Bulawayo Orchestra, there were many tickets left over and they wanted the hall to be full. He was in his school uniform and I was in mine. I don't think he saw me—we were at the back of the Hall of course, and even if he saw me it would have been embarrassing for both of us."

"And then? In 1978?"

Joseph rubbed his nose, looked down at the AK; a long pause. "It was an ambush. They were coming along a dirt road in four Army trucks. One of our land mines exploded under the first one and we opened fire. We killed some soldiers in the first three trucks, but there was a machine gun and it began to fire at us, so we had to gap it, as the White soldiers used to say—we had to get away very fast. But when the land mine exploded, one of the soldiers was thrown out right under my AK. He jumped up and he had glasses and fair hair. I shot him. Through the head. I saw him fall. *I am the enemy you killed, my friend*— Afterwards I told myself I was wrong, it was not him, it could not have been him. Two years later, after Independence, when I was in Harare, starting to work in Mugabe's Government, I went to the Public Library and looked up the newspaper for the day after, and it was there, 'More Ambush Deaths,' but yet his name was not there. So maybe I killed someone else. But I think it was him." He lifted the AK, placed it back on his thighs. "I wanted to be sure. Now I can never be sure."

They sat in silence. The stone fell off Stephen's knee when he turned to Joseph. He reached for Joseph's head and pulled it against his chest.

They were walking slowly because Stephen was limping and in worse pain. The afternoon was waning and "We must choose a place to sleep soon," Joseph said. Stephen looked around them: thorn-veld—sparse thorn-bushes, thorn-trees, dry grass. They would be in the open, would need a fire.

"There is a small hill to the south"—Joseph.

"Right, let's head for it." Stephen was still meditating on Joseph's account of his childhood and youth. *Did it help him to tell me? Yet I am glad he wept. I didn't think he could weep.*

And *I think I am free at last of the voices, for the moment at least. Perhaps they have left me because I don't need them any more. But can I survive in this achingly empty silence? Only the distant screech of cicadas now, the crackle of the dry grass, the slurring hiss of my dragging feet. And inside me, this bleak void. No. Surely my voices are me, part of my reality—how can I be* myself without them? I may be an extreme case, because of my personality and education; but surely all of us are composed of words from the past, all of us are echoes pulsing towards silence. So am I wrong to yearn for unity, simplicity? Is that a destructive delusion? And even if it is, do we need it? To survive? Yet our lives and personalities are fluid, ever-changing. Diversity! So— Is that where we must find our selves, in multiplicity, in dancing to the music of a myriad human voices? But I am confused and close to exhaustion. *Dropping—ever dropping—* Too weary even to care. Am I terminally blind now, mentally as well as physically? Or merely mad? *—die that way—* You will see, Stephen. But how *can* I?

Yet I have my memories. An incident comes back to me now, after so many years. I was nine years old; a boy in my primary-school class had died—I never knew from what, disease or accident. He had sat next to me, we had swapped stamps, he had given me his favourite conker. And I mourned, how I mourned! Wrote his name over and over on scraps of paper, prayed for him every night, wept for him before I fell asleep. And then forgot all about him, until now. I can't even recall his name, what he looked like. All I remember, essentially, is that he lived briefly, and died. And that is you too, Stephen. That is all of us, ultimately. So why— Why search for more, for ultimate meaning?

But I'll try to remember you, Susanna. I miss you. You too will sink slowly to complete absence. But I will try to remember. I don't know how you died, I flinched from asking him about that. And can it matter now? Your parents and brothers, waiting for you, then waiting for news of you, waiting, hoping against hope—I will contact them, go and see them if they wish, talk to them about your courage and generosity and kindness. I will, I promise you I will.

And you too, Paul—surely I can deal with you now. I didn't like you, but perhaps that was my fault as well as yours—you intimidated me with your macho contempt for Queers. But you had courage, and you could have grown into tolerance and understanding and kindness. Death took you too quickly. If there's such a thing as cosmic justice, you surely paid for any sins in those moments before you died. I will write to your family.

The dance, of life, of death— Beyond human comprehension—certainly beyond *my* comprehension, I accept that now. Mystery. Immitigable mystery. But I must believe the dance to be good. If we are to be fully human, we *must* believe that life is ultimately good, whatever the suffering it imposes on us. Remember, remember. Remember the Bushmen, Stephen: the children; the ostrich shells of life-preserving water; the bodies of men and women—painted yellow and red by the flickering flames—moving rhythmically into the harmony of complexity and change which is unity. And what does that mean? Perhaps behind, beyond, within the multitude of voices there is *one* voice, one dominating controlling voice? No, I don't know—that's all I know. I don't know and will never know.

He was suddenly aware that Joseph had whispered fiercely, that the stillness had thickened. He stopped—and looked up at a wall of grey. He narrowed his eyes, tried to force them to focus. Joseph, a few paces behind him, stood rigid.

The massive bulk of the elephant hung over them both. Its ears were flapping slowly, its small eyes glinted, its great head swayed. Two immensely long tusks drooped yellow on either side of a delicately questing trunk. Stephen walked forward. He was murmuring.

The elephant drew into its stillness, lifted one huge forefoot. Poised on the edge of movement— Then surged to the left, trampling thorn-bushes. A heaving diminishing blur. And a stentorian trumpeting ripped the air. And after that—silence. Reverberating silence.

"Our second encounter with a male marauder" Stephen announced, almost cheerfully. "And your leopard, Joseph, makes three. Leopard, lion, elephant. I wonder where the females are?"

"I think we will encounter some of them soon. They are usually more dangerous, so do not wish for them. Female elephants in herds are the most dangerous of all, they will trample to dust any possible threat to their offspring. You would not have survived a meeting with one of them. Why did you walk towards this elephant? You are lucky to be alive—and I am too."

"I knew he didn't want to charge and smash us. He told me so. He just wanted a good reason to go away, so I gave him one."

"You were speaking to him?"

"I told him I was naked like him, and could be no threat to him. That I was a friend. We were friends. I said 'My philosophy of life is the same as *yours*, don't die before you need to.' I said that made three of us. So he saw that we were in agreement, and he went."

Stephen woke with a jerk. What—? The fire was flickering gently. Stars circling overhead. The baobabs clustered around him, hovering protectively in cool moonlight. Strange how I stopped observing the gradual increase of the moon when, just a few days ago, it seemed so important as a measure of time passing. And now I can barely see the moon, anyway. I wonder if today is my birthday? Yes, somehow I think it is. But why should that matter? It doesn't.

Hideous yelping and maniacal laughter. Hyenas. That must be what roused me. And he became aware of another sound, a quiet grumble. He looked into the darkness and saw a momentary flicker define the faraway horizon to the north. Were the rains actually approaching at last?

A movement beside him and Joseph was pulling himself up off the sand. When something slipped softly down against his stomach, Stephen realised he had been covered with his clothes. Joseph must have thought I might be cold during the night—and I *am* shivering slightly, my skin feels painfully tender—perhaps I'm feverish again. And I'm hungry. The last of the roots and vegetables in Joseph's bundle had not made much of a supper. And thirsty.

Joseph moved to the edge of the firelight to piss. Stephen joined him, wincing at the pain in his right foot as he put his weight on it. The hyenas squalled again. And while standing there he noticed the faintest curl of light, harbinger of dawn. Sleepily Stephen put his arm around Joseph's shoulder as they moved back to their places by the fire. Joseph put logs onto it.

As he sat down, Stephen—"Will you listen, Joseph? Not to me—to my beloved Rosenberg. I used to recite his poems, the ones I know, to Susanna. Except one, I don't know why. And now *that* one is in my mind." And I think this is Farewell, Rosenberg bidding me farewell. "He wrote it while meditating on the beginning of the War that killed him. Listen. *'What in our lives is burnt In the fire of this? The heart's dear granary? The much we shall miss?'"* A strange sound burst from his mouth—a squeak, a sob. *"'Three lives hath one life— Iron, honey, gold. The gold, the honey gone— Left is the hard and cold. Iron are our lives Molten right through our youth. A burnt space through ripe fields, A fair mouth's broken tooth.'"* And I too bid farewell, *a long farewell—*

They sat in silence while the eastern light gradually widened. The pan in front of them, beyond their stony rise, greying from black. The dawn chorus.

Joseph suddenly shaking him—"Your spear, Stephen. Where is your spear?"

Stephen laughed weakly. "You've only just noticed? I left it behind when we rested yesterday afternoon."

Joseph shook him again. "How will I hunt? Where will we get food? You are so—stupid."

"I don't want any food. Especially meat. No more killing, Joseph. No more."

"Then we will die, unless I can find roots or other food here. It will be hard, almost impossible, to kill an animal with a knife—even here, where so many animals come to drink. And how can we protect ourselves if we are attacked?"

The pan spread ever wider, glowing into morning. The sun gently penetrated a cloudless sky. The far faint grumbling continued intermittently, counterpointed by birdsong.

"You still have your AK, Joseph. If I had been holding the spear when we met the elephant, if I had been armed, he would have killed us. He told me that. He spared us because I was naked like him."

After a few moments, "I will try to find food." But Joseph did not move. "Are you all right, Stephen? Stephen?"

"Yes. I feel better today, I think. My foot is very sore but you won't need to—" The axe glittered, shuddered. He shook his head, shook the image from his mind. "You won't need to do anything about it. Not yet."

"Stephen. Did you understand? What I said yesterday?"

"The truth. Oh yes, the truth. *Your* truth. But so what?"

"So, do you—?"

"You want to know whether I blame you, whether I still blame you, for what you have done? Yes, I do, I must. How could I not blame you? We spoke of this. I have been trying to think about it. We must all of us take responsibility for our actions or we can no longer qualify as human. That is *my* truth. The morality of my tribe? But—does it even matter whether we qualify as human? I don't know, I'm more confused than ever. But yes, it must matter, surely it must matter. Because if we aren't human, what are we? We cannot be gods, because we are mortal; we cannot be animals, because we have self-consciousness. If we fail to be human, we can only be monsters. You know that, Joseph. I cannot judge you, but I *must* judge you—if only because I am responsible too, even in my passivity. Are pacifists free of responsibility for wars? They can be more responsible than armies."

His voice faded; he paused, swallowed painfully. "Many others are also responsible for what you have done—you are right about that, of course. The men who raped you, Rhodes and the other men who invaded your country a century ago, Mugabe and ZANU politicians in Harare, Daniel's father—so many, so many, uncountable. And that leaves out culture, history, geography, original sin, God knows how much else. As you would point out. But still— you didn't have to rape and kill Susanna and kill Paul. Or do you want me to say that I think you were forced to do those things, that you were insane, couldn't control yourself—that you were inhuman as well as inhumane? If so, I can't, Joseph. If so, life is meaningless. I'm not strong enough to accept that."

"But I am strong enough. Life is meaningless."

"I'm too tired and confused to argue, Joseph. My head aches. My throat—I'm so thirsty, so thirsty. It's hard to talk. And if life is meaningless, why do you care what I think? What anyone thinks? You and Daniel must have discussed these things in your debates. What did he think?"

"That life is meaningless. He persuaded me. We argued about it just two nights before that morning when I was beaten by his father and sent away. We were going to talk about it again, he was troubled. I had told him he was wrong, that one must always fight against evil. I said that I would always fight against evil in my country, even if it meant killing *him*—even him—because he was White and I was Black. But then I realised I did not want to kill him, I would have told him that. But I did kill him. And it turned out that he was right after all."

"Joseph. There's one thing—I wanted to hear you say it, but you didn't. Are you sorry you killed Susanna?" Please. Joseph looked up into the thick baobab branches high above, then down to the fire. Please. The pan lay pale, as sunlight began to pour over it. "It does matter, Joseph. It will always matter to me. I loved her. It does matter."

The sun rose higher. Light spread. Another sunrise—how many have I seen?—and so soon another sunset, another sunset. Still they sat below the sentinel baobabs, while the fire gradually eviscerated itself.

Stephen became aware of a shifting blur on the far side of the pan, heard faint sounds on the small breeze. "What are they? I can't see them. The animals." They are seeking the daily blessing of water—life-giving, death-giving.

"Many. Wildebeest, zebras, buffalo, elephant, many many buck. And lions and wild dogs and hyenas of course, catching and killing stragglers and young ones. We will stay on this side and go that way"—he pointed northwest.

A new sound enlarged, bellowed. Stephen looked up, puzzled, as the helicopter swept over their baobabs towards the pan. A military helicopter, green and brown.

"Stay still"—Joseph. "Do not move."

The helicopter circled the pan, thudded back towards them, surged on over the baobabs.

Joseph stood up. "We must go. Put on your clothes."

"No. Do you think they saw us?"

"Put on your clothes."

"No."

∗ ∗ ∗ ∗ ∗

They came down to the river at mid-day. The Zambezi again, it must be, descending slowly through its wide valley towards the Victoria Falls. A gash of blue and green in the dun flat landscape, harbouring trees in leaf and bloom. Numerous water-birds inhabited it. Stephen gazed blindly at its rich darkness between the trees lining its bank. The Garden of Eden. Another Garden of Eden.

"Is that a bird, just there, quite near?" Stephen pointed at a blur of grey.

"A heron, we call it *itsheme*. And there are two hamerkops near some lechwe and waterbuck, *uthekwane*. And a fish-eagle, *ihunkwe*. And those very big ones, they are storks, can you see them?"

"Hardly at all. The glare—my eyes—" My voice barely a croak.

"Are you hungry? I am hungry. Shall I look for food?"

"No, let's go on." We are near. I know we are.

"Do you want to lead the way again? It is easy along the river. I will warn you about trees."

"And lions and other predators?"

"There will be no need. In the middle of the day most animals are resting."

"No, you lead. My foot is so sore. Can I hold your hand?"

They went on, slowly; following the river downstream into a copse of mimosa thorn-trees in bright blossom. Then five tall black-barked mushuma trees. Stephen stopped, under their welcome shade, his right hand still clasped in Joseph's left. "There's one more question, Joseph. I forgot to ask it earlier. My final question. All right?"

"I promised to answer all your questions, Stephen."

"Did you kill him?"

Joseph frowned in puzzlement. "Paul? Daniel? You know I—"

"Not Paul, not Daniel. Daniel's father. The farmer who gave us a lift—who took us to you. His name is McGregor."

"Yes. We killed him. And others. His wife and the son Abraham—I gave the order, they were killed in the farmhouse while I waited with Mpofu and Ndlovu for McGregor. We knew he would return that afternoon, the cook told us. We shut the second gate on the farm road, so he had to get out of his bakkie to open it." Spear and axe.

"Did you—?"

"I executed him. Mpofu and Ndlovu held him. I cut his throat. With your spear. I wanted him to know who was killing him. Then he fell and I executed him."

"With the axe. And so—"

"And so the farm, the land, belongs to my people—it is theirs. My father, he is an old man now, they said he was living in a hut on another farm—and Mpofu and Ndlovu, my cousins, I told them to take my mother and sister with them, and my sons, and they will own the land, all of them, together. It was their land, *our* land—and now it is our land again. Nobody can ever take it away from them."

"Nobody? Not even Mugabe? And Daniel—?"

"Daniel is dead, Stephen. The land is for the living."

Voices. Human voices, thin in the distance. Sounds of splashing. "Where are they?" he whispered into Joseph's ear.

"Stay here. I will look." Joseph was back quickly. "I think we may have been seen before we came among these trees. Or maybe the helicopter— But I should have noticed, we were exposed sometimes to the other side of the river. They are talking, looking across the river, looking through their binoculars to where we were walking. I could not hear what they were saying, they are too far away—the river is wide."

"Who are they?"

"It is one of those lodges for rich American tourists, I think—so they can watch animals, take photographs. They are excited about what they have seen. There are some elephants in the river, washing themselves, I could see them—maybe also hippos— But the tourists are frightened to come closer to the river, I think—whatever they saw."

"Perhaps they are only interested in the elephants? Perhaps they didn't see us."

They walked on, Joseph making sure they were concealed from any watchers across the river. The day was oppressive now, darkening. A far rumbling. Violet and purple clouds massing on the northern horizon.

"Can we stop, please?"—Stephen, gasping. "My foot—I need to rest it. My feet! Unless you want to carry me. And I'm very thirsty."

They went slowly down to the river to drink, Stephen leaning against Joseph. Then they sat shaded by a tall mukwa tree until early afternoon. Its strange decaying seeds, bristly cores frilled with pale green membrane, surrounded them—as once before, Stephen recalled.

He dozed. Joseph watched him. When he opened his eyes, "I will look for some food to eat" Joseph told him.

He came back with roots and berries. "You eat them," Stephen whispered. "I can't."

While Joseph ate, Stephen leaned back against the tree, caressing a mukwa seed and gazing vacantly up at the sifting foliage above him, his eyes narrowed, bloodshot. Flies were buzzing round him. Mosquitoes had appeared too, now that water was nearby. And tsetse flies. He no longer tried to brush any of them away; he endured their bites.

Joseph looks exhausted. Stephen leaned towards him and registered, almost with surprise, the emaciated face, its cheekbones and lips jutting through shiny skin, sketchy beard. His clothes and cap filthy, and his hair. And his arms—dust and dirt caked over sweat. The sunglasses and AK are the cleanest parts of him, they define him now, their aggression sustaining his weakened bones and shrunken muscles.

And I? I must look even worse, a scrawny scarecrow. But do I exist? I ache, therefore I am? Or am I merely a ghostly inhabitant of Joseph's dream? Stephen's eyes dropped down to skinny arms and legs, pulpy red flesh streaked with blood and dirt, swellings from the multitude of insect bites. Painful swollen feet. *—unaccommodated man— poor, bare, forked animal— the thing itself—Humanity must perforce prey upon itself—Poor naked wretches—* Still with me, Shakespeare? I thought all my voices had abandoned me to the silence of my self. But then, I am an *Englishman*.

He slept, uneasily; shifting, groaning.

Joseph shook his shoulder. How many times has he wakened me like this? Stephen looked up into the sunglasses, into the tiny enigmatic face that was his but not his.

"We should go on now, Stephen. Are you all right?"

Where to? But does that matter? There is no end. *On and on, on and on.* There is no end. He got to his feet, slowly, painfully, with Joseph's help.

Holding Joseph's hand, he felt the ring hard against his fingers—Paul's mother's ring. They looked at each other. Stephen unclasped his fingers, pulled the ring from Joseph's forefinger, dropped it at their feet. Then he raised both his hands to Joseph's face and drew off the sunglasses. Your naked eyes, the brown irises, black pupils; illimitably deep—mysterious, beautiful. "Joseph." But what was there to say? What do I want to say, what *can* I say? "Joseph." That I can't hear your voice, even though I tried; that I have never heard your voice, never? That we are both men, we are both human. "Joseph." That we are both human, and I can't hear your voice. That I hate you. That I love you, that I hate you. That I hate you, that I love you. That I love you.

After a moment, Joseph took the sunglasses from him, put them back on. He took Stephen's hand and they moved on very slowly, side by side, near the riverbank.

Rumbling. Closer? To the north, cumulus clouds massing. Closer? A flicker of lightning. And another. Low rumbling.

Stephen was limping painfully. He stumbled. Joseph's hand tightened on his.

It was almost evening now. They emerged from a copse of trees and the river was there; swinging away from them, glinting softly in thick red light.

Stephen pulled his hand free, staggered forward.

"Stephen." But Joseph's hand on Stephen's shoulder was shaken off. He followed silently.

The river broadened here, one stream flowing sluggishly into a great dark pool. Stephen reached its edge. Above a gallery of trees opposite him, the clouds were now mountains, a range of purple mountains. Streams of lightning spilled off their flanks. They spoke in a low voice—menacing, consoling? Ambivalence is our name. We bring life, we bring death.

From the pool poked a multitude of tiny ears, tiny glittering eyes, slits of nostrils. A herd of hippos. Occasionally one would surge upwards, snorting, bubbling, wallowing; then subside into muddy somnolence. A bucolic scene; peaceful, almost humorous.

Stephen strained to see the hippos. Then in the silence he heard the crocodile. It was on the opposite bank of the pool, a great green log. Its head rose. It stared unblinking at him. It began to slide forward. It reached the water.

Veins of silvering light spread softly across rich purple.

The crocodile was swimming, its tail thrashing.

Thunder rumbled gently, ruminative.

The crocodile forged on, ripples slapping now against the bank at Stephen's feet. It spoke to him again out of silence, its huge approach.

A blur of sudden movement among the trees on the other side of the pool.

Behind him Joseph was raising his AK.

Shouts.

Stephen stepped into the black water, holding out his arms. Here I am, he wanted to say that— Here I am—but his mouth didn't open and there was no time.

As the crocodile lunged, haloed by a seething froth, three shots from behind Stephen ripped the red evening. *Corrode, consume—*

Stephen's body lifted forward, slipped sideways. He was dying as the crocodile reached him.

The soldiers fired eleven shots. Four of them struck Joseph as he fell. But he was already dead. He had placed the barrel of the AK in his mouth and fired, once.